# Betrayal in Brooklyn

A NOVEL BY

## W. J. REEVES

This is a work of fiction. Names, characters, places, and incidents are either products of the author's imagination or used fictitiously. Any resemblance to actual events, locales, or persons, living or dead, is entirely coincidental.

W. J. Reeves
reeveswj1944@yahoo.com
United States of America

Cover art by Stephanie Ryan

# Acknowledgments

I would like to thank my wife Cathie for her support these many years. I would also like to thank Stephanie Ryan for creating the cover and preparing this novel for ebook publishing.

# Preface

Betrayal in Brooklyn, set in a gritty, urban world, is about a man who has become the hunted. Richie Bucceroni is trying to rebuild his life after the murder of his wife and child when another killing arrives on his doorstep. As Bucceroni investigates, he discovers he's now the target of the killer. Fast–paced, action–filled, Betrayal in Brooklyn moves to a thrilling, violent conclusion.

# Chapter One

It was a day like most days—life punching, me ducking.

Maybe Atlantic Avenue wasn't the best place for an early morning run. Too much flotsam, too many of the down and out still up and about. But there I was, minding my own business, running in the street instead of on the sidewalk, keeping out of the way of early birds on the way to work, not looking for any trouble. Which, in Brooklyn, is usually when you get it handed to you.

True to form, there it came: trouble with a capital T. Three skinheads, complete with tattoos, chains, leather; no doubt on their way home after an ill–spent evening. Three creeps, just the type for Geraldo to interview. The leader saw me. I was easy to see. An all–red tank top and blue and white striped shorts covered two hundred fifty pounds of aging Italian beef.

He was a big guy, with a shiny pinhead set on a bull neck who probably put steroids on his Cheerios. He whacked his chain into a parked car for practice, stepped into the street to block my way. He said nothing. The other two formed a mutant duet:

"Cut him, Ice!"

"Take his fuckin' face off!"

Up to that I ran, like a pastrami in a piranha tank.

Mr. Ice took his shot, missed; the chain whipped into his own leg. He howled. The other two screamed up a storm: "Come back ol' man, we'll kill ya!"

I swerved around them and took off, moving my ample ass.

A thought crossed my mind to go back and kick the respective rear–ends of three Neanderthals half my age. I let the thought cross. I had better things to do, like teach my class. I ran faster.

Up ahead loomed my college, which didn't really look like a college. No winding walks, no watchtowers, no quad, and no ivy. All of that's at Williams, where the Wall Street types get educated. My college is ten stories, straight up, square. No spires. No stone lions guarding the gate. No gargoyles at the gutters. It's strictly an institution where the proletariat comes to get taught by yours truly.

Bright and clean, the college stood out like Steve Nash on the all–star team. Behind it are old, dirty, burned up, broken down buildings, and a lot of driftwood. Full blown gentrification hasn't yet arrived at this part of Brooklyn.

I kept my peepers peeled for any other A.M. Brooklyn street killers in the market for a moving target who looked like Mussolini doing an Uncle Sam imitation.

Looking up, I saw someone staring at me from an open window high up in the college, but I couldn't make out who it was. Looking ahead, I saw a panhandler outside a package liquor store owned by an old Korean named Dim "Buffalo" Pang.

The panhandler was glad to see me. He stepped into my path, talking a mile a minute. I debated about running him over, decided against it. I came to a stop, feeling the strain in my ankles.

"Hey big man, got five dollah for a vet? Vietnam, man, Vietnam."

I took a second to get my breath. I was face to face with him. Me, reeking of sweat; him, just reeking. His eyes were bloodshot. His breath could've provided illumination by alcohol light for a month.

I formed a question, found air to get it out.

"In... what?"

"Wha' you mean?"

"Army, Navy, Marines, Air Force, Coast Guard, who'd you ... serve... with?"

"You think this fuckin' Jeopardy?"

"You think I'm fuckin' ...Chase Manhattan?"

"Fuck this shit."

"Woof—woof."

"Wha'?"

"Bow—wow," I said, pointing over his shoulder at what was heading our way.

Mr. Pang's dog, big, black, fur—up had escaped from the liquor store and was now doing some end—of—the—world growling while it searched for fresh meat.

The ex—Green Beret scrambled away around the corner with the old Korean's pet killer in hot and heavy pursuit.

I stood stock still just in case the monster had a yen for seasoned Italian food.

Mr. Pang appeared. He was about half my height. He had a considerable club in his small, right hand.

"My dog. He go where?"

"Your dog. He go there," I said, doing a tomahawk motion, gesturing toward the corner.

Mr. Pang ran after his dog.

The dawning of another day at the Urban U. The professors at Amherst don't get to see such sights.

I punched in my code to open the steel gate next to the entrance which was also protected by a steel door. Inside I went. Safe and reasonably sound.

No one was in the lobby. No bums, no skinheads, no one. Just lovable, increasingly old, me.

The hot, late fall day had worked in combo with the running to set off some major league perspiring. Thinning hair on end, sweated through my workout togs, very high on the odor meter, I didn't exactly look or smell or feel like Princeton material.

The spanking new elevator took me to the sixth floor. The door opened. I stepped forward and chest—bumped into a classics professor named Walter Brzenk, a new hire, from Princeton no less. This was his first year in Brooklyn. He wobbled back. I'm not the best choice for someone to bump into.

"Sorry," I said, watching the young professor right himself.

"It's okay. Come with me. There's something going on outside, Richard," he said, looking down at me over his bifocals.

"Richard" isn't my usual moniker. Rich or Richie is what I answer to. My wife called me Richard, but she doesn't do that anymore.

"Like what?"

Brzenk leaned past me and pushed the down button for the elevator.

"A couple of police, plus Mr. Pang and his big dog. It's something around the corner. I could see all of them from my office window. Come with me, this might be spicy, a real slice of city life. Life verite." He said, his voice high, meaning he probably was a tenor.

I looked up at Brzenk while we stood in the hallway.

"Hey, Walt, don't say words like 'verite' out loud, ok? People might think you were a gavone."

"Excuse me."

"A schmuck?"

Brzenk was a redhead, a real carrot–top. Green eyes stared down at me. Behind them was a blank. No flicker of understanding.

I tried a different culture.

"A muhjdoob."

Still nothing. This boy had his work cut out for him in Brooklyn.

"Richard, you've told me about how mean these streets are, so let me see firsthand," said Brzenk, smiling at me.

The smiling bothered me. If there were cops on the scene, then there was trouble. Trouble in Brooklyn is a lot of things, but none of them are something to smile about.

Now was the time for a sharp guy to say "no thanks" to life verite first thing in the morning in a crappy neighborhood. Now a sharp guy should say he had a shower to take, a speech to rehearse, an element to discover. Only a jerk would tag along to see life verite.

The elevator arrived.

I got on the elevator. Down we went.

Outside, we turned left and walked to the corner of two questionable streets. I could see, and hear, Mr. Pang jabbering at about seventy–eight rpm to a beat cop who was standing next to a squad car. There was a loud back and forth going on between the big, Irish cop and the little, old Korean.

The cop looked our way and saw a tall, skinny professor decked out in a kinda white linen suit, complete with an orange and black ivy league tie and next to the Nassau Kid was me, half a foot shorter, mucho pounds heavier, still in a sweat drenched running outfit. A guido making out to be Carl Lewis.

"Hey, Richie, you tryin' out for some team?" said the cop.

"No, I work around here. Wha's goin' on?"

"Real bad over there. Real bad. You come. You help with my dog," interrupted Mr. Pang, putting his small right hand on the cop's large, hairy arm, then tugging on him to get the cop moving, something which the big Irish didn't like a whole lot.

"Hey, Pop, hands off. I can walk all by myself. Don't need no seein' eye dog. You keep your mitts to yourself, ok?"

The cop turned and talked to me.

"It's a bad one, Richie. Dom Mancini's on his way. You want to take a look?"

Detective Dominick Mancini was an old pal. The beat cop had recognized me because Dom used me for expert witness work.

Brzenk and I trailed the cop and old man Pang down the street. Ahead of us, the Irish's partner was roping off an area in front of an abandoned building. I knew the area. This was strictly a stay–the–hell–away–from place. A lot went on at night in these buildings, most of it not very nice.

"What do you think it is, Richard?" said Brzenk, excited, having himself quite a time getting a peep at the underbelly of Brooklyn.

"We'll know soon enough," I said, trying to sound serious. I put a hand on Brzenk's arm.

"Let me give you free advice. Button your lip, take your look, then leave. These are cops. They got a job to do. Us, we're just takin' in the sights."

"Got you," said Brzenk, pulling away from my grip, walking faster so that he could keep up with the cop and Pang. My words of warning were already out his other ear. Profs are like that. They only hear the tune they play.

In front of a dingy doorway, Pang's big, jet–black, bad–ass dog was pacing, doing tight, little circles, growling, sounding like death about to happen. Pang wrestled the Terror of Inchon away, using both hands, and the cop helped out by giving man's best friend two healthy swats with Pang's club to make sure it moved.

All of this should've warned Brzenk that whatever was up there to see wasn't going to be pretty, but he was hot to trot to see Brooklyn life in the raw. He wanted to treat himself to a good long look.

He got one.

Inside the doorway, the man propped up against the wall was straight out of Psycho. An ear to ear grin frozen on his face made him look like Norman Bates's mother, the eyes wide open and staring, the eyebrows arched, the lips peeled back, showing a gap where one of the front teeth should be. Down the chin was a dried blood trail. He looked stiff as a board, like a statue, but this was no work of art. He'd been made into a nightmare.

"Why's he smiling like that?" muttered Brzenk, who all of a sudden didn't look quite so chipper.

Looking at the dead man, my mind played tricks on me. For a moment, I wasn't here on this crummy Brooklyn street getting too good of a look at the smile of death that'd been etched on some unfortunate's face, but I was back in the past, back in my own past, standing in an emergency room where a cop was asking me if the mangled shapes on the tables were my wife and my son.

"Richard, what's happened to him?" said Brzenk, who didn't sound well.

Before I could answer, the Irish came over to me.

"You know this guy, Richie? Look here, he's got ID from the college over there. That's where you work, right?"

"Right," I said, choking down the urge to gag. No matter how many times you see stuff like this, it's never easy to take it in stride. What the cop showed me made it even harder to keep from heaving.

The college photo ID turned the grinning corpse into a student. His name was Edwin 'King' Gomez, and, up until now, he'd been taking my Introduction to Chemistry course. The King moniker was on account of his other job, which was to supply daily dope to the students. He had been an A student.

I had kept my eyes glued on the picture, but now I forced myself to look again at the original. My mind was going a mile a minute. Brzenk was wrong. The 'King' wasn't smiling. The dead don't smile a lot. That wasn't a "smile" spread over his face. It's called risus sardonicus, and it happens when the jaws get paralyzed. I know all about which poisons could stick a death smile like that on someone's kisser. That's what I lectured about as a professor. That's also what I investigated for Detective Dom Mancini.

"Richard! It's Edwin Gomez! He's in our classes, officer!" said Brzenk, looking down over my shoulder. I opened my mouth to shut him up, but the cop had something to say.

"Not no more he ain't. Richie, when Dom shows up, I'll tell him you was here. You be around all day?" said the large Irish.

"We'll be here. We have to teach all morning," said Brzenk, doing a lousy job of lip buttoning.

"I'll be in my lab. Dom knows where to find me," I said.

The cop turned and left us.

It was now just us three: Me, Brzenk and the stiff stiff.

A fly flew down, landed on the late King's chin, worked its way down, searching for a fresh drink.

It was the fly that did it.

Brzenk went from green to greener.

"I don't feel so good," he said, turning toward me.

I kept him turning, hoping to get him facing the curb. I'd got him halfway when he let loose.

The first projectile of puke made the street. I had him by the arm. The tall Princeton Ph. D. leaned into me and fired what was left of his breakfast onto my bare leg.

Brzenk fell away from me to his knees. On the dirty pavement, he knelt and heaved. This went on for some time. He must've gone to some bargain breakfast buffet in the neighborhood.

Finally, he was done. I helped him up, and he went again, this time onto my chest. It just goes to show you, you head out in Brooklyn in search of life verite, and the next minute you're covered in hot, chunky vomit.

"Sorry," said Brzenk, his voice hoarse.

"It's ok," I said, glad that I had a shower in my lab. Today, I'd need it.

"Can you walk?" I said.

"I think so," said Brzenk.

I got a slippery grip on his arm where he'd projectiled himself and started us in the direction of the college.

"This is what you told me about... really something... What do you suppose we'll have to do... Do you think we'll be questioned?" gasped Brzenk as I frog marched him away from the crime scene.

I walked us faster. Brzenk was still high as a kite even after the heaving. The sight of the dead man had worked on him like a pop of cocaine. His face was double flushed, one from puking, the other from excitement. The words tumbled out of him. Brzenk was still having something of a great time. Brzenk had a lot coming to him.

Even though this wasn't the best of times, I hit him with the truth.

"Look, Walt, this is no game. You better go clean up, then get in your office, sit down, clear your mind, check your files, make some notes about you and Gomez and how you got along. The cops'll have a shitload of questions and you better have some answers."

"I don't get what you're saying. Why would I have to take notes? Why are you telling me this?" said Brzenk as we reached the parking garage side door of the college.

I used my key, got us inside. Stopped. I talked slowly and clearly.

"Put two and two together. You're a professor. A student is found dead right next to the college. Ok, so far? So, as soon as the cops get their act together, they'll remember you blabbin' that Gomez wasn't just any student, but that he was one of your students. This startin' to add up for you?" I said, my eyes boring into Brzenk, trying to make an impression. I succeeded.

Brzenk got the point. The dawn of day finally broke in his mind. He'd been having fun, trailing after cops, seeing what happened on a Brooklyn street, having a high old time, like he was in an episode of Law and Order.

"You mean, someone might suspect me? I barely knew the boy. He said very little in my class. I had no trouble with him—"

"Ease off, Walt. No one's said you did anything. All's I'm telling you is that there's a dead student back there, and that he's one of ours. The cops are gonna want to know chapter and verse about him."

"And we'll be the ones to give it to them?"

"That'll be us."

We went inside the clean, quiet and cool college, which was a whole lot different from the shithole where some tidy killer had dumped "King" Gomez. We climbed the backstairs to avoid contact with any A.M., eager–to–learn students, of which there were not many.

Brzenk and I made our way up the stairs, he with his lips now securely buttoned, me huffing and puffing, using the steps to get my mind back in line.

The whole stairway was a really bright orange with shiny black metal railings, but the newly painted walls had already been re–decorated. Graffiti in big, black, bold letters slashed across the orange paint. Some of it, actually most of it, was students just having fun, but there was overwriting done by gangs. This was serious, the walls doubling as billboards, announcing whose head would get opened and for what reason. Third floor, fourth, Brzenk still silent and pukeless. Me, plunging upward.

One wall notice did catch my eye. It was right next to some filth out of a stand–up's routine, beside a few bits of wisdom from Howard and over a detailed drawing of a private part. I stopped stair–climbing, waited for Brzenk to come up to me.

"Why've you stopped?" he said in a curt tone.

I said nothing in reply. I pointed instead to a neatly printed sentence on the orange wall.

LIVE BETTER THRU CHEMISTRY–POISON DOC BUCCERONI

"Is it always like this?" said Brzenk.

"Naw. Usually you can't tell this place from Dartmouth, except on those days when we got life verite." I said, trying to lighten up Brzenk.

Brzenk didn't laugh. Tough crowd. We'd reached the sixth floor. Brzenk went toward his office. He didn't say goodbye. I headed for my lab.

I now walked slowly. This was turning out to be some day. Before I'd been shown the worked–over remains of one of my students, I'd been planning the speech I had to give to the faculty. I was a full professor from the main campus, on loan to this downtown branch, and a dean had tapped me to lie to the faculty about their job security. I'd told him that my major in college had been organic chemistry and that I'd opted not to minor in lying. This had all been said using my really deep, professorial voice. He'd repeated his request. I decided that maybe some jokes would be a good way to start my Power Point.

It was still early. I had a morning's worth of work ahead of me. My speech to the doomed faculty was now the least of my worries. I knew the 'King' had presented himself as a higher up in a Hispanic gang known as the Latin Monarchs. The King had the franchise to cram the college with crack, whack, sniff, ice, jolt, blast and the junk of the month. I had a line on him and was about to present my case to my old pal Detective Dom Mancini.

Someone'd beaten me to it.

# Chapter Two

My lab's my home away from home. Set up the way I like it. Neat and clean, which is what I was now. Showered. De—puked. Powdered. Hair slicked back. Three—piece made—for—me suit from Oversize. Inc. Power tie. Shiny shoes and sharp socks. I looked great, I woulda been a wow at Cornell.

The morning was winding down. It wouldn't be too long before the cops came calling about Edwin the late King. I took a seat behind my large oak desk.

My lab was wall to wall with enough chemicals to do in the better half of Bensonhurst. Heavy metals like lead and thallium and mercury were there, also cyanide crystals and arsenic. In the lab, I had scopolamine and even curare which was strictly legit and labeled d—tubocurarine.

But neither curare nor cyanide can fix a death smile on a face. Strychnine could do that. Strychnine's meant to kill rats. Nasty stuff. Sets off muscle spasms that take life right dead out. I'd researched strychnine. When Cleopatra was giving some thought to snuffing herself, she did a lot of experiments with poisons and one of them was strychnine. She gave some of it to a slave girl and watched what happened. That must've been something to see, muscle contractions so strong that vertebrae can crack, and when the squeezing was over, Nadina the Handmaiden's pretty puss had a grin of death set on it. You ask me, Marc Antony should've stayed the hell home, got on Caesar's good side, found himself a nice Italian girl who could make good pasta e fagioli.

King Gomez had gone out the hard way. Two minutes of hell.

Plus, the killer had left a signature. Pulling out the King's trademark gold tooth was part of the Brooklyn gang trade; someone had gotten a turn–on by watching a human being contract himself to death. So, on the loose, right next to where kindly old Doc Bucceroni was educating the sweaty masses was a sadistic, chemically proficient gangbanger.

I rocked back in my chair, and it was right then when my day got even worse. I know the lab like the back of my hand. One of the bottles had been moved, not a lot, not enough for most people to notice, but I wasn't most people.

In one of the locked glass cabinets in the lab was a bottle labeled brucine, which was like strychnine. Like, but not completely alike. Brucine's a poison to slip into a drink. It's odorless, tasteless, a perfect chemical weapon. I should know. Brucine had been the feature of last week's lecture attended by the King. He'd been taking notes like a house on fire.

Someone up to no good had been in here. Someone had gotten through a locked cabinet without breaking the glass. Terrific. I'd told Brzenk to check his dealings with the King in order to protect himself. Good advice from Saint Richie the Wise. I should have a heart to heart with myself. Sometimes, street dealers cut cocaine with strychnine, but brucine was something else again. If it turned out to be the reason for King Gomez's untimely departure, then the police would do a Q and A with the closest source for chemical weapons—the death cabinet of Professor Rich Bucceroni, Ph. D.

The phone rang, breaking into my train of thought, which had me on the way to Attica. A voice started right in talking with no greeting. It was my dean, an academic joke named D. Douglas Fenner, who I'd never gotten along with. One reason was that we both did work in kinda the same area, but, not to toot my own horn, I'd made some noise and was a full professor while, in terms of noise, Fenner was a mute, a noiseless nobody who'd never published much of anything of note and who was, at age sixty, still an associate professor. College teaching's like a monarchy, a few on top living the life of Reilley, and a lot at the bottom working as adjuncts and getting paid peanuts, and a good number like Fenner, stuck in the middle, going nowhere fast and getting no respect, especially from me.

The voice on the phone proceeded to dole out orders:

Come to my office.

In 30 minutes.

Police are here.

They want you.

Be on time.

Click.

All of this had come rapid fire with no chance for me to interject anything, boom boom boom, sounding like Tonto imitating Hemingway and then concluded with a hang–up, leaving me with a dead phone in my hand.

I put some pressure on the inanimate object in my mitt like it was Fenner's skinny neck. Fenner was one swell sweetheart: no class, no manners, no publications, no nothing—that's probably why he made Dean.

The cops were on the premises.

Great.

And they wanted to talk to me.

Shit.

Rain ticked against the window, I hadn't noticed the change in weather. I'd been too busy taking care of business by finding murder weapons. I stopped throttling the phone and went over and looked down at the dirty street six floors below. So much for a nice day. Clouds had rolled in, darkening the world, making Brooklyn look gray and nasty.

A river of decay ran right up to the college, and the pièce de résistance was the corner street which featured broken bottles, butts, paper, plastic, potholes, condoms, crap, puke, blood and, today, one stone dead student/crackpusher.

"The rotten core of the Big Apple."

This line I said aloud. A sharp metaphor. World class. I have a way with words. The Dante of Dekalb Avenue, that's me.

I look over at my well–ordered, everything in its place desk, which had next to it a metal filing cabinet with years of work inside it. Lots of work, good stuff. Added all up, they had given me something of a reputation, maybe not Stanford quality, but still it was significant. There were dozens of files, all in manila folders. Also, inside another cabinet, put away, hidden behind lock and key, was a clipping from the TIMES. A front page item. Carmella Bucceroni, aged forty–two and her son Richard Jr. aged six. Pushed from an IRT platform into the path of an incoming train. Killed on the spot. No witnesses had come forward about the pushings. In another folder was a map, photo–reduced, of the subway station. There were also lots of pictures, taken of crowds, standing, waiting for a train to arrive. That was my hobby. Riding the trains at night, trying to get a line on who did it. A waste of my time. Not a chance in a million I would ever find the bastard.

It's one hell of a world. My wife had been a sweetheart, my son a marshmallow. Both of them nice, never a bad word for anyone.

It'd been a day just like this. Rain coming in. My wife had gone with my boy to do some shopping for his first day at school. I should've been with them. I would've driven them, but I was elsewhere, ignoring the Seventh Commandment, sex trolling, ugly bumping with one of my fellow professors.

When I got home after an afternoon of sinning, my old pal, Dom Mancini the cop, was there. Bad news, Richie. Pushed off a platform. Run over. I had to go and identify what was left of them. Hardest thing I ever did. My wife was all ripped up. Other people in the room saw her. With no clothes on. The little guy had been underneath her when they fell on the track. The emergency crew had some trouble separating the parts; some of my son was mixed in with my wife. A mess. Dead because some piece of shit punk got a rush seeing someone torn apart by a subway car. What a world. The good get it; the bad get their kicks.

All of this rolled through my mind, which was strictly doing me little good in preparing to meet cops, who would be after my ass. I spend too much time thinking about this. Thinking and rationalizing are bullshit. If I'd kept my dick in my pants and been where I was supposed to be, then all of this wouldn't've happened.

My mind needed some attention, so I focused on getting out of the dismal past, coming to the dismal present, which, at this moment, wasn't exactly a bowl of cherries. Death on my doorstep I need like John Gotti had needed wiretaps.

Someone came into the student part of the lab, which was set up for classwork. I was sure I'd locked the door. My lab held the chemicals I used in my research. I keep everything under lock and key.

"Hey, Richie, you back there?" said a gruff voice, which I recognized. It was ok; I'd given a key to this person.

"Yeah, come on back," I said.

A man walked through the student lab into my lab and over to me. A short, wiry man with slicked back, black hair who looked liked he needed a second shave. The man's suit was on the wrinkled side. From under black eyebrows, two cold, dark eyes fixed on me, no blinking, the gaze steady, eyes which had seen a lot of the world's troubles. Not a big man, but not someone to cross. He'd always been like that. Detective Dominick Mancini and Professor "Richard" Bucceroni went back a long ways to when we were on the street together in Bensonhurst. Back then we had not a clue as to where we would go in life. We'd both come a long way from Eighteenth Avenue.

"You're here about the guy outside, right?"

"Yeah, you got troubles," said Mancini, his voice rough, scratchy, like someone who smoked too much.

"I know, I saw him. Deader than Joey Gallo."

Mancini lit a short, thick, maduro cigar without asking, something which could've blown us both to kingdom come if the gas had been on. He sat down across from me.

"The patrol cop told me you was out there. Why?"

"I get here early. Another professor and I saw something going on in the street, so we went for a look–see. We got an eyeful. He couldn't take it and..."

"Yeah, well, you're gonna get an earful in about fifteen minute' cause I got to question you upstairs"

"Just me?"

"Naw, I gotta do all the professors who had the spic in class. I've been with your boss, an old fuck named Fenner. Dr. D. Douglas Fenner he calls himself, like I give a shit about what he calls himself. So, I been goin' through his files, something which he don't like me doin' a whole lot," said Mancini, blowing smoke my way.

"Medical examiner see him yet?"

"He's workin' on him now."

"I think I know what he'll find."

"Oh yeah? One look and already you know what killed him?" Dom blew more smoke my way across the desk. It was not the best of cigars he was puffing on and polluting my lab with. The stogie must've set him back thirty, maybe forty cents, if that.

"Hey, I'm a genius, what else is new?" I said, lightening the mood, trying to cover my nervousness.

"So, ok, Einstein, let's hear it."

"That ear to ear grin and his bein' rock stiff came about 'cause of poison, and this could be it," I said, moving while I talked, taking down the strychnine and setting it on the desk. It was a small bottle. It didn't look like a killer.

"What's that?"

"Strychnine," I said, repeating the name so that Dom could copy it into his notepad, "It's rat poison..."

"Why the fuck some clown take rat poison?" interrupted Dom, looking closely at me.

"Someone might cut cocaine with it. Gomez was a pusher. Maybe he was a user too. He'd snort it up and he'd be ass deep in trouble quick and no way out."

"Strychnine in the cocaine. I'll tell that to the M.E. He'll appreciate the tip. He likes for life to be simple."

"If he wants it complex, I've got that too."

"Oh yeah?"

"Yeah, it could be this," I said, walking over to another bottle on the shelf, which I tapped with one of my large fingers.

"What's that?"

"Brucine. Nasty stuff, have to be careful how you handle it. I wrote a paper about it three years ago. Remember? I showed it to you. This stuff is tasteless, you could slip it into booze and the unsuspecting would drink it right down. I'm missing some..."

"Hey, Richie!" Dom cut in, "Don't say shit like that upstairs. Me, I know you for Mr. Fuckin' Honor Bright and, yeah, I remember you showin' me your fuckin' paper, so I think you're a big cheese, but my partner who don't you from Adam, he 'll see you as just another jerkoff professor. You give him an opening like that and he'll have your balls. Look, as long as you don't shoot off your mouth, you'll be ok..."

"Some fuckface sayin' I'm not ok?" I said, feeling my temper letting loose. I'd had it with all of this, first tossing about in the past about my family and then being about to be hot seated.

"Wow, Richie, cool down! No one's said fuckin' nothin'. Yet. I'm here to help you, ok?" I shut up, put my hot Italian temper back in its cage. Dom was right, he was sticking his neck out giving me this head's up.

"Look Richie, down here you're a bigshot professor, and everybody shuts the fuck up when you open your mouth, but upstairs, with me and my partner, you're just somebody who had somethin' to do with a dead tamale eater. Upstairs, I'm gonna treat you like everybody else, then..."

"You mean I'm gonna get your hardass treatment?"

"Bingo! See you ain't so stupid after all. You're gonna sit there and take it like a good boy. When this investigation gets goin' then, you and me, we'll have a private, just us, talk. I'm gonna have trouble gettin' anything out of these professors. A bunch of prima donnas if ever I saw one. Already your dean, this Fenner guy, is resistin' my lookin' over the files he has on all of you. So, what I want is for you to go upstairs, give me lots of yesses and nos, don't do no showing off, and then afterward you help me get a line on this place."

The door opened. In walked my lab assistant and my student intern.

Mancini stopped talking. His eyes locked onto my lab assistant. That was normal, everyone gave her a good, long look, until they saw all of her face.

Candy Dwyer smiled at me. She had long, full blonde hair, a golden tan and pink lipstick on full Kim Basinger lips, a comparison which shows how much I was her senior. The whole lab began to take on the scent of her great smelling perfume. She had her good side toward Dom.

The intern was the exact opposite of Candy Dwyer, but Nikki Nateal was also a knockout. Nikki was short and black and dressed in tight, ripped at the knees black jeans, with a black tee–shirt knotted above her navel. Her glossy black hair was pulled back and tucked under a black bandanna, making her look like Li'l Kim with even more attitude.

Both women carried purses. Inside Candy's was a .38 Smith and Wesson while Nikki had a Ruger .22, which was just right for her small hand. Where she'd gotten hold of it, I could only guess; its owner was probably decaying in the trunk of a '76 Buick in a back street in Fort Greene. The two women were two beauties, but they were also deadly and well equipped to take care of themselves in the questionable parts of Brooklyn.

"Holy God! Now you got two. You in here alone with them every day?" said Mancini, stage whispering to me as Candy and Nikki got down to their day's work

"Every day," I said, smiling at Dom.

"Nice job you got," he said, talking to me but watching the two women bustling about. "Ok, I gotta go, see you in a minute. Hey, short and sweet answers, no professor bullshit; nothin' about that brucine, ok?"

I had planned to tell Mancini more about the late King's former career as a drug pusher, but his attitude had thrown me off, had made me think about what I was going to say in front of this other cop, who I didn't have an in with.

I went with Dom to the door. Candy and Nikki were back in the lab lining up the day's work.

"There's something you need to know," I said.

"Like what?" Mancini relit his cheap cigar, something which must've produced a pleasing taste in his mouth, he drew on it. I pointed to the NO SMOKING sign which was there to save lives, especially mine.

"That's what you want to tell me? You gonna make me sit in the corner?"

"The stiff was a pusher. Big time. I've been after him," I said, the words rushing out.

Dom said nothing. He dropped his cigar to the floor, squashed it, made work for the janitors.

"What you got?"

"Mostly two and two together stuff. He took my class. Really interested in the chemistry. Always there, never missed a class, on time, in the front row, taking notes. I talk about cocaine, do a lesson on crack..."

"This you keep the fuck to yourself!"

Mancini caught himself talking too loud, looked over at Candy and Nikki, lowered his voice.

"This you tell no one! Upstairs, you come with this shit and next you'll be uptown gettin' your ass reamed out."

"You want what I got or not?" I said, keeping a damper on my temper.

Mancini nodded, took out another cigar, motioned for me to step into the hall. We found a spot where we could talk. We stood close together. A student, or a dean, or a professor, would have to stop and stand by us to hear what we were saying. Clever on Dom's part. Privacy in the middle of a lot of coming and going.

"So tell me," he said, running his non–cigar hand through his black and gray hair.

"This is drug central down here, lots of fucked up kids, smoking it all over the place. There's money to be made, real money—this Gomez didn't dress like he was from a project," I said, rapid fire, trying to get it out before I was cut off and yelled at.

"And he took your class?" said Dom, calmly.

"Yes."

"Anything else?"

"I kept a record." From an inside coat pocket, I took a list and handed it to Mancini. It covered the times I'd seen Gomez dealing, the names of students, other dealers. It was pretty complete. It went back to the beginning of last term, which was when I'd gotten a handle on all of this.

Detective Mancini took the paper from me.

His dark eyes bore into me.

"Let's get perfectly straight on this. This is just between us. Just us," the words clear, the tone measured.

"A clam?"

"Strictly. The knockout know about this?" he said, motioning with his head back to the lab where Candy was setting it up for the students.

"No," I said quickly. Candy was one of my projects. She was someone I thought needed some protection. There was no need to have Dom get after her too. If I could, I'd keep Candy out of this mess. That was a good place for her to be.

"Good, keep it that way. Nothing to nobody but me," he said quietly.

Some students got close to us, talking, heading for the biology lab which was across the hall from where I set up shop.

"Thanks for this," said Mancini, stuffing my report into a side pocket of his really wrinkled jacket." See you upstairs."

I watched him go. Mancini's foul, illegal, cigar smoke trailed after him as he made a path through the swarms of students, not looking to the left or right, parting them, going his own way. They knew who he was. Students always know who the fuzz is. None of the students said anything to him or about him; they just got out of the way.

Dom was about it in terms of people I really trusted. The two of us went back a long way. At one time, as punks, we'd spent most of a day's twenty–four hours together. Gone after girls. Drunk our share of booze. Boosted cars. Rolled drunks. Gotten into fights. One in particular I remembered because I'd been knocked out cold. I'd taken on a huge Irish, three hundred plus pounds of Gaelic nastiness and I'd done ok at first. Bobbed and weaved and fought the giant like he should've been fought. Marciano would've been proud of me, taking big time shots on my elbows, shoulders, on the top of my hard head. Then I'd gotten cocky. Tried to follow up, in I went. Too close. The Irish sapped me. He'd waited for me to get within his range, pulled metal wrapped in leather from his back pocket and laid one on between the eyes. The world went black. I could still hear, but I couldn't see. I was on Queer Street, like Patterson after Johanson clipped him. Dom had stood over me, striking out with a blade, keeping the beast at bay. Dom had kicked me in the ribs to revive me.

"Come on, Richie, get up! Get up! We got work to do!"

The world was still fuzzy, but Dom's kicks brought me back, the darkness cleared. I could see a little bit. I shook my head to wipe out more of the mist, rolled close to the griffin, my razor out, grabbed an ankle, divided his Achilles into two distinct sections. Dom stepped in. Went to work. Dom carved up the basement. The westie wannabe was strictly a soprano after Dom was done with him.

I was damn glad that Dom was on my side. Brucine used to snuff a student; crack being dealt hand over fist at the college; and me, a chemistry professor who'd made a considerable career writing about how to do someone in with chemical weapons. Any other cop than Dom handling this case and I'd be in for the third degree, big time.

My mind was going every which way, glad that I'd given Dom what I had about Gomez, worried that Candy and I could get nailed.

# Chapter Three

The door to my lab opened and Nikki Nateal walked my way. In her hands was work to do. Library searches.

"Off to the library?" I said.

"She's workin' me hard," said Nikki in a soft voice, so soft that you had to lean into her to hear it, which was probably her purpose. She was in that respect like a co–ed from Bryn Mawr, only Nikki wasn't rich, white and spoiled.

"Good," I said. Candy made use of her intern and in the bargain Nikki learned a thing or two.

Nikki fixed her large, brown eyes on me. She was one of my gambles. Half into college and on the way to a straight life, half into a street gang known as the One Percents, which was as unstraight as could be. Nikki could go either way. I was investing some time in setting her on the good path. I expected a call from the Pope any day now to praise me for my largesse of heart, maybe call me in for a one–to–one audience.

My intern went down the hall and turned left. That was wrong. The stairs were to the right. I followed her, kept my distance, saw her walk into the office, without knocking, of Professor Ross McClure, English department. So much for a work ethic. Nikki Nateal was taking a sex break. "Mac" McClure had added new meaning to the term "office hour." Those English professors are like that. Horny bastards. It must be on account of their reading all those dirty books.

I decided to go to the fifth floor to see if young Walter Brzenk was heeding my advice. I do that a lot. Throw out advice, distribute wisdom, then check on the heed quotient.

Using the back stairs, I went down one flight, moving fast, in a less than good mood, dressed to kill, opened the door, stepped right into the middle of it. Seeing what was going down, I hit a red button which was supposed to alert the three hundred fifty pound security guard in the basement that something was amiss. His name was Lester 'Beef Patty' Norwood, and he spent most of the duty time working out co–eds on the large metal desk in his small, hot office. I hoped he was taking a break, maybe smoking a cigarette. The nicotine would make him alert. He'd need to be alert.

Ahead of me there was taking place an interdisciplinary, multi–cultural exchange between Ms. Rowanda "Sista" Simmons and Ms. Chiyon "Sandra" Sung. Their educational endeavor touched upon rhetoric, colonial history, anatomy, and karate.

The two fighters were ringed by students divided upon racial and ethnic lines. Young black males with gold teeth stood next to black females attired in classic rapbitch, tight black spandex, muscle tee–shirts and behind them, towering over everyone, stood J. P. Carlisle, the boyfriend of Nikki Nateal and the head of the One Percents. His dark eyes were fixed on his opposite number among the Asians, a slender, young fellow wearing a white dress shirt, slim black tie, black slacks tight at the ankle, and pointed black shoes who was on the college's roster under the name of James Kim but who was known about the place as Jimmy Fisheyes. Mr. Fisheyes was also at the back of his part of the crowd where he could stare down Mr. Carlisle. The Asian crowd was mainly composed of prepped out Asians, but there were other young men dressed in white and black like their leader. Fisheyes' gang was called the Seoul Brothers. These two had more or less a Mexican standoff at the college. It was best not to come between them. J. P. and Jimmy Fisheyes looked at nothing in the crowd or at the fight; they only had eyes for one another.

"Bitch," said Rowanda Simmons, doing some Sugar Ray side to side, feinting at the other girl, aiming at the eyes.

"Slut," said the small Korean girl, eyes wide, hands stiff, ready to strike.

"Slant," said Sista.

"Gorilla," said Sandra.

This was going quite well. I wished I had a tape recorder, get all of this down verbatim, send it to one of the colleges that want to call themselves "Diversity University." Better yet, hold an open house in my class where all of the tribes of Brooklyn were confined to a few square feet. Quite a sight to see, the students voluntarily sitting in a ghetto of their own making—Russians with Russians, Indians over here, Haitians over there, Asians up front, Puerto–Ricans at the sides, Italians in the middle, young Israel from the yeshiva in one clump, boys from boys high in another.

The melting pot?

Not quite.

Young Ms. Sung set her left foot, pivoted, came in fast, her right hand closed, a spinning back fist, well executed, Anderson Silva would've approved, La La Land in an instant if it landed.

Rowanda Simmons blocked the backfist with her own right hand, shifted weight, put a short, straight, from the shoulder stinging jab into Chiyon's nose. Blood spurted over the girls face. A whoop went up from the black sector, accompanied by some over the head, hand circling. I wondered if Arsenio would be interested in a tape of this, help him to make a comeback. Not likely, I'd have a better chance of impressing Dana White.

"No way karate gonna save your fuckin' yellow ass, you goin' down," said Rowanda, following up with a right cross, driving back the smaller girl.

The elevator door opened. Out stepped Beef Patty, pants on, fly open, exposing blue boxers with red whales painted on them. He grabbed the Korean girl from behind, scooping her up in one huge arm, lifting her off her feet. She scratched his cheek, drawing blood.

"Motthafuck!" said Mr. Patty, moving his large forearm under her chin, trying to choke her.

"Le' me go! Le' me go—" said the girl, the words trailing off as the chokehold set in.

"You goin' all right, your sweet li'l ass goin' outside!" gasped Beef Patty, wheezing out the words, pulling the wiggling, writhing girl with him back into the elevator.

The door closed. Good. Now it was just me and fifty students hell bent on attacking one another.

"Any you slants want a piece of me?" Rowanda said, sweating, her eyes sweeping the crowd.

I made a path through the Asian students, using my shoulders, coming face to face with them, ready to take on all comers.

"We have class now, Rowanda," I said in what I hoped sounded like a professor's voice. The words coming out, but fear was behind them.

"She fuckin' asked for it, Doc," said Rowanda.

I was close to her now, I could've pulled her away, back into the stairwell. Bad idea. Black students have a thing about white hands touching them; it was words which would get me out of this mess.

"Well she isn't going to give you a quiz."

"No lie, we gonna have a quiz?

"Italians never lie, it's part of our code," I said, smiling broadly, trying to be avuncular.

That got a laugh from the black half of the circle of potential violence. Rowanda smiled at me. Turned. Headed toward the elevator.

Her audience drifted away. Half of my problem left. I was rolling.

Jimmy Fisheyes said something rapid fire in Korean. The other half dispersed, leaving just three people in the hall. There was J. P. Carlisle, six feet four inches of black power who looked like he could run down a cheetah, break its neck, then eat it raw; there was Mr. James "Fisheyes" Kim who looked liked a cobra sizing up lunch; and then there was me, an aging, amiable, Italian chemist who'd lived nearly half a century and who wanted maybe another two or three decades before he had to check in upstairs. I would have to draw upon all of my extensive, professional, educational background and my considerable cultural knowledge to resolve this situation. I needed a wise saying to break the tension.

"So, now what?" I said. John Dewey would've loved me.

"This, this is a waste of time," said Jimmy Fisheyes, whose voice was deep, ignoring me, talked to J. P.

"I can't always control them. They are the ninety–nine percent; I am the other," said J. P., in a rumbling, really deep voice.

"I cannot control Mr. Pang next door. He is my elder; I must respect him," said Fisheyes.

"I can. I don't." said J. P.

Jimmy Fisheyes smiled a deadly, I can kill you smile, then backed slowly away. J. P. left in the opposite direction.

I was all alone.

It was good to be alone.

"I am all alone, and it is good," I said aloud, sounding like Hemingway on a bad day, this done to help my pounding heart back down from triple digits, which threatened to split my chest.

"You're not alone," said a clear voice from right behind me.

It was Candy Dwyer, standing next to the doorway for the stairs, her hand still in her purse where she kept her pistol. She turned, took her right hand out of her purse, opened the door, held it open for me, taking pity on the terrified.

"I bet they don't start the day this way at Brown," I said over my shoulder as I scurried back to the safety of my non gang–infested office.

# Chapter Four

"How'd you know there was a fight?" I said to Candy, now that we were safe and sound back in my lab, which was full of chemical weapons.

"You had the alarm wired into here, remember?" she said, smiling, showing bright, white, even teeth.

"Oh yeah," I said, like I still had a functioning memory.

Growing old is great. Hair loss, waist flab, eye spots, "speak louder" please, all of this along with recall brain cells dying by the dozen.

Candy went back to work, setting the day's lab experiments, doing them all just right, careful, precise—she had a good pair of hands. Looking at her, too many men might think that her blonde head was full of fluff. They'd be wrong. She'd finish her Ph. D. this year. She had a good shot at being a big shot.

I stopped musing about Candy's fabulous future and came back to considering my less than promising present.

I was getting too old for what just went down. Today, Rowanda had done what I'd asked. Tomorrow, she might stick me just to see the blood trickle down a white body.

"There's been trouble down here. King Gomez was found dead. I saw him up close, right next to the building," I said, to Candy, drawing her into it, forgetting what I'd promised Dom about keeping her out of it.

She stopped her work.

"Bad?"

"Dom Mancini's on the case."

Candy's light grey eyes locked on to me. She'd removed her safety googles. The lights were on in the lab. They lit up her bad side. I didn't look away.

"You're ahead of me. Gomez is dead, Mancini's down here. Fill me in," she said, speaking slowly, clearly.

"The King was snuffed. Someone poisoned him. His face told it all. I'd bet on it being strychnine or brucine that did the job. This is Dom's beat, so he came calling, so I gave him what I had about our number one pusher, and I told him what I thought had gone down. Also, I think someone got the brucine from in here," I said, speaking slowly, giving my report for the day.

Candy turned, walked away into my lab. I tagged along after her. She went right to where I kept my chemicals.

"You're saying the bottle has been moved?" she said, taking care as she picked it up, still wearing gloves.

"It's out of place and it's been opened. Whoever did it thought I wouldn't notice. Mistake on their part, Captain Queeg, he kept an eye on the strawberries."

"I'll inventory the whole lab. There may be more that's missing." She said.

"Good idea."

"We've got to watch Nikki," Candy said, putting down the brucine and turning to face me. She was not a short woman, so she didn't have to look up very far to get into my face.

I made a noise in my throat. Sub—vocalizing was a specialty of mine. Darwin could've made a pile of dough exhibiting me.

My face no doubt took on the aspect of a frown, for Candy wrinkled her brow.

"We've got to. She's like I used to be, she's half and half.

Candy, as usual, was right. One minute, Nikki Nateal was a streetcrazy, backing up J. P. Carlisle, in someone's face for dis'ing the One Percenters, the next she was a budding scientist, doing searches and right now, this instant, she was doing a desktop do with a forty—five year old professor of English who specialized in dialogical criticism relative to Victorian pronouncements about morality, none of which I really understood, but I did get that a married man should keep his noodle in his pants and not have office flings with what were basically kids.

"She was here off and on during the summer Maybe she set up shop, maybe the shop's still in operation," said Candy, continuing a line I didn't want to hear.

"So what happened to Gomez?"

"One, she killed him. Nikki made the brucine into a cocktail and got him to drink it. That's what your paper on it detailed. Two, he killed himself," said Candy, reminding me how involved in all of this I was.

"You just lost me."

"Do you know how skillful our Mr. Gomez was as a lab student?"

"You know about him, not me. Probably nothing special. He did well on the exam part of the course, he..."

"Up on his lab procedures?" said Candy, interrupting me.

"This a quiz?"

"No. It's just that someone of great wisdom once told me that all lab students should be robots. Gomez was at best an ok lab student, I know, I watched him, he was always in a hurry, so all that needed to happen was him to get careless with the brucine."

"I get old all of a sudden! Shitballs! Two minutes and already you're ahead of me in this. I better go and read over my own lecture notes." I said, starting to sweat.

"One sip was all he'd need. Absorption would kill him just as sure as if he'd drunk a killer cocktail," she said.

Candy was nearly on the money. Brucine had to be handled with kid gloves. Better yet with cast iron gloves. Touching it gave the poison access to the nerve network. Absorption might take a little longer than ingestion, but the result would be the same. A person's own muscles would put him/her/it out of the air business.

"But why was he handling it in the first place?" I said, running my hand through my hair.

"Who knows? These Monarchs are sado–power gang freaks. Brucine would've been a new weapon to Gomez, but he may have been just careless enough with it to poison himself. Look, Rich, this is pretty basic. Nikki and the King were on a collision course. Maybe the head of the monarchs was going to take out a One Percent just to send a message, to let them know that no one was going to stop the dealing down here. You tell any of this to Dom?" said Candy. She talked to me like an equal, which is what she was. Candy was sharp. I needed to listen to her.

"I just gave him a report, a list of the times I'd seen Gomez on the job and with whom. I also told him I would say nothing to you. He was here bright and early to help get me through the interview with his partner. Something which I'm about due for."

"They going to question me too?" she said, her voice taken down a notch.

"Probably."

Candy turned away from me, walked over to the window in my lab. The rain was coming in hard now; it beat against the window, did its best to clean up Brooklyn. I figured fifty days of hard rain could wash off Brooklyn's top layer of grime. Outside, someone was working in the rain to haul away King Gomez's rigid remains.

"You've got to watch yourself down here, you got to watch your step. This is just getting started, and we're right where we shouldn't be," I said, switching into avuncular mode.

She went quiet on me, leaning against the window sill, looking at me, no longer smiling.

I could hear what she wasn't saying, like how Dom Mancini might link her up with King Gomez, something he could do because Candy had also been a streetcrazy, doing guys, taking my class, turning my lab into a factory for a hot, of the moment drug. Candy had paid a price for trying to live in the fast line. A dealer had sent two thumb–busters to pay her a visit. They'd used a hot iron, leaving her with half a face. She wasn't easy to look at. The scars were deep. I'd paid for a plastic surgeon, but she still wore her hair combed over to hide her mutilated face. She'd come to work for me, gotten her life in line. She spent a good portion of her off–time looking for the thumb–busters. I pitied them if she ever found the scum.

"What should I say if I'm questioned?" said Candy, her voice even and calm.

"That he was one of our students, that he was in your lab section. Period. Take your grade book. Give Dom facts and figures. Nothing more."

"Dat's it ? Dat's all I should, like, you know, say, or what?" she said, deliberately mangling the King's English, breaking the tension that had been built up.

The way she spoke was an ongoing joke between us since at one time we'd both talked in basic Bensonhurst. When I went to college, I took a speech course with an old professor named Murray T. Lipschnitz, Ph. D. who'd drilled the 'dat's' out of me. I'd paid for Candy to take a tutoring class with the old fellow even though he was now retired. We both talked beautiful now. We could go to Princeton and order an egg cream and no one would know us from the natives.

"Yeah, talk just like that, tell 'em you're Rocky Balboa's kid sister, Babalou."

I looked at my watch.

"I'm late. I'm due in the dean's office. Fenner wants me."

"I bet he asked you real nice to come see him."

"Yeah, real nice, like calling his dog so he could beat it. I don't think he loves me. I may pee on his carpet."

"I get the feeling he doesn't love much of anyone. You be back here before class?"

"No, I'll go right to class after I'm finished with Fenner. I'll see you at six. You hold down the fort here."

"Yes sir," said Candy, executing a salute, then smiling at me.

She had gray eyes which seemed to change color. Sometimes they were dark gray, at times light gray. Candy was like that. She made men look more than once at her. It was just that when they looked too close they could see what had been done to her.

"You're a lippy kid. If you weren't the best, I'd fire you," I said.

She saluted again and this time clicked her heels. Then she delivered some more bad news.

"Oh, one other thing, lots of people know about what happened to the King," said Candy.

"Like who?"

"Mac stopped me in the hall and told me. He said some student told him."

"Why didn't you tell me this before?"

"You were talking, I was listening."

"Ok, I got to go. Fenner is waiting."

"Have fun. Don't kill him," said Candy, starting to work on the experiments again.

Leaving the lab, I walked briskly down the hall to the elevator. Ahead, waiting, I could see Brzenk, the new hire, presumably over this puking, talking with a big blond guy who wore khakis and a pink short–sleeve shirt, the kind with the little animal stitched on it. This was Dr. Ross McClure, the professor of English, Mac to his friend, of which I was one.

Mac's office hours "affair" with Nikki Nateal was not a wise move on his part. Nikki and her big boyfriend J. P. Carlisle were One Percenters, crusaders, seeking the grail of power for their people, which boiled down to their functioning like feudal warlords. The One Percenters and the late King's Latin Monarchs had the same pyramid structure, the elite on top, the subjects on the bottom, with the only difference being that the King turned on the kingdom while the One Percenters cleansed the borough of junk. The killing of Gomez had the trademarks of a One Percenter rubout; he sold dope to the ninety–nine percent of Nikki's race who had not yet seen the light. He, therefore, would be removed, be made into an emblem, then displayed for all to see. Sweat started at the back of my neck. Nikki would have to be watched. Mac had better watch himself. He had a reputation for preferring co–eds of color. Nikki was moving in on him. The college had a new sexual harassment policy which covered everything from the sex act itself to ogling, but all of that was for the real college at the main campus. Down here sexual harassment didn't really register on the crime meter, but the One Percenters had their own ideas and could make Mac mend his ways.

"Going to preach today, Richie?" said McClure.

"Yeah, at the First Church of Fenner," I said, laughing, knowing that Mac was busting my chops about my fancy, made for just little me suit. I didn't dress casual like most of the professors did, many looking like they were at no place special. I didn't get a Ph. D. to go around dressed like I was gonna play a round or two of golf. Of course, with my suit on and my tie and what not, I did look more than a little like Vinny "Two Bananas" Bimbano from Eighteenth Avenue; but what the hell.

The three of us took the elevator down to the fourth floor. Brzenk didn't say much more than "Hello." I figured he was probably lining up his legal defense, maybe thinking about hiring the best to represent him.

"The dean call you in, too?" said McClure.

"Yeah, he phoned, told me to show up el pronto," I said, using some Spanish lingo.

"I'm in after you," said Mac, "then it's Walt's turn. I guess they'll see everybody. It's all about Edwin Gomez. I heard you and Walt were out there, right?"

"On the spot. We got too good of a look at him," I said as we got off the elevator. Brzenk has his lip buttoned.

The three of us went down the hall and into an office which had DEAN D. DOUGLAS FENNER stamped on it in big, brass letters to let everyone know who was in control of this place. A secretary nodded at us, told us to sit down, then buzzed the dean.

The grilling that Dom Mancini had warned me about would take place in Fenner's private office, which was no shabby affair. Brzenk and Mac took seats like boys about to see the principal. The secretary, who was slightly younger than dirt and permanently crabby, told me, snippily, to go in.

I knocked on the office door, and it was quickly opened by someone nobody liked. This was Winston Wiant, a Ph. D. but not a professor. Wiant was a higher education officer, which meant he got to be present when Fenner fired someone for cause, or not.

Wiant was a weirdo. He had his black hair clipped short on one side but long on the other and long on top with the long half falling down on the short side. He was always pushing it off his forehead. Cold, dead, black, shark eyes shone out of a fish belly white face. Nosferetau of Nostrand Avenue was what Candy called this creep.

He looked at me like I was something in a Petri dish. He was not on my good guy list. I knew what list he had me on. "He's here. Bucceroni is finally here," said Wiant to whoever else was in the room, his voice high, squeaky, like fingernails scratching across a dry blackboard. This boy was a real charmer. I unclenched my fists, made a mental note to punch the walls in my own office for a half hour after this was over.

Dean D. Douglas Fenner peered over his bifocals at me as I walked into the room. Fenner was as tall as Walt Brzenk, only he was nearly sixty while the young professor was somewhere in his thirties. I didn't like anything about Fenner, including his hair, which was too long and made him look like that hippie lawyer William Kunstler. I hadn't liked anything I'd read about William Kunstler either.

"Ah, yes, Dr. Bucceroni, have a seat, have a seat, the officers here wish to ask you some questions," said Fenner, the eyes behind the glasses cold, unblinking, his face spreading into a smile, reminding me of snapshots I'd seen of Mengele, who was supposedly overly polite to his doomed patients.

Fenner sat down at a big, oak desk which was in front of a large, glass window, and Wiant took up a position next to him. A lamp threw light directly into my eyes, making it hard to see. Dom Mancini took over, smoking a cigar, and blowing some pollution my way. The other cop came over and stood by my side, in case I tried to break out. This wasn't going to be a lot of fun. I wondered if they had a rubber hose or maybe they'd shoot me full of a truth serum like scopolamine or maybe hotwire my gamunga.

I concentrated on Mancini's questions, keeping my answers short and sweet and to the point so that I wouldn't get my thick neck deep into trouble. I walled off the truth in my mind and focused on lying. I had lied to the dean at the main campus about not liking lying because when push comes to shove I can lie with the best of them, especially when someone is hell bent to hang me. In a situation like this, the truth has to be put into a special compartment in the mind. Then I pretend like that room is red hot. When I get close to the truth, I run away from the heat.

Mancini bored in. Had I known Mr. Edwin Gomez? For how long? In what capacity?

I steered clear of telling him how my eagle eye had been focused on the King for over a year. I gave Dom facts and stats strictly from my classroom knowledge. Dom said nothing about drugs. I said nothing about drugs. Drugs were not a topic for us. I wondered as I lied how much Fenner knew about the King. Probably not much, for Fenner didn't venture far from his plush office.Over Mancini's shoulder, I saw Fenner and Wiant staring at me. Two iceburgs. Himmler would've loved the two of them. They hated me, and were hoping I'd slip up. I decided to also punch the door in my office for a half hour.

Mancini kept at me. Had me go over my story, giving me a chance to slip up. I gave him a boatload of yes's and no's. The other cop put in his two cents. They persisted. The only good thing about all of this was that I wouldn't have to stand up and lie to the downtown faculty about their job security.

Right now that seemed a whole lot easier to do.

# Chapter Five

The door to the office of the distinguished Dean D. Douglas Fenner was opened for me. I stepped through, a thought came to me, I stopped in the doorway. The door hit me in my left shoulder.

"Umph!" exclaimed Winston Wiant, who'd tried to clip me in the heels in the process of closing the door. Instead, my short stop had resulted in the heavy door making contact with Wiant's thin, beaky nose.

I smiled, then continued. Maybe the day would turn out ok after all.

Inside, it hadn't gone so bad. Thanks to my pal Dom Mancini, they hadn't laid a glove on me. The questions had gone nowhere. All routine. No zeroing in about the possibility of strychnine or maybe brucine from the lab of yours truly making its unmerry way into the neuronal pathways of the late, scumbucket, Edwin "King" Gomez, no picking away at me until I fingered him as a crack pusher and spilled the beans as to my lab being a crack factory and my lab intern being into urban renewal.

Outside, Walt Brzenk had been joined by another professor, the two of them had worried looks set on their pusses. They had something to worry about. This downtown concrete college was provisional, and having a dead student found in the street with reaching distance of the school wasn't so good for public relations.

None of the professors here had tenure, including Fenner. He'd been forced to take this job. If this school went under he went with it.

A lot of the professors had shot themselves in the foot. Not long ago, about ten of them had gone marching across the main campus, chanting that the college president was a racist, fascist pig for his stance on immigration. Right out of 1968. Tell off the guy at the top. Eat it, prez. Right on. Times change. Today, professors get it in the neck for doing that. I'd bet good money he had a dossier on each of the protestors. I was mostly sure that the president would axe the whole crew and dump the building and its occupants.

In my humble opinion, most of the professors at the college were on their way to the academic ashheap. College teaching's pretty much a one shot deal. One chance for tenure and those who don't make it get a one way ticket to nowhereland and end up driving a cab telling the fares all about Hegel. Once professors are canned, they have about as much of a chance of finding another tenure track job as Tessio did of getting off the hook. And in the real job market? Who'd hire a professor? We're not really good for much of anything other than teaching. Most of us are hair splitters, guardhouse lawyers, pains in the ass really, not exactly what the world of work is interested in.

The professor next to Brzenk was an art historian named Annie Porter. She had curly red hair and eyes which seemed to be light green. She had on perfume which smelled like strawberries. I knew all too much about how she looked and how she smelled.

Annie showed me a picture she had just drawn. It was my head on the body of a bear, which was down in a pit and, from above, Fenner, Wiant and the two cops were throwing rocks at me. There was a sign next to the pit which read:

THE BEAST MUST BE WICKED TO DESERVE SUCH PAIN!

Mac looked over her shoulder at the picture.

"Browning. Only you got part of the line wrong. It's brute not beast. 'I never saw a brute I hated so/ he must be wicked to deserve such pain.'

"That's the way it goes."

"Yeah," I put in.

"Well, well, well, two intellectuals," and Annie, "and here I thought you boys were just all triceps."

"I am," I said.

"We is," said Mac.

She smiled at us, showing really white teeth which had a gap between the front two. When she smiled, like she was doing now, she flicked the tip of her tongue in the gap. I had seen her do that too many times for my own good.

Annie Porter was short, maybe five foot one, and she was dressed in a conservative grey suit. This was the complete opposite of her usual uniform of jeans and tee–shirts, which she dyed herself.

I now took a closer look at big Mac. His clothes weren't rumpled; he had no lipstick smears on his kisser; he looked like a normal professor; he didn't look like a guy who spent time in his office doing teen–age girls.

For each of the three, this getting fired business was a different story. Brzenk was a single guy, young, full of himself; he'd told me he had the right stuff to find another college teaching job, that he'd come here only because of some research he was doing in the city. Annie Porter was another story; in her forites, this job was the last chance for her. Art historians aren't highly employable. Not that she was a dope or anything. Some time ago, we'd co–published a paper on the chemistry of art forgery. She knew a thing or two about science.

"What was it like in there, Richie?" said Mac.

"Pretty intense. Mostly chronology. Where were you and when and why. That's the way they're doing it."

"Who's in there?" he asked.

"Two cops, plus Wiant, and the dean."

"I'm sure Dr. Wiant put you at ease from the onset," said Brzenk, standing up so that he had his back to Annie and Mac. He opened his eyes wide, then shifted them toward where Mac was now sitting with Annie. He did this three times. Maybe he was having a fit.

"Oh yeah. He looked at me like I was a specimen," I said.

"'The eyes that fix you in a formulated phrase/and when I am formulated, sprawling on a pin/pinned and wriggling on a wall.'

That's our boy Wiant, the poet must've had him in mind," said Mac from the couch.

"You're right about him, Mac, and the dean's even worse. A couple of weasels," I said. Mac laughed nervously.

Annie Porter was looking at me. Her eyes went cold, and her smile dropped off when I dumped on Fenner, but she said nothing.

"But there was nothing more than their asking you to explain where you were this morning?" said Mac.

"They'll want to know if you had Gomez in class and they'll want to know if you've been down here at night," I said.

Mac got up from the couch, walked over and took a drink from a fountain in the office.

Checking his watch, he said, "I better get in there or they'll send out the S.S."

Mac knocked on the dean's door and Wiant ushered him in.

I left Brzenk and Annie Porter behind and went to teach. I had with me no book, no notes—just chalk.

Rounding the corner on the way to the classroom, I saw J. P. Carlisle talking earnestly to an island black man who was a dead ringer for the late Bob Marley.

"What the fuck you doin'?" said J. P., his voice deep and nasty, a voice which meant business.

"Hey, mon, my brother, cut me a break!" whined the island black's voice, squeaking, edged by fear.

J. P. hit him in the throat with two large stiffened fingers, then grabbed a handful of locks and slammed the head of the smaller man into the wall. J. P. repeated this slamming twice more, with the last slam producing a bloody nose.

"This jus' a warning," said J. P. twisting the island black's face close to his own.

"I said this jus' a warning, you hear me! Answer me, motherfucka!" said J. P., his voice rising. To my mind, this was a tad unreasonable on J. P.'s part. A man with a potential ruptured larynx and a possible broken nose often experiences difficulties in articulation.

The island black bobbed his head in agreement to J. P.'s arguments. J. P. looked my way. He released the small, black, battered man who weaved away in the direction of the restroom. J. P. went into my class in order to receive his higher education from good old me.

J. P. was on the job. Other crack/dope dealers would move in on the late King's territory, missing nary a beat. Dope dealers wanted it all and wanted it right, like immediately, now. They would have their hands full with J. P., who was strictly business when it came to getting after whoever or whatever was pushing to the other ninety-nine percent of his own kind.

Looking over the classroom, I saw J. P. Carlisle sitting in the very back row, in his usual seat. The rest of the class was the same as always except that one of their classmates was on ice downtown. J. P. was wearing dark glasses, gold around his big neck, dressed all in black, six foot four, about the size of Lawrence Taylor. Those who think that selling drugs is going to be easy street to the big money should come here, have a little chitchat with J. P. I would introduce them, then sit back and watch.

J. P. smiled at me. I smiled back. J. P. was probably thinking that he could kick the ass of his aging white professor. Maybe he could. Then maybe not.

I took a deep breath before I started teaching. This was no picnic as a job. The main campus had pawned off remedial students to the downtown branch. The students were a problem. At age eighteen, they could not really read, write or figure at any acceptable grade level. They were about as well suited to college as I was to being a flamenco dancer. Teaching them was not a day at the beach.

This was my only halfway decent class. It was full of kids who'd flunked out of BU and had to slink back to Brooklyn. They were down here because their parents didn't want them around the house. In front of J. P. in the Italian village was a fatso of a white kid named Tommy Rosselli, dressed in baggy pants, a rock concert tee-shirt and sneakers which must've set him back a hundred bucks or so. His parents would be very surprised when Fat Tommy got busted or turned up dead. "Not my Tommy," they'd say or "He's a good boy.

Never did drugs. There must be some mistake." Parents like that kill me. They've got zero idea about the life their "boy" is living, and the reason is that they don't want to be bothered. They play Russian Roulette by ignoring their offspring and then their ass is amazed when they're down at the morgue getting their last earthly glimpse of Junior. I'll tell you this; I still had a son, I'd spend some time helping him out. Another kid was in the class's Jewish ghetto. He was also a straight ahead, dead on crack popper, dressed just like Rosselli, only his name was Aaron Weinstein. Prejudice doesn't exist for crack dealers. Christian or Jew, all would be sent on a one way trip to Whackoland.

I resisted the temptation to go through the motions of teaching, to flip on the automatic professor pilot, make like a toll–taker at the Verrazano bridge, do the routine, mark time until I could collect my paycheck. The students were not wholly interested in what I was saying, like, ya know, science is not my thing, so why can't I take my major classes and skip this bullshit.

I could've given them what they wanted, which was an easy to follow slowly paced lecture, which I would test them on with an exam that a gerbil could ace. The only student other than J. P. who was really paying attention was a Spanish kid named Peter Ramos, dressed in a white shirt and tie, hard–working, a straight arrow, the mirror opposite of the late King Gomez. A nice, black girl named Lystra Morris was another hard–worker. Both of them would write down all that I said; they might even ask me a question.

The rest of the class was sleepers, back row talkers, POST readers and one Asian girl doing her long nails. They said nothing; they queried me not; they just sat there, waiting me out, doing time, like they were serving thirty days for disorderly conduct.

I took a chance. I asked a question.

I got an answer.

"I dunno."

I worked a problem on the board. I instructed a student in the front row to copy the procedure into her notes.

"I forget my pen."

I gave the student a pen.

I asked a student to read from the text.

"I forgot my book."

I gave the student a book.

I bore on in splendid isolation.

The class ended and I waited for the next class to arrive. This would be remedial math. This would not be fun.

The students arrived in different degrees of lateness: somewhat late, really late, overdue, not on time, coming for a cameo. Those there were bookless, paperless and minus pencil, calculator, and initiative. This was the class that Rowanda Simmons "attended." It'd been Candy's idea to give quizzes, and it was that handle I'd used to deter Rowanda from a further maiming of her Asian counterpart.

Twenty–five sets of eyes stared at me, radiating hostility, hating me for making a big deal of adding, subtracting, and fractions, which in Taiwan would've been mastered in the fourth grade.

The class got restless after the quiz as I worked the problems for them on the board. Most of them were hungry and some of them were between hits of some type of foreign substance. I was illustrating for them the way to determine area and I happened to mention that Manhattan was an island.

"Say what," said a tall, skinny black kid named Barry "Three Balls" Ashby. "Three Balls" had a four inch flattop and made use of his time in class asking girls around him for a blow job, this done when he wasn't reciting some rapcrap to a pal next to him in the black sector.

"Manhattan's an island," I repeated, unaware of where this discussion was heading.

"What kinda island?" said Three Balls.

"Land in the middle of water, that kind of island." I said, smiling a sickly smile.

Three Balls paused for a moment, thinking; I could hear the rusty gears turning.

"Yeah? It an island, why it don't float away?"

I searched my rich storehouse of teaching techniques. I selected levity.

"The bridges hold it back. Also the tunnels. If Manhattan starts to move out to sea, they stop it."

"Hey doc, you think I'm dumb?"

"What is thirty–six divided by four?"

"Eight."

I went back to teaching what I was supposed to be teaching, zipping my lip about geography.

Rowanda Simmons got up and left. I didn't stop her; I felt like joining her. She was on her way to the restroom. It was time for her to take a hit of something bad.

The class wore on. Minutes seemed like hours. I kept on talking to myself, providing all of the enthusiasm, keeping them on task, staying the course—getting nowhere fast.

The students asked no questions. They talked among themselves; they stared blankly out the window. I knew what this type of behavior would get them; I knew where they'd end up. I'd run across them, out in the bottom of the barrel in the workforce, behind the counter at Blimpie's, searching for someone to blame. They'd greet me, some job, huh? Life sucks, Doc, know what I mean?

"Yeah," I'd say, "know what you mean, make that two large fries with my cheese and bacon burgers."

Finally, I was onto the last problem. The door opened.

"Doc, come quick! Someone cut Rowanda!"

The class stampeded to the door, making it impossible for me to exit. I waited my turn while maybe one of my students bled out, then followed the class down the hall. On three of the five classrooms I passed were posted notices on the doors announcing that classes were cancelled for Monday. The college allowed ten such days a year. After one hundred sixty were accumulated, they died with the school year, so the other professors were out ten times a year, on either Monday or Friday. I never missed a day. Richie the Reliable, that's me. I was expecting my good conduct medal in the mail any day now.

Outside the girl's restroom was a crowd of students. They were in my way.

A loud, deep voice said: "Get the fuck outta the professor's way!" J. P. Carlisle. Like magic, a path opened up for me. The students let me in. If they could've seen what was inside, they would've been glad to let me through.

Rowanda "Sista" Simmons had been tied by the neck to one of the stall doors. Her toes were barely touching the ground. Every time she tried to put her feet flat on the floor, she was choked by a silver chain around her neck. Her right hand was covered with blood. I hit the alarm button to alert Beef Patty.

"Put these on," said a voice close to me.

Candy had come into the restroom. I took the rubber gloves she was offering. With them on, I lifted Rowanda, and Candy removed the chain. That gave the girl some oxygen. She used it.

"Fuckin' bastards cut me! Where my finger?"

I lowered her to the ground. Candy worked a tourniquet onto the girl's hand.

"What goin' on, Doc?" said Beef Patty from the doorway.

"Get EMS, Lester, she's lost a lot of blood."

"Already called 'em. they on the way. God Damn!" Beef Patty's epithet preceded his announcing of a discovery. "Look here, Doc! Here her finger!"

It had been a neat job. Sista's index finger had been severed at a joint.

"She's going under," said Candy, who was closest to the girl's head. Candy was wearing a white lab jacket which was now spotted with red.

"Let me in there," said a new voice. I recognized it as belonging to the woman who headed EHS at the college. She got a lot of business.

Candy and I moved out of the way. This was a job for professionals, not well—meaning professors.

Outside, the hall was full of noise.

"Get your asses back!" roared Beef Patty, who made himself into a human wave and moved the students away from the restroom. Candy and I walked quickly back to our lab.

"Seoul Brothers?" she said as soon as we were safe and sound inside."Looks that way," I said, going to the sink at the back of the lab, turning on the tap, taking off the outer layer of blood, then stripping off the rubber gloves. My fancy suit would need a thorough dry–cleaning.

"Jimmy Fisheyes wasted no time," said Candy, who also cleaned up.

"This was a great opportunity for him. All the other Koreans saw Chiyon get her lunch handed to her. He got even for all of them. This'll gain respect for his gang."

"He put a new 'slant' on things," said Candy, continuing her turn at the sink.

"Good one, make sure you write that down. We'll send it to Letterman," I said.

"So, other than that, how was class?" asked Candy, removing her red and white lab jacket.

"Three Balls doesn't know that Manhattan is an island."

"Three Balls doesn't know what an island is."

"That's probably true."

"See what happens when you ask culturally biased questions?"

"I see."

"How'd your meeting with our esteemed dean go?"

"Swell. He and Wiant were very kind and sweet."

"I bet they were."

"They call you?"

"No," said Candy, her tone changing.

"Good. Don't volunteer. It's not an experience to pursue," I said, watching as she started to clean up her own work. Gas/mass. TLC. Candy was the real deal when it came to doing science.

"You about done?"

"Yes. Go look in your lab. Dr. Brzenk brought you a message."

"Brought me? He have a problem with the phone?"

"See for yourself. It's on your desk. You'll like it."

On the desk was a letter with my name typed on it. The letter was sealed, also taped, and as an afterthought Brzenk had stapled the edges. I took it back to Candy.

"You open this?"

"Yes."

"Good girl. Notice any white powder on your fingers?"

She laughed.

"He say anything when he dropped it off?"

"He just asked me about ten times when you'd be back. He followed that up with 'This is just for Dr. Bucceroni,' which I took to mean as 'keep your mitts off, kiddo.'"

"Then he left, then you opened it, read it and re–fixed it."

"Correct."

"What would I do without you?"

"So he's playing cop," I said, reading the letter, after ripping it open and snagging myself on one of the staples.

The letter went like this:

Rich, FYI. I've done some work. Maria Perez, the girlfriend of you know who is involved with a professor!! Call me. I've got more to do on this today. Call me at home. 780–5199.WB.

"He's Sam Spading it," said Candy.

"Christ, this from Walt Brzenk. His idea of detective work is who killed Oedipus's old man."

"And he said nothing about Gomez and drugs?"

"No, he thinks he's got a hot tip because he's found out about professors and students getting it on."

"He's got a lot to learn," said Candy.

"Yeah, he does. Let's just hope he doesn't get his throat slit in the process. He said nothing else?"

"All that he did was to go to the fridge and take his running bottle."

"Why did he do that? That's for Sunday."

"He just took the bottle. He must've been going to run. Which is what I have to do now," she said, glancing at her watch.

"Be careful, the streets'll be worse for a while. One killing seems to give the creeps ideas, sets off the border liners. Anything from your inventory?"

"Someone's been in here. I've changed the locks on the cabinets and the door. Here's your new key," she said.

"Who made these?"

"The janitor. He got a blank from the dean's office."

"Anything other than the brucine suspicious?"

"Someone was cooking crack. Probably students."

"Let's hope the key switch slows them down. Where you going?" I asked.

"Dinner. I'm meeting Jim Doyle. You know him. He works at the police lab."

"You gonna tell me why you're meeting him?"

"I want to see Gomez's autopsy report."

"That makes two of us."

"I've got a lot of other questions for him about the work we're doing for them, some back cases; eight to five he'll tell me about the King without my asking. If not, I'll fill him up with Harp, then ply him."

"I don't want you to do this."

Candy said nothing, putting away the drugs she'd been using, locking her cabinet.

"You're out of this. Stay out."

"Are you in?"

"Yeah."

"Then so am I."

"I thought I was the voice of authority around here."

"Who'll handle this if I don't?"

"Dom. He's in charge."

"Dom's a drunk."

"But not nearly as bad as he used to be. This last year he'd gotten almost back in line."

"Someone once told me that words like 'nearly' were just bullshit, that there was either 'was' or 'wasn't...'"

"Look Candy, this is close to home. This is going to be bad. This use of brucine, that means a creep is out there."

"'Facts before theory.' That's another statement of wisdom from someone I respect. Right now, we don't know up from down. Right now, for all we know Gomez OD'd on some of his own almost pure."

"This is probably a turf war between the One Percenters and the Seoul Brothers, we don't want to..."

"'Probably' means nothing. Let's find out what actually happened." She said, then checked her watch again.

"I'm late. Got to go. If I find out something I'll call you on your cell."

With that, she left, and the lab became dead quiet. All that remained of Candy was the scent of her great–smelling perfume.

# Chapter Six

In my own lab, I got to work on a set of student notebooks. I'd
have to grade them before I could do my own work. This was
part of what the city paid me to do. After five minutes, I moved the
notebooks to the back of the desk and stared at them for another
minute or so. I divided them into three piles. There were still a lot
of them to grade.

I phoned Walt Brzenk. No answer. His tape was on. I wanted
to tell Brzenk to take a cold shower, down six or seven Xanax,
watch a dirty movie, or do anything but free–lance detective work
in Brooklyn, at night. Instead, I told him I'd be there later in the
evening.

"Rich, you here?"

The voice was Annie Porter's. She was in the student lab. I
wondered how she had gotten inside. Candy had left, closing the
door behind her. The lock had been changed.

Annie Porter came over to my desk. She smiled at me. I sort of
smiled back. I didn't like her getting in here—loose ends bother
me.

"You busy?" she said.

"No, just grading the notebooks. Not too bad. The semester's
about over. They're not so bad."

"Doesn't Candy do those?"

"She's not here."

"Gone for the day?"

"Yeah," I said, as I listened to her two questions.

Annie sat down across from me. "So, Rich, what do you think the police will do now?"

"More of the same."

"You mean we'll be questioned again?"

"Yeah."

"Doug told me I wouldn't be questioned again."

Warning bells rang in my ears, making hearing difficult. "Doug" was Dean D. Douglas Fenner. The dean and I were not Rich and Doug to one another. I had other names for him, like scumball, piece of shit, turd whalloper, any of those, but not Doug.

"That's nice," I said, smiling at her, switching on my lying button.

"Yes, I didn't like the police, especially that little one. He wasn't very polite," said Annie, her green eyes fixed on me.

"That's the police for you," I said.

"Did you know Edwin very well?"

More questions from her, but what was their source?

"No."

"I did. This is a tragedy. His death from cocaine overdose illustrates the desperate lives led by the disenfranchised."

"That's true," I said, shaking my head, placing a look of sympathy on my meaty Italiano face. I said nothing about what I really knew about King Gomez and his adventures as a drug dealer. Annie Porter was here on a fishing expedition, and I could make a calculated guess as to who the head fisherman was. I had no intention of being reeled in.

"Do you know the little cop?"

"Not really. We went to the same grade school a long time ago," I said, polishing my lies.

"He wants to look at all of our records. He's really interested in Mac."

"He is?"

"You know, of course, that Mac does girls all the time in his office."

"He shouldn't do that," I said, looking concerned.

"He's doing Maria Perez. You know who she is, don't you?"

Her questions were becoming sharper, more focused, making lying more difficult.

I did know the little Hispanic girl. Maria Perez was the love interest of the late King, and one of his distributors. Her place of business was the girl's can.

Annie went on without me answering.

"Doug told the police about Mac. Doug said that he had knowledge of many other cases of Mac's sexual misconduct."

My blood pressure surged. This was like Fenner. He had dead meat on his doorstep, and he was fingering one of his own faculty for doing the deed. Not that I approved of Mac and his student screwing. Some time ago, I'd warned him, but he'd brushed me off, fed me some crap that he was just counseling them. Candy had told me that Mac was addicted to sex. I hadn't asked how she came by that assessment, but Fenner's accusations were out of left field. Fucking co—eds was pretty low on the moral meter, but it was a jump to start pinning murders on Mac.

"So, that's how it's going. Doug thinks the police will be interested in Mac primarily and not the rest of us. Doug thinks Mac's in big trouble."

"That's too bad."

"Not really. Mac's a sexist pig. He's used these girls as if they were his personal harem. He's getting what he deserves."

"Well, all of this will be settled one way or the other," I said, producing the most innocuous sentence I could.

"What do you think happened to Edwin?" said Annie, coming back on line with questions.

"No way of knowing. The cops didn't fill me in."

"But you know a lot about drugs. Do you think it was a cocaine overdose?"

"Probably. These disenfranchised kids, you know, they're sitting ducks for those up to no good."

"Rich, let me be straight with you. You know J. P. Carlisle and Nikki Nateal, right?"

"Yes."

"Doug thinks they're drug dealers. He told the little cop that's what they were."

I nearly laughed in her face, for Fenner, the fucking moron, had gotten it dead wrong. J. P. and the One Percenters were ass kicking after drug dealers. They were the exact opposite of what Fenner suspected. I now wanted Annie to get the fuck out of my lab and leave me alone. I needed to talk with Dom Mancini. It sounded like Fenner was burying the three of them. Mac had asked for trouble, J. P. could take care of himself, but Nikki was something else again. Nikki was someone on my help–out list.

"Nikki's ok..."

"Doug thinks she..."

"Maybe Doug is wrong.

"He's deeply concerned about this school and..."

"Look, Annie, Mac has no business doing what he does and J. P. I don't know anything about, but Nikki works in here—she's ok."

"She may have used your lab to make crack cocaine," said Annie, cutting to the chase.

"That another of Fenner's 'thoughts'?"

"Yes it is. He told the little cop that you were being duped. He said you'd had a bad time of it with your family. He said that you had a tendency to take on students who were lost causes and try to save them," said Annie, talking fast, using a lot of 'he saids' which unfortunately for me contained more than a little truth.

"I do my job," was all I could manage in retort.

"Rich, I know what you've been through, so does Doug; but we also know that this death has to do with drugs. Your lab could've been used to make crack, that's what Doug said."

I'd had enough of "Doug said."

"What's the rest of this conspiracy theory? That Mac is some kind of Fagin, mind fucking kids into doing what he wants? That Nikki's one of his 'gang?' That they sold bad dope to Gomez? That this is a drug war with a professor as one of the generals?" I said, finally losing my temper, which gets you strictly nowhere; any outburst with more than one "that" in it is just me ranting to myself.

"You're pretty close to what Doug told the police. I just wanted to fill you in; I'm on your side, you know," said Annie, keeping her cool, making me sound like a jerk.

"I'll check out my lab. Anything unusual, I'll get back to you and the dean," I lied.

"Do that," she said. But she wasn't done talking.

"We haven't seen much of one another for some time."

"I'm not the best company, Annie."

"You know my phone number, right?"

"Right."

Annie smiled her sexy smile at me, got up, came around the desk, leaned into me, kissed me on the cheek. She was close to me, like she had been before, her breath warm, the smell of her perfume, the red hair which was nice to push your face into. All of this set off my memory. Past and present got confused in my mind.

Annie straightened up, smiled again, left, leaving me behind with more bad thoughts. Her whole speech had sounded canned, like she'd been programmed to check me out. Fenner had sent her on a spy mission. Annie wasn't like she used to be. She was no longer a hippy–dippy, wearing DEAD tee shirts, talking about some new weed she'd come across. Deadheads don't get uptight about sex, and they don't change costumes from a Woodstock uniform to a buttoned down dean look. She even talked different, in whole sentences, no "like," no "you know," no "bummer," no "far out;" Annie was now strictly into deanspeak, which was short sentences and the use of questions and imperatives. She wasn't on my side. Annie was in Fenner's camp. Targets were being lined up. Some poor bastard was going to be selected as the guilty party. I needed to talk to someone I trusted. Only two people fit that bill—Dom was one, Candy was the other.

I returned to the marking of the lab notebooks, an activity which occupied me for maybe sixty seconds. Too much swirled around in my mind. I needed a diversion. Maybe I should go down to the fourth floor and throw Fenner and Wiant through the window. That'd be diverting. Instead, I decided to go and work out. Make my body healthy, get a grip on my brain, that'd be wiser than killing my boss and Vlad the Impaler's nephew. I thought well of myself for that decision.

In my office, I kept a workout bag, with shorts, shoes, top, Ben Gay ointment, socks, and a towel. The clothes were still wet from the running I'd done in the morning. That was nice. Go to my club to work out wearing sweated through clothes. Should be fun; I'd keep downwind of the other members. I took the workout bag, left the lab, used the backstairs, keeping my ear peeled for riots.

In the parking garage, Beef Patty was sitting in his office, gearing up for nightwatching—he double–shifted which meant he slept most of the second shift. I wondered how many co–eds he had scheduled for work outs on the slick surface of his silver desk, this he would do after he woke up.

The big man looked up from his desk to see me enter the garage.

"Where you goin', Doc?" he asked.

"To work out," I replied.

"It still rainin' out there."

"I got a raincoat."

"Gonna come back here?" he said.

"Yeah," I said.

"Gonna work late?"

"Yeah."

"Me too."

I knew all about Beef Patty's late night working. I made a mental note to use the door to the lobby when I came back. I didn't want to see any more evidence of sex at the Urban U.

I went out into the twilight streets of Brooklyn.

# Chapter Seven

The health club was a few blocks from the college. Not so bad at this hour. I had a fifty–fifty chance of making it without being set upon by street warriors. The rain helped; a slow drizzle, humid, unpleasant weather, poor working conditions for killers. It was windy; the breeze blew the drizzle into my eyes making it difficult to see what was coming my way.

The club itself was in a place where the young and up and coming came to worship themselves. I walked along, fighting to avoid letting my guard down. That was the problem with Brooklyn: there were no safe streets, there were just less dangerous streets. I could get jumped at any time out here in the world of gentrification as I could back at the college.

Outside the club, at the door, was the underclass, waiting just for me. Maybe I'd open my workout bag, smell him to death.

"Hey man, got some loose change?"

"For what?"

"The United Negro College Pizza Fund."

I laughed. That was a good one.

"You think that one up all by yourself?" I said.

"Yeah I did, big man. So you got anything for me?"

I gave the street Seinfeld five dollars.

Mac and I had talked about Brooklyn. He gave me his literary view, quoting books I'd never heard of. All I know is that there are two worlds. At the doorstep the losing class but inside was the leisure class, at ease, at a shrine of itself. We were supposed to be in a recession, but I could see little change in the dynamics of Brooklyn—violence, street peddlers and those with bucks—that pattern hadn't changed with the bad times.

Inside the club, upwardly mobiles were using the Nautilus machines and sneaking secret peeks at themselves in the many mirrors ringing the room, making sure their buns were getting steely and their triceps were being properly cut, while outside was some poor slob panhandling for a cheap meal. Disraeli—that's the guy Mac talked about. What was true today had always been true. Mac knew a thing or two. I just hoped he could wise up about where his dick was leading him.

In the clean, white locker room I changed into moist, red running shorts and a mostly wet tank top. Being in my gym bag all day had done wonders for their odor. I was very fragrant and would be a big hit with the yuppies who wiped down the machines after they'd used them and regarded smell as beneath them. I took out the tube of ointment and rubbed it into my calves and thighs. The Ben Gay complemented my sweaty clothes nicely. I smelled swell.

# Chapter Eight

Upstairs, a step class was going on at one end of the room. A tall, thin woman in a tiger striped outfit was putting about twenty people through their paces. She made a big deal out of it, acting like she was at Paris Island, a drill instructor getting in the faces of raw recruits. The young and the rich ate it up; tough exercises for tough people in a tough town. I'd lay nine to five that none of them have ever bent their backs in a real job in their whole life and that they couldn't make it halfway down a dark street in Brooklyn without getting roughed up. Being a hardass on Wall Street was one thing; getting into someone's face on Flatbush Avenue was another.

The rest of the club's room was laid out into Nautilus and free weights. Nautilus is bullshit, in my humble opinion. Sometimes, the old ways are the best. Lifting real weights with no pulleys was the real way to get strong. Isolating muscles sounds good in a brochure; in practice, I think it's hot air crapola.

I eased into my workout, stretching for a good fifteen minutes, big movements done slowly, no hurry, fat gives, muscle tears. I don't have a whole lot of fat. I used a life cycle, twenty more minutes, starting slow, working up to my heart's target range, keeping myself in air. Fat can't be burned without oxygen, so I worked to stay aerobic. I broke a good sweat before I started my routine. The new sweat mixed nicely with the mornings sweat. I was something to sense. My odor could bring down a gnat at ninety meters with no problem.

Today was an arm day. That's how I work out. Arms, legs, chest. Every other day. A procedure to keep me on the straight and narrow.

62

I used the bicep machine, ignoring the Nautilus instructions, loading it up with as much weight as possible, plate after plate, doing only a few reps. That just teased the muscles, so I headed for the free weights where I did curls with a bar standing up, curls with a bar seated, curls with barbells standing, then sitting, back to the Nautilus machine, the arms pumping up, my head clearing, back to the weights, more curls, veins popping out; no step exercise for me, this was vintage guido. No one from Eighteenth Avenue would call "stepping" exercise.

I had come here before with Annie Porter, who always wore a black leotard, which apparently had been created to show off her rear quarters. The designer must've known her onions because Annie always attracted some serious prolonged eyeball time. Annie hadn't discouraged the men from looking either. She'd spent a lot of time on floor exercises, sit–ups leg raises, plus considerable bending over, toe–touches, then arms over the head emphasizing that no bra was being worn. Next there was work on her hamstrings on the Nautilus, moving her calves up to her back, calling attention to the leotard, which was doing its best to cover her.

I'd teased Annie about her turning on the nine to five high–end business crowd since she was pretty much anti–capitalist, and she'd protested by asking whatever did I mean. Then she'd used the inside thigh machine which set off some major league oglinSweat was rolling off me now, making the machines slippery. I tried to wipe up after myself, but whoever followed me might do well to bring along a large sponge.

Finishing a final bicep set in which I lifted the machine's entire rack of weights, I noticed a young, well–put–together guy, dressed all in white, including a white headband. The man was next to the Nautilus, watching me, a smile on his face.

"You're Rich, aren't you?" said the man.

"Yeah," I managed because I was kinda out of breath.

"You used to come here with someone didn't you?" More questions. Everywhere I went people had questions for me.

"Yeah," I said, bracing myself for the man's continuing inquiry which was a none too subtle attempt to get a line on Annie.

"What was her name? I've forgotten."

"Vito" I said.

"Vito?" he said, furrowing his brow, his smile fading.

"Yeah, Vito Scopolamine," I said.

"Are we talking about the same person? You've come here with a woman, short, redhead, really in shape," he said, which showed that this was another leotard conquest by Annie.

"That's Vito. Short, red–headed, really well–built, a looker, but one of those, know what I mean, a Swedish slice job," I said, giving the man a friendly nudge in the short ribs. All–whitey seemed to tire of the conversation because he walked away without saying good–bye.

"Good–bye," I said. All of this I could see as funny now, but these workouts were how I got hooked up with Annie. Workout, then we'd talked, discovered how interesting we both were, then go to a bar, more talking, then a touch or two, the holding of a hand, then, finally, to her place and to her bed. So that'd been where I was, in the sack with Annie, getting it on, while my family, my real life, lay ripped up on a dirty subway track. My mind now forced these thoughts into the remote parts of my memory, but then I started to focus on my immediate consideration. This was the problem I was having, it took nothing to set off the memories of what a four–letter irresponsible jerk I'd been. There's a price paid for being a jerk. I was now paying mine.

I went back to working out. I was now messed up mentally, so I decided to do triceps and take tomorrow off. The same strategy applied. Warm up with the machine then pump with the free weights. It felt good to work out. Working out left me no time for thinking. That was good, but my mind switched the troubles with my past to my present difficulties. I'd dead–ended with my theory about King Gomez. Dom was right: treat this death like a guy fucking up with his own drugs—no more no less. There was no need to bring in elaborate musings about brucine or scenerios involving strychnine. Dom was handling this. He was a cop. He handled this all of the time. I was a bullshit free–lancer, a professor who didn't know up from down about killings in the real world. On paper, I was a crime solving wizard. In reality, I was a rank amateur. I checked my watch. I had an hour of lifting to do. Sixty minutes without thought.

# Chapter Nine

The rain was coming to an end in Brooklyn. I looked around. The water hadn't begun to touch the dirt. Which goes to show you that Mother Nature has no stature in the borough. I made my way carefully, eyes going every which way, back to the college. No one asked me for 'five dollah.' No one called into question my masculinity or screamed at me. One cabbie did make an observation about my knowledge of the traffic laws of Brooklyn. Since I was crossing with the green light, I thought about telling him to eat it, but, since I wanted to live and not die with tire tracks on my jaw, I said nothing. At the end of a block, two decked out hookers made a half–hearted attempt to convince me that, in their words, they were "double the price, but double the pleasure," but I just smiled and kept walking. They didn't call after me, so I must have looked normal.

The farther I walked the less civilized Brooklyn became. Around the workout club were cafes, shops, stores, decent people out and about, but, heading toward the college, the crowds thinned, no cafes, no boutique shops, no police guarding the best of western civilization. The streets got even dirtier. There was less light. There were more hyenas. It wasn't the type of place I would recommend for a pleasant evening stroll.

Approaching the college, I had the sidewalk largely to myself. Viewed from the outside, there were only lights on in two of the college's ten floors. Not much of anybody was around. No one was out and about. I began to having a respect for the wisdom of "no one."

It started to rain again. But I didn't start to run. In the first place, I was pretty tired from working out and the other was that running brings you up on trouble faster.

No students really stayed at the college at night. Night school was a hard sell. The risk of life was a high price to pay for a higher education.

I walked past a store, which was diagonal to the college. The store was open into the evening. That was good. That way, the muggers could be sure that their victims had just bought something and weren't empty–handed. Half of the street light were out. I had seen a cop there once, some time ago.

The farther I went, the closer I was coming to the dark and deserted street, the urban desert, where King Gomez had met his maker, or been introduced to the Devil.

At the deli on the corner, I bought a large, regular coffee. Not much business. Harry, the owner, was not around. One shabby old man was nursing a drink, stretching out how long this purchase could keep him off the streets. He was eyeballing a newspaper on the counter, which he was probably looking at as a blanket for the night. The old man smelled like he'd shit himself. The other diners, few though they were, had given him a wide berth. It was great; life in the best city on the planet, make a wrong turn, get on the wrong block, run into a mutant who'd cut a face for pocket change. Even if someone managed to live to a ripe old age, this was what was in store. A foul up in life, a fall down the job ladder and the end result was to wind up sleeping on the sidewalk wrapped in the sports section, Lupica's observations serving as a pillow. Maybe someone should come here, give the old guy some stimulus money.

I could feel Brooklyn putting on its night face. Those who'd spent the day pursuing an honest living were getting the hell away and heading home. Taking over the streets were the hunters, the night stalkers, the pushers and pimps, the type of scum who keep TV news crews in business. And out in all of that playing Lenny Briscoe was a Princeton Ph. D. who knew all there was to know about Sophocles and dead nothing about the streets. Dr. Walter

Brzenk was school smart but street stupid, just the type to get himself ass–deep in trouble.

I forgot about my decision to use the front door and went around the corner, walking wide, this done just in case some street slime was waiting to nail me. Ahead, it was dead dark; the rain had eased off again, leaving behind fog. I could see no more than fifteen feet ahead. Godzilla would be hiding there. If so, he had better watch himself; there were monsters in Brooklyn who would have his large lizard ass for lunch. Stepping into the doorway at the side of the college, I stepped on something.

"My space! Get the fuck away, motherfucka!" screamed a voice.

The ragman got a good look at me and decided to let me pass. I opened the door and quickly stepped inside. Beef Patty's office door was closed. The rag man pounded on the door. Apparently he'd decided to talk to me.

"Wha's that?" said Beef Patty, coming out of his office, buttoning his pants.

"A bum," I said.

"I take care of his ass," said the big man, moving past me. He threw open the door. I heard the ragman scream as Beef Patty took care of him.

Now, back inside the college, I used the backstairs, not the elevator, to my lab. Elevators are bad news. Once on one you can't get off, which is a polite way of saying you're trapped with whatever is with you.

I was now feeling less than sharp. Being back at the college had set off bad thoughts. Something was going down, I could feel it. The high from working out, the thoughtless activity, was wearing off and I was back to thinking about what the death of Gomez meant. I was in the middle of something, but I didn't know up from down. I was feeling slow and stupid. Brooklyn was no place to be stupid in. Greenwood cemetery was full of the stupid who hadn't seen something coming at them. I climbed the stairs, my fancy black shoes making the only noise. No one appeared to be down here but me. I was alone at night in a place where a killer was on the loose. Good thinking on my part. Maybe later I'd go to Bushwick, stand on top of a wrecked car, give a speech telling the locals that Malcolm X had been a fake–phoney–fraud, and see what happened. I climbed faster. There were too many questions for which I had no answers. Jimmy Fisheyes and J. P. Carlisle were cleansing society of its many ills. Had one of them taken out Gomez? Annie Porter had a key to my lab. How? The dean was nailing suspects for the cops. Mac was a suspect. Could Mac be part of this? And what about Nikki Nateal. And what about Candy? Did Fenner know about her? Nikki and Candy, two people I was trying to take care of. Father Bucceroni, the knight from east New York. That was me. The more I thought, the less I knew. Lots of questions and all of them whirling around me and my lab and a dead drug dealer who'd been squeezed to death.

# Chapter Ten

In the hallway outside my lab I stopped, listened. It was dead quiet. There's only one thing in Brooklyn worse than noise, and that's no noise. Silence wasn't golden in Brooklyn; it was the calm before the storm of violence.

The hair went up on the back of my thick neck and stayed up until I was in my lab with the door locked. I hung up my raincoat and put my gym bag back in the closet. The clothes were really something in terms of odor. Maybe I should wear my gym clothes all the time, protect myself with bacterial warfare.

I started to work, but not on the student notebooks. I needed to know just what I'd announced to the whole world about the killing qualities of strychnine and brucine. In back of my file were papers I'd forgotten about. There was one, on scopolamine, that I now remembered well, how I'd been working on it at home, putting on the finishing touches, hard to concentrate with little Rich playing with a friend, and I'd given Carmella a hard time about how I needed peace and quiet, went on and on, getting louder and louder about how important this work was. Gotten totally bent out of shape. Yelled at her, yelled at my kid, and his little friend, too. Jerk. Now, here was that paper published, reviewed, and now forgotten, at the very back of my file, a piece of work that even I no longer remembered; but I had my peace and quiet. Good for me. Jerk.

The paper on brucine was full of good ideas, written in a short, snappy style. Brucine is a resolving agent. It can denature alcohol and oils. It can also be deadly.

Clear as a bell. Easy for a killer to comprehend.

I closed my eyes, brought up a vision of the last time I'd taught this material. I'd done my road show. Linus Pauling brought in a bottle of brucine. Handled it carefully, explained how it was central to the separation of chemical mixtures into their component parts. Then I'd held up a wine glass, shown how it could be coated with brucine. First rate drama. Branagh, he was nothing compared to me. It was just that his acting never resulted in murder.

There was more bad news in my paper. A killer cocktail can be concocted by adding liquor to the glass to exploit the solubility of brucine in alcohol. There would be no smell, no taste and no way anyone could survive who gulped down the deadly drink. Not only was I clear, but, looking back on it now, I was planting suggestions, a great idea, giving the young citizens of Brooklyn detailed instruction about taking out the unwanted. I should get the Ohaus Award for my teaching of such stuff.

Nikki Nateal had audited my class for that lecture, in the front row, copying down everything I'd said. A good lecture, easy to follow. An easy to read paper. All of this in the file cabinet in my lab. Nikki, my lab assistant, had access to the paper and to the chemicals. Good for me, making life simple for a killer. I was probably on the short list in Stockholm.

Sweat formed on my forehead. There was more. And it was also trouble. The paper also had chapter and verse on strychnine. That I'd taught last week and in the back row, paying attention, taking notes, had been one Mr. J. P. Carlisle. Nikki and J. P., just the dynamic duo to receive clear instruction about chemical killing. I formed a theory. Nikki and J. P. snuffing Gomez for dealing drugs to the Ninety–Nine Percents. Nikki needing a weapon. Strychnine, maybe brucine: everything anyone ever wanted to know, courtesy of R. V. Bucceroni, the kindly consultant to chemical killers.

It was hot, humid; the rainy night was seeping its nastiness into the lab. The window had an air conditioner in it and I flipped it on. The room needed oxygen. I left the lab. Out in the dark hall, I could breathe, and I went for some water, past the elevators, on my way toward the office of Professor Ross McClure.

His office door opened.

I froze in the dark hallway, plastered my large self against the wall as an Asian girl came out of Mac's office and stopped ten feet away at the water fountain. She spent some time cleaning out her mouth, and, while she was performing that action, something black fell out of her purse onto the shiny, white floor. After she'd finished with her oral hygiene, she picked up her black panties from the white floor and moved toward the stairs at the other end of the hall. Mac was more predictable than the browns offense had been under Belechick.

She left. I took her place at the drinking fountain. Then I thought for a moment about what she'd just done, I nixed the idea of a refreshing drink of NYC water.

"Burning the midnight oil, huh, Richie?" The voice was right behind me.

It was Mac. I hadn't heard him come up behind me. I was asking for it. Wandering around down here, alone and about as aware as a deaf dumb and damned old dog. I was asking for it all right, and in Brooklyn such requests are usually granted.

"Jesus, Mac! Scared the shit out of me! Better watch myself or I'll get Japped."

"Japped? Good word Richie. We need more of that. Good old WWII racial slander."

"Hey, I try, you know, divide the races, maintain prejudice, that sort of thing." I said, trying to be funny, this done to hide my fear.

"A dirty job, but someone's got to do it," said Mac. He continued: "So, anymore news? Cops done with us?"

"Yeah, no one's around."

"You think they're done? They question us again?"

Those two questions weren't like Mac. Something in his voice, not his usual tone, this was nervous, uptight, but Dom had told me to keep what I knew under my hat. That's what I'd told Dom, except for telling everything under the sun to Candy and letting her get ass deep into the middle of this whole mess. I needed to work on following instructions given to me to the letter. Here was another chance. Mac had started off being a wise ass, now he was getting to what was really on his mind.

"Depends on whether our answers added up. That's the way they do it. Run through everyone once. Get the facts, then line the facts up. If they come back to us it'll be because they think there an inconsistency," I said.

"Hope they don't come back. I'm not big on inquisitions. What're you up to? Working on your Nobel?"

Mac was changing the subject, which was ok with me. I wasn't too good at fending off those I thought might be guilty of something.

"Going through my work, been reading something about brucine. It's an old paper of mine, you remember it," I said, being subtle, focusing on my excellent detective skills. The Continental Op would've loved me.

Mac's blue eyes fixed on me. He paused, said nothing for a few seconds, which seemed a long time.

"Sure, good stuff. You used to do a lot of stuff like that, didn't you? I've been grading papers. Like pounding sand in a rathole. This job gets me down," said Mac bending over and taking a long drink. I was going to tell him not to, but I couldn't figure out how to introduce the subject.

"You ready for our race?" I said, now my turn to change the subject. I wasn't in the mood for a bitch, woe is me session about teaching down here, and I also wasn't about to ask Mac about his sex life. I didn't have the time or the inclination. Learning about how many times a day he did it would take some time, like a maybe a year. Mac must really be a sex addict to keep on doing what he was doing with the co-eds with the cops swirling around the place.

"Dempsey ready for Firpo? Bears shit in the woods?" said Mac.

"Dempsey was down three times in the first round. Lucky as hell to win. The ringside reporters pushed him back into the ring. As for smoky, he uses a john because bushes give him a rash," I said.

"I'm in shape. I'm hot stuff. Olympic material. Can do four minute miles. Ten, twelve of them. Been sandbagging you and Walt, your ass is in trouble," said Mac.

"Second liar never has a chance. You got me. I guess I won't go."

"You got to. I want to beat you, then rub it in. Take out an ad—The Italian Stallion has ass kicked. Send the results to Fenner," said Mac.

"I don't like him much. Send them to Wiant, I think he loves me."

"Yeah, I noticed he's got a thing for you, that's probably why he wears his hair that way, just for you alone," said Mac.

I enjoyed this back and forth. It filled up my life a little. Mac was ragging me about this fifteen kilometer road race we were going to run. Mac had gotten me into running, Candy had approved, thought it was a good idea, which it really wasn't. I had too much weight on me. The pounding involved in getting into running shape took years off my back and knees. By the time I was old and grey I'd be doing a fifteen kilometer in a wheelchair. Walt Brzenk went along to these races too. It was something to do.

"You done for the day? I'm on my way home," he said.

"No, I've got some more to do. Then I got to go see Brzenk." As soon as those words were out, I regretted it.

"What about?" said Mac, sending me into an area I didn't want to go. I plunged ahead, forgetting who I was talking to.

"He thinks he's Sam Spade. Called and told me that he had something about all of this," I said, getting myself in deeper and deeper.

"Like what?" said Mac, not smiling.

"Who the fuck knows? Look, Walt got himself a snoutful of mean streets today. He's having fun. So, I'll go listen to him. He's got a lot of beer at his place. He talks, I listen and drink his Bass. Not a bad deal." I said, trying to trail this conversation off into nowhere.

"Walt's a funny guy. This morning, he was really tight–assed about being interviewed by the cops and Fenner. Didn't want to talk to me about any of it," said Mac, starting to sweat. Was the sweating just the result of the humid hall or was he revealing that something was amiss? Only Sherlock Holmes could figure out that one, and I was no Sherlock Holmes.

"Mac, Brzenk's like a duck out of water down here. This is all new to him. He thinks he's a professor and that this is an A college. He's got a lot to learn," I said.

"Let's hope he's a fast learner. See you," said Mac.

He went toward the elevator; I went back to my lab where I no doubt could put all into perspective. Inside, I sat down at the computer and made a new file for Dom Mancini. I wrote up a clear and concise report for him. This was a layout on what I thought about J. P. Carlisle, starting with dope dealing and ending up with murder, why he would know about strychnine/brucine, how he would use them, who'd told him and how, the whole nine yards. I said nothing about Nikki Nateal. Looking at the report I thought it was a pretty good job, considering that half of it was a lie. I was focusing on J. P. and not on Nikki. Whether I would get away with this separation or not, I didn't know, but I decided to cut my intern a considerable break. I got up Dom's machine on the phone and faxed him the report. He was out, no doubt really solving crimes; my report would be waiting when he got home, which was usually late. A good day's work on my part. Figuring out crimes, giving lady justice a helping hand.

The lab I closed down in a special way, putting clear tape on some gas valves, arranging the chemicals needed to make crack so that I could tell if they'd been moved even a hair. Someone came tonight to cook some crack; tomorrow, I'd know about it, and then? I had no "and then.Outside, in the hallway, the place was absolutely stone quiet. I felt like yelling just to convince myself that I was still alive.

In the parking garage, there was noise. From behind the closed door of the large night watchman came loud panting and squealing as Beef Patty worked over a co—ed. Love at the Urban U. was hard to explain to those who'd never been there. There were no songs appropriate for it. No tunes about the moon, no reflective pools, no lasting lyrics, no awakening beauty ditties. What there was, was a girl offering explicit instructions about how she wanted to be done, which weren't poetic. As for Beef Patty, the only sound he was making was some kind of guttural animal grunting.

I turned the key in my car. Nothing. I tried again. More nothing. I cursed the Toyota Motor Corporation for a while, turning the stale air blue, using epithets embarrassing to me if anyone heard them. I would now have to walk. I would now have to take a bus home.

I slammed the door of my import. That helped. Maybe I should kick the car's foreign ass. I went out through the side door, looked for the ragman, maybe I'd kick his destitute ass. No sign of him. Beef Patty had really "taken care" of the bum.

The only place open outside was Fat Harry's deli on the corner, which was a 24 hour operation. An Indian kid was running the deli at this hour. I waved at him. He waved back. The kid no doubt glad to see me. Fat Harry's was robbed about once a month. Harry had lot of turnover with his work force.

Heading for Brzenk's, I passed old man Pang's liquor store, and his big, black, butt–ugly, ass–devouring Doberman got a whiff of me and growled, it no doubt frustrated that it couldn't get a healthy piece of me. The temperature had hit eighty degrees during the day, and it hadn't cooled off a whole lot. It was still raining softly.

I was wearing an extra large rain slicker, which my wife used to say made me look like a Bronx Zoo bear. The baggy coat flapped against my legs. The streets were empty. Just fine for a night walk. Out here, being a professor didn't mean diddly–doo squat. Out here, I was just one big piece of white meat.

Heading north, passing dark deserted buildings, I was all eyes and ears. Ahead of me, it was really dark, no street light, thick fog, a battalion could hide around here. Two voices started in, one deep and loud, the other mostly whining. I soon recognized the dialogue.

"Fuck that, motherfucka, I done tol' you!"

"Don' hit me man! Come on!"

The whiner was knocked into the side of an abandoned car, a big guy dressed all in black came after him. He was followed by a short, black girl.

I faded into the deep dark of a building.

Thump. Thump. J. P. used his big boots, punting ribs, doing a real number on the other guy. Nikki Nateal said nothing.

I watched. More life verite. Too bad Walt Brzenk wasn't here. He could rescue the whiner. Talk to J. P. and Nikki. Reason with them. Maybe read some Aristotle to them. "Why thank you, Dr. Brzenk," they'd say, "you be one interesting motherfucker. You also one dead motherfucker." Slash into Walt, slit his nose, maybe nip off his balls, make Walt into one tall street trophy.

J. P. was doing some serious injury to one of the crack dealers, that's how I read what was going down. I crept away from the three of them, went on down the street. This was no man's land, no place for this man. I'd made a mistake in helping out Nikki. It looked like she was in league with all facets of the One Percenters. I'd taken a chance that I could straighten her out like I'd done with Candy. The right Reverend Richie had struck out. Maybe I should get out of the straightening out business for good and all.

Brzenk's brownstone was in an ok part of Brooklyn. Not fancy, but not in a jungle which was being gentrified. Here a tax paying citizen of King's County had half a chance to make it home alive after a hard day of work, which weren't bad odds these days.

I held the buzzer. Nothing. Now what? Shit and misery. Now what? Walk back to the college? To my lab? Be all alone? Check out Crack, Inc.? No thanks.

I slopped my way over to where I could grab a bus to my house. Helping me get good and wet was a car full of punks which came down the street fast, splashing water from the gutter, splattering me with runoff water. Two slime balls, one of them in front, one in back were leaning out the windows, holding bats, their hair chopped to baldness, lots of skin showing. They screamed at me: "Eat it, faggot, we drown ya, then we fuckin' kill ya!!" I said nothing in reply, they sped away, "wilding" they call it, black creeps, white, brown, yellow, they all do it. Load up a car or go on the subway, pick out someone they're sure they can take and then let themselves go, rape, rob, kick the shit out of the helpless, the weak, and the old. The twenty–first century is going to be a great time to live in.

I made it to the bus. Score one for Bucceroni. Ten blocks of night walking and no flesh wounds. Hooray!

I had the bus pretty much to myself. There were two white kids doings some pretty heavy, not really meant for public viewing, making out, the guy licking the girl's ears with his red, moist tongue; a foxy looking black girl, dressed in not much, was talking to the driver, and at the back was some no doubt vet, in fatigues, a nutzo look about him, like he wasn't sure where or who or even what he was. It wasn't a long trip, maybe twenty minutes to where I lived.

Off the bus and walking down the street, I wondered where the hell Walt was. He'd insisted that I come see him now, when I'd arrived, no one there, an empty house. Strange.

The place I lived was nothing like where the college was. Trees here, big homes, lawns taken care of, pretty quiet too, which was thanks to organized crime. In Brooklyn, not only does crime pay, it keeps the peace. On the corner of my block lived a wiseguy. I minded my own business. He minded his. We see each other, we nod a hello. My wife used to talk with his wife—that had been a while ago.

My house is large, three full floors, a lot of real wood in it, all hardwood floors, high ceilings, the real stuff for mouldings. This was a place I couldn't afford now if I made fifteen times my salary, and I made a nice piece of change. My old man had bought this house a long time ago. Got the money doing what the wiseguy on the corner now did. I'm the spitting image of my old man, but I wasn't anything like him. Anthony "Baby Ducks" Bucceroni had taken one path—the crooked one—I'd chosen the straight and narrow. This house was what he'd left me and my mother after he'd picked the losing side in some family squabble and been dumped in the East River.

The big kitchen was done all in white. I took off my slicker, pulled off rubber boots, put them all away neatly and walked slowly upstairs to the second floor, my footsteps echoing in the big, empty house. On the second floor, I started my routine. I checked one room, a little boy's room, neat, with bins of toys on the floor and bunk beds at one end. A nice room, but no little boy. I left the room and carefully closed the door. A master bedroom was next, a big room with a king sized bed. I opened the big walk–in, cedar–lined closet and looked at the silk dresses, neatly hung, and I ran my hands over them. On the dresser were a woman's comb and perfume and pins and sachets—a woman's stuff, but no woman. I said, "I'm sorry," to the empty room.

This was too much house for me. Why I stayed here I didn't know. This was a crypt. Memories of the dead were everywhere, carefully preserved so that forgetting was impossible. Only a sicko would live in a house like this. A part of the third floor had been converted from an attic to one small bedroom. A single bed was under the window, made up, pajamas under the pillow. Pretty bare. Not much in there to make me remember.

I hung my suit up and threw the shirt in the hamper. The tie went back on a rack. The shoes were put where they should be. Precise. A ritual. Another routine. More time killing. I had no time to kill. I had work to do.

I put on black sweats and a black tee–shirt. My subway sleuth outfit. Ride the New Lots trains. Look for subway shovers. Dream about getting one in my bare hands.

With the lights out, I moved to the window. Candy lived a few blocks away. In the winter, with the leaves down, I could see into her house, but the leaves hadn't yet fallen in Brooklyn. The rain was really coming down again.

One car drove slowly by. A woman was hurrying along the street coming from the avenue. Someone was probably waiting up for her at home, wondering where she was. She walked very fast, head down, bucking the wind and rain. Something in the way she walked made me stare at her. I'd been a husband, a father. One shove had changed all that. Who was I now? The image of King Gomez's face, the death smile, flashed across my mind, filling it full with death.

I phoned Candy. Her tape was on. I had her cell but I didn't want to look like I was tracking her, which I was.

I picked up the late news of Fox 5. The usual. Robbery. Head Bashing. Assault of the old. Abuse of the young. The Giants holding their own, the Jets on a roll, the Rangers and Knicks starting their seasons. One item just in. A jogger, age in his 30s, found dead in Brooklyn. Heart attack the apparent cause of death. I was half–listening, this just another item in the daily list of pain and suffering. The jogger was a professor sat the Urban U. His name: Dr. Walter Brzenk. No longer half–listening. I was all ears now, but that was all they had.

I called the precinct. Not much more for me. The same details as on the broadcast were all they could give me. The jogger was a professor, been running on the promenade in Brooklyn heights, collapsed. Someone there had tried CPR, but it hadn't worked. The professor had been rushed to an emergency room. That's all they could tell me.

I left the house, leaving my pistol behind. I wasn't ready for that. Yet.

I wheeled my second car out of the garage. It was an old Plymouth. A big car. I'd bought it for my wife who had been a pretty poor driver. It wasn't used much anymore. I hated driving it. The smell of it inside brought back memories of my family.

Out I went, making for the emergency room, driving fast through the wet, Brooklyn night streets, lining up facts as I drove. Two deaths in one day. This morning Walt and I had been right there when King Gomez was found. This evening Walt was dead. In between he'd done some snooping around. Cause and effect or just coincidence? Walt's dying from running didn't make much sense to me. He was a forty minute ten K runner, not the type to keel over while doing a few easy miles.

I drove faster. At the hospital, there might be some answers. Then I needed to talk to Candy and lay out all that I knew. And then? Now I really had no "and then."

The driving wasn't easy. Bad weather, bad road and Brooklyn drivers. Not the best trifecta in the world.

# Chapter Eleven

B rooklyn Hospital was pretty close to my house, a short trip, should've taken me maybe ten minutes tops. An hour it took. One hour. Sixty minutes. Forever.

Mother Nature had decided to assert herself. Heavy rain. Two of the highway's eastbound lanes were flooded. Which, in Brooklyn, constituted an emergency of some major magnitude and required restraint and reason on the part of the borough's hard working citizens on their way home. That was a problem. There's about as much reason and restraint in Brooklyn as there is integrity in Washington.

A gal in a Honda cut off a guy in a Volvo with Jersey plates, which got her the horn from him, which occasioned a one finger wave from her to him, which in turn effected his throwing a can of something at her windshield. Two questionable looking kids drove a white caddy into the floodwaters, stalled out, jumped out, ran away, causing me to suspect that the vehicle's true owner might be elsewhere.

Most of Brooklyn squeezed from three lanes down to one. My old Plymouth was a tank. I gave way to no one. Patton should've seen me.

An old, fat faced man in a blue Nissan tried to cut in on me from the right. He failed. Down came his window.

"Learn to drive, ya fuck of a motherfucka!" he screamed.

He was a pleasant looking older fellow. Spectacles. White shirt, light tie. Looked upstanding. Probably a CPA. Maybe a degree from Baruch, with a wife he didn't beat, grandkids he took to Mickey D's on Saturday, and a dog whose bone he threw on a regular basis. A pillar of the community. Just the type who should exercise reason and restraint. I waved at him. He jabbed his finger, vigorously, at me—which he did because he didn't know what a great guy I really was.

Life didn't become a whole lot easier after I was off the highway and onto a parkway. Still bumper to bumper traffic, all trying to go south, which shouldn't have bothered me since I was northbound. The problem was that the usually worthy denizens here were also not temperate.

A bus pulled in front of a gypsy cab, which plowed into it, denting the left side. The driver and the cabbie got out and got into it. Not a bad fight. More action in sixty seconds than some pros do in thirty minutes. The difficulty now was that all of the morons heading north slowed down to rubberneck at the wreck and the boxing exhibition. Time ticked away.

The parking lot of the hospital was jammed, no place for me, three times around until some visitor decided visiting hours were over.

Heading toward the hospital, the rain again easing off, I was noticed by a homeless, who was residing under a backhoe, its operator having left his machine behind, an action which occupied three parking spaces.

"Hey, big fella, you got five dollah?" he said.

A hand reached out, grabbed hold of my cuff. I lost it.

"Hey, scumface! You fuckin' want to lose your fuckin' hand!" I yelled, feeling my considerable neck bulge. He released his grip. I went on my way. So I'm no saint, so sue me.

Brooklyn Hospital is no place for the sick. Here, the sick got sicker. I ever get sick, I'll shoot myself while I'm riding in the ambulance. Better to die by my own hand than go out the hard way in Brooklyn hospital.

The emergency room was a zoo. Patients using the floor as beds, the smell of disease, moans, screams. One young stud with a guido haircut was holding the hand of his stabbed girlfriend. He kept yelling over and over: "We got a situation over here! We got a situation over here!"

Which may have been true, but no one gave a shit and she would just have to wait her turn. The young fellow should've saved his breath and told his little sweetie to bleed slower.

This was where the underclass went when it needed a doctor. This was also where a lot of dying took place. The back rooms did a very brisk business each night, keeping on ice Brooklyn's dead until the undertaker could take over. This was the place where I'd been forced to see the ripped up parts of my own small family. This was not my favorite place.

At the nurse's station, I was recognized.

"Doc Bucceroni, why you here? You sick?" said Malvina Moore, the night duty nurse, better known as "Heavy Duty" on account of her tonnage. She'd been one of my students, plus her boyfriend was Lester "Beef Patty" Norwood, the unfaithful night watchman at the college. LOVE AND THEN SOME was what Candy called them. She was right; as a wrestling tag team Heavy Duty and Beef Patty would be too much for Slash and Axe to handle.

"No, Malvina, I'm ok. I'm here to find out about another professor. Dr, Brzenk. Dr. Walter Brzenk. He died this evening," I said, leaning close to her to cut down on the din of the crowded room.

"He back there. Frien' of yours?" said Malvina, pointing down the hall toward the ice rooms.

"Yes," I said.

"Too bad about 'bout him. Young Doc Wooley say he had a heart attack. It come on while he was runnin', kill him on the spot, that what young doc Wooley say," said Malvina.

"Donald Wooley's on duty?" I said. That was a break for me in case I wanted to do some snooping around, which I did. Wooley had also been one of my students, but at the main campus. He'd been in a chemistry class for pre–meds. Malvina had taken a science course for nurses. She got to spend all of her long, working nights in the emergency ward of a Brooklyn hospital. Each and every one of her nights was full of yelling, bleeding, crying, and dying. It was some job she had.

"Yeah, but he be draggin'. Shamela here too. We all here."

Before I could answer her, Malvina had to go care of some business.

"Stop that!" she screamed at a small black boy who was throwing spitballs at an inert patient on a cart, for all I knew pelting the dead. She advanced on the kid, like a water buffalo lining up a rabbit.

"Who in charge of this boy? Somebody better be or else Malvina take over. You want me to take care of you boy?" said Malvina.

The boy looked up at Heavy Duty, looked at three hundred pounds of agitated black nurse dressed all in white bearing down on him and he backed away, heading toward his really pregnant, really young mother, who was nodding, listing to one side in her chair, head resting against the cool, dirty white walls, in heroin land I'd bet, out of it. Malvina walked back to me.

"Say, Doc, want to axe you somethin'. Lester, he jus' call me, sound like somethin' botherin' him. He say he may come see you. You know what about?" she asked.

"No idea," I said, hoping I wouldn't get in the middle of a love feud. I wasn't entirely sure I could whip either Malvina or Beef Patty.

"Well, he off tomorrow, maybe he catch you on Monday," said Malvina, getting back to the large pile of paperwork on her desk.

I walked away from the emergency room back to where they kept those who hadn't made it through the night.

Outside, standing in the hall, talking to Shamela Hall, was Donald Wooley, who looked like he'd been without sleep for about a week. Bloodshot eyes. In need of a shave. Handling about five cases at once.

"Hello, Dr. Bucceroni," said Shamela, her voice soft, looking good like she always did, big, brown eyes, skin like honey, long, long legs. She could've doubled for Beyonce any day.

Shamela and Malvina had both been in my chemistry for nurses, Malvina making it through by copying from her friend. Wooley had been in the pre—med chemistry class I used to teach. Right now they were all in the same boat, but Donald was just paying his dues. Soon he'd be in the money while Heavy Duty and Great Looking would work their lives away at the bottom of the heap in Brooklyn.

"Hello, Shamela. Hello, Donald. I'm here about Dr. Brzenk. Where is he?" I said.

"In there. Was he a friend of yours?" asked Shamela Hall.

"Yes," I said, even though I wasn't sure that he really was.

"Sorry. He was dead when he was brought in. There was nothing to be done," said Donald Wooley, his voice sounding fatigued.

"You take his temperature?" I said, feeling silly the moment that was out. Donald was now the doctor; he wasn't my student anymore.

"EMS did. Nothing. 101. The slight elevation caused by the running. It's what I would expect," said Wooley, answering my question like I wasn't out of line.

"You think it was his heart?" I said.

"Looks that way."

"Who'll run the sample?" I asked.

"Me, or maybe the medical examiner. Why?"

I turned and looked at Shamela Hall. I smiled. She smiled. I waited. It took a while.

"See you later, Doc. I got my rounds to run," said Shamela, finally getting the point.

"See you, Shamela," I said.

She left.

"Walt Brzenk didn't have a bad heart," I said.

"Neither did Jim Fixx," said Wooley.

"Yeah he did."

"You know what I mean. All you runners think running cures everything. Who knows what he had?"

"Ok, so he'll probably have blood that's on the high side for minerals, but that's just because he was exercising..."

"You looking for something?" Wooley interrupted.

"Yeah," I said looking my former student dead in the eye.

He hesitated for maybe a second.

"Should I ask what?"

"No.""This going to involve me?"

"No."

"You need urine and tissue?"

"Yeah," I said.

"Wait here," said Wooley, who then walked away.

He went down the hall and into a lab. I walked into the room where Walt Brzenk was laid out.

It was an all—white room. Brzenk was there, he was really tall, his legs were right up to the end of a white cart, the legs dead white, partially covered by a white sheet. He hadn't really been my friend. I hardly knew him; I'd interviewed him for the job with a lot of other professors; he'd come across as ok. He just came on board, getting his first taste of Brooklyn. He was just one of those professors that I taught with. On his way to being fired. Come the summer he'd be gone. Never see him again. Over the years, dozens of people like Brzenk had drifted in and out of my life. He came from a completely different background than me. Running was about all we had in common. He hadn't been a friend.

Brzenk was naked. On the floor was his green, running outfit which was soaking wet. It was ripped where they'd cut it off him.

Alone with Brzenk, I felt it coming up inside of me, tried to stop it, couldn't. It all came out, not crying, I was a long way beyond crying, heaving up, burning, hot, coming from deep down in me. I made it to the sink in the room, put both hands on each side and threw harder than Doc Gooden used to.

I washed up, cleaned myself, splashed cold water on a hot face, drank some water, a mistake. Started up again. My retching was strong enough to register on the Richter scale, shook me apart. A first class farewell I was giving, puking my guts out while Brzenk lay there in his next to last resting place.

Finally, I was done. There'd been a time when I'd wished I was dead. It'd seemed easier to be dead than to remember what I'd done. Bullshit. This here was the real thing. Dying scared me. I'd hate for that to be me, lying there stone cold white dead, being stared at in a too—bright white room by a guy who wasn't even a pal.

Hard to swallow, my throat seemed tight, the muscles stiff, my Adam's apple rock hard. Outside, in the hall, it was better. The hospital was quieting down, not so many incoming, those there being sedated. Facts weren't adding up for me. Brzenk's dying like this made no sense to me. There would not be another time to get straight on the facts. I went back into the room.

Next to the running outfit was his running belt, but there was no running bottle in it. I knew about these running belts. I had one, so did Mcclure, so had Brzenk. They were good for long races. A runner could put his own water in a bottle, stick it in a belt, and have a drink whenever he wanted one. Brzenk's bottle was gone. Where was it?

The door opened.

"Dr. Bucceroni, you're wanted up front," said Shamela Hall, ignoring the smell I'd made.

"What for?" I asked, not liking that she'd interrupted my train of thought.

"Malvina is trying to deal with the professor's people; she's getting nowhere. She said to come get you."

I was not happy to be taken away from this room. But maybe doing something else would further clear my mind. Looking at Walt was turning me into a basket case.

I got on the phone with Brzenk's parents, who must've been about a thousand years old. They were in separate rooms in their house, each with a phone. Conversation with the two of them was an adventure. I would get through to one about what had happened, then the other would start telling me about something Brzenk had done when he was ten years old. It took me at least a good hour to receive their permission to send the body back to Walt's home state.

After dealing with the two ancients, I burned up the phone lines with a mortician where Walt had come from. His first concern was who would pay. He became more oily when he learned the parents had bucks and Walt had insurance. He also expressed an interest in Brzenk's height. Maybe long coffins fetched a heftier price.

After I resisted the temptation to call the mortician a greedy, ghoulish, no class, soulless piece of snail shit whose mercenary pus—

covered balls I'd like to rip out and stuff in his fucking pointed, hairy, yellow scum ears, after I didn't say that, I thought our exchange went well. It was actually an easier job than I thought it would be. Brzenk's body would be taken to a local funeral home, prepared, then shipped back to this home.

I got a quick education in the dead business. The living think their dying will interrupt the world, that everything'll stop for a while because they're gone. Not true. Brzenk's being dead in one state and being laid to rest in another was no big deal. The funeral director said he'd enjoyed speaking with me. He asked for my name and address.

"Dr. Winston Wiant. 1125 Rugby Street. Brooklyn, New York, 11210," I answered quickly.

I thought about investing in a wire tap. It would make for a nice evening to listen to our college's resident vampire talk to this backwoods stiff stuffer.

And then there was nothing to do. Searching for something else to occupy my mind, I remembered the water bottle. I tried to find out what had happened to it. This was something to do, but it turned out that no one knew anything. The doctors had seen no bottle. Neither had the nurses. I talked to Shamela. Never heard about a bottle. Malvina. Didn't know. The ambulance driver said no bottle was there when they first came upon Walt. Nobody knew nothing.

I thought about going to the promenade and searching for it. I thought about crawling around Brooklyn at 2 am, using a flashlight to try and find a small, dark green plastic bottle. I came to think not a whole lot of that thought. I was making work for myself, playing detective.

I went looking for Donald Wooley. We met in the hallway.

"Here it is, "said Wooley, handing me a plain brown paper bag.

"Thanks," I said.

"I never gave you this," He said.

"Gave me what?" I said.

"Right," said Wooley. He walked away from me.

I left the hospital, headed toward my car, giving the backhoe a wide berth. I had no interest in interrupting the sleep of the panhandler.

Getting into my car, I sat my broad, aging rear end down in water. Some dope who I knew intimately had forgotten to close the driver's side window. Not a big job closing a window, able to be done by almost anyone with half a brain.

I'd thought the rain had stopped. My soaking wet pants informed me of the error in judgment I had made. I summoned up the strength to curse myself thoroughly for being an idiot. This I did for some extended time at a considerable volume, but my swearing didn't dry out my pants.

I looked up at the heavens. A front seemed to be coming through. I could see breaks in the clouds, and the wind was picking up, coming in from the west.

The drive home was a picnic compared to the time it'd taken me to get here. The avenue was clear of angry, in your face motorists, the belt pretty empty. Not many people were out at this late hour. Not much was left of the night. I was used to these late hours, the truth being that sleep didn't come easily for me, that's one of the other reasons I rode the subways at night. With the weather letting up, the storm moving away, it looked like tomorrow, that is, today, would be a great day. But not for Brzenk. It was over for him. Good days, bad days, they no longer figured in his existence. I wondered what would become of him. Now that was the sixty–four thousand dollar question. What was next in line once you'd been edged out of life? I hoped it was ok. Being dead should mean a good, long sleep with no nightmares. At least I hoped that's the way it will be. Never can tell, though. For all we know, the nightmares will just be of a different kind.

I felt my mind stir. Someone had gone after Walt. I could feel it. A dead on street killer was at work, someone who always took the straight line. Anyone in the way was on the way out. Two deaths. Bam Bam. Gomez, then Walt. The King was dead, Brzenk saw him, he wrote me a note about something he'd found out. And then he was dead. Cause and effect isn't always the answer but right now it worked for me. More bad thoughts came to the surface. Someone else had seen the King Gomez. That someone had received the note from Brzenk. That someone ran a lab which had in it the probable murder weapon. That someone was no doubt next on the hit list. I felt sweat form on my head and it wasn't from the night, which was cooling off. Now was the time to get extra sharp. The only way to deal with a killer is to be two steps ahead and not one behind.

My car hadn't taken me home. I couldn't go back to that house of the dead past. I was in front of Candy's. I locked the door of my car and walked to her place, hoping that she was alone. I knew that she'd be up. She also had a problem with sleeping. Sometimes we'd talk into the night, me making up stuff to keep her on the line. She told me she didn't sleep more than three or so hours a night, that she'd always been like that, never got sick because of it.

I rang the bell, got cold feet, wanted to run the hell away. Instead, I searched my mind for something funny to say, something real witty like: "Please let me in, I'm fucked up and can't go home."

Something like that should do the trick.

# Chapter Twelve

Standing outside Candy's place, ringing the bell, I felt more and more like bolting and going home to memory central. Her house was only a few short blocks from mine, all brick, three stories, very nice. She'd told me that the money to buy it came from her father's life insurance. She'd also told me how her father came to be dead. One night, he'd been doing his job as one of New York's finest, which consisted of his stopping two guys for doing forty–five mph on a thirty mph parkway. He'd pulled them over, walked up to the car, asked for a license and registration, all of this strictly routine, and he'd gotten two straight in the face. He had leaned into the window, made it easy, a sitting duck. He'd died right then and there. The two vermin got thirty months thanks to a sharp lawyer and to some sloppy work by the arresting officer. Candy was looking for them as well as the scum who'd redone one side of her face. Candy and I didn't talk about this stuff. What was the point of talking? The past wasn't for us. In the present was where we tried to live, except for those nights we spent hunting for those who'd fucked over us, turned our lives into a hell that even Dante couldn't imagine.

Her large front door was framed by two sets of glass panels. I ran the bell again. This would be my last ring. I didn't want to stick my nose into her after–hours business. I'd done enough poking around in her life. I had stood in this very place before, at about the same time of night. In my hand was the evidence that Candy had used my lab as a drug factory. I was pretty hot under the collar. Some piece of slime had been with her. He'd opened the door, no shirt, pants with fly open, no shoes, no socks, where's Candy, what the fuck you want old man? a right to the balls an elbow across the throat you'd like to maybe rephrase your comment I said. Him, I'd sent on his way after he found his shirt and pants the shoes I'd said fuck it to, he'd now need some repair to his essential parts. Candy, I'd then talked to, real Dutch Uncle stuff. Candy's first reaction was fuck off, her second was to offer sex, her third tears, her fourth acceptance. From her house right then and right there we'd gone to a detox center upstate where she'd cleaned herself out. From that moment on she'd become a new person.

Doing that had kept me from going off the deep end. Back then I was having a hard time of it. Getting Candy into the straight and narrow wasn't just for her sake. Bailing her out had been done as much for me as for her. Other than that, a lot hadn't changed for me since then, like my midnight rides on the IRT, dressed up all in black, looking like a ninja on steroids, pretending to be a stumble bum, waiting for the skunks who'd got my family to come after me. I'd ride the trains also at rush hours, trying to fit in with the crowd, dressed differently, be all eyes and ears, trying to laser in on some pusher whose rocks went off when a commuter sizzled on the third rail just before the number four sliced through him. That was something I couldn't let go of, like tonight, which was what I would do if Candy didn't answer her bell. It was nuts to ride the subway in the hopes of sniffing out an old trail. It was nuts. Which is maybe what I am at times.

A front light went on, and there was Candy giving me the onceover.

"We don't want any," she said, smiling. I tried to smile in return. She must've noticed how sickly my smile was.

"I called, you weren't home," she said. She was wearing some type of white robe, her blonde hair was fluffed out. She looked good, like always.

"Brzenk's dead," I said, blurting out the words, pleased with myself for doing a good job of delivering bad news.

"Come in," said Candy.

I followed her inside, closed the door myself and then up to the second floor. I looked around as I climbed. Candy had herself a nice place. Classy. Totally different from my house, which was done in early gloom. This was all in white, lots of glass, everything going with everything else. I should hire her to redo my house. Living in the dark does a number on your mind.

On the second floor, Candy had a sitting room, with a white carpet, white couch, white loveseat, a white brick fireplace set between two big glass panels. There was a fire burning. I sat on the couch. Candy curled up on the loveseat.

"You heard me say Brzenk is dead?"

"I heard you. How?" she asked. Beside her was some paper. She'd been up working.

"I just came from the hospital. They said it was his heart. He was found dead on the promenade. No signs of violence. He'd been running. His heart went. Strictly Jim Fixx." Rushing out the details, throwing a lot at her in one outburst.

"That's what the doctor said?"

"First of all, the doctor was Donald Wooley. He gave me as much of the nine yards as he had. He also gave me some samples, which he wasn't supposed to do."

"Urine and tissue?"

"Yeah."

"Looking for?" she said, staring at me with her gray eyes.

"Something that'd take him out and fool everyone into thinking it was the running that killed him. Walt could run forty minute ten Ks. I had a hard time keeping up with him. It doesn't add up. He wouldn't have been running that hard. This was a slow day for our training. He was just working out. It wasn't all that hot. It doesn't make sense. I've been down at the hospital, getting no answers. All I did was to handle the funeral arrangements. I've got a lot of facts, but no theories," throwing more detail at her, most of it jumbled and tumbling out on top of itself.

Candy got up and went to a small bar in the corner of the room to get us a drink. She poured scotch for herself and for me a glass heavy on the Jack Daniels, light on the ice. She handed me the drink, then sat down across from me.

"Success to crime," I said, raising my glass. It was an old toast, one that Dom Mancini and I had used as teenagers back in Bensonhurst.

"Success to crime," said Candy, sipping her scotch.

"Let me tell you something about Brzenk," she said.

"Like what? " I said.

"Like he was a squid." This was Candy's term for someone who tried to hit on her.

"Oh boy. When?"

"Last week, when he was preparing for his first classroom observation. Strictly pitiful. Asks me if I need a ride home. It's raining about an inch a minute. Yes, ok. Thanks. So he drives me home. Stops, left hand on wheel, right hand on my leg. Can I come up? Can we talk?"

"But he lived?"

"Yes, but after I hit him, his libido was probably put on hold. I also told him I could have his whole family killed. I was very Bensonhurst."

"Why didn't you tell me?" I said.

"You see the way your neck is bulged out, you notice what you're doing with your hands?"

I put down the pillow I was strangling.

"Anything else? You ever have any more trouble with him?"

"There was no 'trouble,' he was just being a man."

I gulped my drink. Strong. JACK DANIELS VERSUS THE MIND MONSTERS. It sounded like a WWF main event. Walt was put back into the place of the normal. The dead are always regarded as holier than thou. This didn't mean I wasn't sorry he was dead, but it also meant that a saint hadn't left the land of the living.

"So Walt was a creep, too. That means two creeps got killed in one day," I said.

"You don't know that he was killed; you just know that he's dead," said Candy.

"Thank you, Watson," I said, saluting Candy with my glass, then gulping down more brain cell killers. "You're right, but this has the look of someone taking care of business. King Gomez, a thug of a drug dealer, gets it on our doorstep. And he gets it in a way straight out of yours truly's lectures. Strychnine, maybe brucine. A good choice of a chemical weapon. The M. E. can be fooled into categorizing this as the result of adulteration. And Walt's right there, sees him dead, decides to become Dr. Detective, goes on the prowl, finds something, wants to see me with his evidence. Then, bingo, he ends up dead. Another death with a fast and easy explanation. He was running, he died, case closed. But the big question is, did he get on someone's hit list, the same someone who dropped Gomez?" I said, making a long speech, rushing it all out in front of Candy.

"There was no mention of strychnine or brucine in the M. E.'s report," said Candy, speaking slowly, then sipping more of her Johnny walker.

"Said who?'

"Said the M. E. Jim Doyle said that he was full of cocaine. Case closed," she said

"But I told Dom about the strychnine and the brucine! I spelled it out for him. He thanked me for the tip," I said, having agita, which I did a lot.

"Could you be wrong?" said Candy.

"The way Gomez looked. I would've bet a month's pay on a poison. You get a copy of the report?" I asked.

"Couldn't. What I got was just from talking and drinking with Doyle while he tried to suggest other things. I didn't want to let him know what we thought. But I'm not done. Tomorrow's a day off. Doyle's not at the lab, so I'm going to go there. I've got some work of ours to drop off. I'll try to see if I can find the report, see what they did," she said.

"Good. See if you can get a tissue sample. Maybe they just didn't test for anything other than cocaine, maybe they were told to do so."

"That's not possible. This is New York, not L.A. Here they're pretty careful with evidence."

"But is this really evidence? Dom said this was not big deal, then maybe they did a quickie. So do what you can. Dom wants this all nice and neat. A lot of times he gets pissed at me for giving him complicated explanations. To him, this is just another drug killing, one dealer cutting out another or one dealer doing a poor job of cutting. How Gomez died is nothing to him. Me, I'm giving him a chemical killing. Cocaine overdose; easy to explain. Strychnine poisoning, a lot of college professor bullshit."

"But you think you're right?"

"I've shot my big mouth off. Laid out chapter and verse on how to kill someone, told anyone who was alive in my class who wanted to listen. J. P., he's a listener. All he had to do was to put what I preached into practice," I said, trying to calm down.

"And Nikki?"

"Looks that way. Like you said, she had a key to the lab this summer. I ran across her and J. P. this evening, pounding some dealer into the sidewalk. Maybe all this One Percenter stuff is for real, maybe J. P. is the man, and Nikki is riding with him," I said, then I gulped some more Jack Daniels.

"And Brzenk would walk into all of this blind as a bat. He'd set himself up. He'd ask the wrong questions, of the wrong people, at the wrong time and in the wrong place," I was talking faster and faster. The sour mash was loosening my tongue. The question was, was it also scrambling my brain?

I looked at her as she pushed blonde hair back from a golden forehead. So Doyle was after her too. She smiled at me, and her grey eyes seemed to sparkle. Her teeth were white against the pink of her full lips. She had the most beautiful one half of a face I had even seen.

The other half was not so nice to look at. The two scum who'd worked her over had dug in with the tip of the hot iron, ripped through nerves and muscle. Not only was the one side of her face scarred, it didn't move. It was like fifty percent of her face was dead. It was my fault she'd been hit. The creeps had wanted her to keep her drug factory open for business. After Candy had come back from upstate clean, they'd paid her a visit. There had been two of them.

One of them was still alive. For now, Candy had a long memory. I wouldn't want to get on her bad side. If she found him, she'd kill him, dead on the spot, no ifs, ands, or buts about it. I'd done some research, found out the two weren't connected, all bullshit on their part strictly a line used to scare people. The two were on their own. I'd told Candy, she'd gone hunting, one she'd found. I didn't try to stop her. Someone did that to me, I'd search the ends of the earth to get a shot at him. Revenge in Brooklyn was a big deal. She was just paying back for what she got. "I've got to run these samples I have from Wooley. I've got to find out about Gomez," I said

"You're not going to the college now?" she said.

I didn't need to tell Candy I was a piss poor sleeper. I hated sleep. It opened me up. Asleep I couldn't keep the clamps on my memory. Sleep made me vulnerable to the past. Dreams weren't sweet for me; they were nightmares. My mind dredging up debris I'd tried to forget, tossing and turning, coming awake drenched in sweat, my hands working as if I had hold of the bastard killer who'd shoved my life off a subway platform.

"You can stay here," said Candy, smiling at me. There'd been no funny business between us. I had cut her a big break, but I hadn't done what other men had done to her in the past, which was to demand a piece of her in return for their favors. To tell the truth, I was kind of dead in that department. My last time hadn't even been with my wife. Her dying had killed off that part of my life. It's not necessarily healthy to do without, but that's what I was doing.

"All I'll need is a pillow, and a sheet," I said, glad that she'd asked me. I really had no place to go. Candy got up and walked down a white hall while I removed the end pillows from the white couch.

"I don't sleep much. I'll be up and gone early," I said when she was back with the pillows. She didn't say anything for a moment, like she was thinking I had better slow down and get a grip on myself before I was out in the bad world playing at being Marlowe.

"Get me up before you go. We'll need to talk more," she said.

We looked at one another. Living in the present meant that we had to forget what had happened in the past. Easier said than done.

The past had at me, and probably her, each and every day, and every time she brushed her teeth or hair Candy got a too good look at her reflection and saw what had been done to her.

She walked away to her room. I got into the bed I'd made up on the couch. I kept my clothes on. I lay back, alone, but knowing that Candy was just down the hall. This was better for me. At home, I'd had have paced the floors, talked to myself, did a real number on my fucked up mind. I felt myself getting sleepy. Maybe it was the quart of J. D. I'd drunk. For once, sleep came easily. For once, I felt safe. My swirling mind shut down and I was dreamless.

# Chapter Thirteen

My deep, sweet sleep lasted an hour. The booze had done that. Booze was bad for me. It shut me down but not for long. Sixty minutes in a drug stupor, that was all my memory gave me. Then the nightmares came on. Maybe I should write to Jack Daniels, tell them to up the proof.

I got up quietly. Not having to dress in the dark helped me to be silent. I checked to see if Candy was asleep. She was, out like a light. I'd give some serious money to someone who could make me sleep all night.

Outside, there was still something left of the night. Cold now. My car hesitated before turning over. It probably wondered what the hell I was doing up at this hour. That made two of us.

I headed for the college. Brooklyn was a ghost town. No one but us sharp ass amateur detectives were on the prowl. I wanted to see if anything was going down at my lab. Poirot would think well of me.

The street by the college was empty, the homeless gone somewhere else in search of warmth, the hookers done for the night, the pre–teen stalkers resting up for another day of crime at their junior high school.

I parked a block away from the college on an all dark block. Harry's deli was open and, surprise, Harry himself was behind the counter.

I decided to get some coffee and listen to Harry, which is what you did around Harry since he thought he was the sidewalk Socrates of Flatbush.

I wasn't the only one who'd decided to talk to Harry.

"So you think the One Percenters are a big deal?" Dom Mancini was saying as I parked my bulk next to his small frame.

"Big Deal? I did not call them a big deal. I established that their philosophy revolved around violence," said Harry in an aggrieved tone.

"Hello, Professor," said Harry to me. He then went to get me some of his coffee.

"You early for work?" said Dom, helping out his sarcasm by looking at his watch.

"I'm checkin' out my place."

"You want a job on the force?"

"You always this friendly?" I said, shoving aside the temptation to tell Dom about Brzenk. Dom already had his hands full with me and the brucine and the King. Right now didn't seem like the time to start offering him theories about the way a classics professor may have met his end.

"Look, Richie, I don't need you puttin' in your two cents. I'm gettin' close to crackin' this whole thing,"

"J. P. Carlisle high on your list? That what you and Harry were talkin' about?"

"Nothin' wrong with your ears, is there? Yeah, as a matter of fact, the knuckle dragger is right up there at the top. He's something, that guy. These One Percenters is bad news."

"Harry explain them to you?"

"Yeah he did. Somethin' wrong with that?"

"You know what goes on upstairs here?" I said.

"You mean the shunt business he runs with the chink?"

"Pang is Korean."

"Big fuckin' deal! Chink, gook, slant, Charlie Chan, king foo, chow mein, what the fuck is this, some professor jerk–off bullshit? What difference it make what I call him? You frontin' for the U.N.? The little old bastard is a shunt artist. Him and fat stuff here get the snatch at your place to hike up their skirts for some fuck shots, then do tongue numbers on one another. So yeah I know all about this. So what?"

"Here you are professor, this should be conducive to your conversation," said Fat Harry, setting a cup of Joe before me.

"Conducive? What the fuck does conducive mean?"

"You know, Detective Mancini, I think you do know words like conducive, I think you know many things," said Harry, laughing a fat man's laugh, a belly shaker, causing ripples that went up to his chins.

"That's me, a fuckin' philosopher. I'll tell you one big word I know. DOUGHNUT. How's that for a big word?"

"You would like a doughnut," said Harry.

"I would like even two doughnuts," said Dom.

Harry pushed off from the counter, using his meaty arms to start his body rolling, aiming himself for the far end of the counter where, under a greasy glass cover, he had week–old doughnuts whose glaze wasn't the work of the baker.

Dom's dark eyes didn't follow Harry. They flicked toward the college. He had a good view of the front of the college. He was sitting with his back against the slick, blue vinyl wall of the deli. To his left was a large window. A good spot. No one could get behind him. No one could come at him unnoticed. Dom had always been like that. He wasn't about to let someone get the drop on him.

Without craning his neck, Dom could see the windows of the first six floors next door. The whole college was still dark. No crack cooking, no co–ed banging, no gang warfare, nice and peaceful, just like it was at Swarthmore.

"Here, Detective, enjoy. This is on me," said Harry, returning with the two doughnuts, their edges wet from his sweaty hands, wheezing the words, even this short trip an aerobic event for the porn and pastrami purveyor. The descendent of Apollo waddled away, with his right hip making contact with the counter.

Dom took a large bite of one of the big, glazed doughnuts. He seemed to swallow it whole, then chased it with coffee. Wrong choice for a beverage. Liquid plumber would've been better.

"So, what you got on the One Percenters?" I said.

"Lardass told me they're here to straighten out the Ninety–Nine Percent."

"That'd go down how?"

"Burn a crack house, shave the head of a street whore. Last year they cut off the dick of a pusher who set up shop in a schoolyard."

"How about killin?'"

"They kill, they leave a callin' card."

"Like pullin' out a gold tooth?"

"Yeah and like settin' him out for everyone to see. You 'bout done askin' questions?"

"Jesus! There you go again, your prostate botherin' you?"

"It's late. I'm on the job. What excuse you got for bein' in this shithole at this hour?"

"The One Percenters, they got a headquarters?"

"Headquarters! This ain't IBM. These fucks is all over Brooklyn, some of them even go to college."

Two transit workers came in. Harry served them coffee. Harry inclined his big head toward Dom. The two got the point. They'd wait, get their porn later.

"I'm not so sure about Nikki Nateal. She may be ok."

"Bullshit, she's the gorilla's pussy."

"She works for me," I said, trying to keep my cool, knowing that Dom was laying it on thick and foul just to get my goat.

"Answer me this. She fuck that big, blond professor?"

"Yeah, she does," I said.

"She's a sweetie ain't she?"

"She's a kid."

"She's a gorilla's home base cunt."

"Look Dom..." I said, finally having had it, I started to lose my temper.

"Hey, Richie, let's cut the shit, ok? I know you're tryin' to find a life for yourself down here with these kids, but, in my mind, this Nikki nookie is linked up with a big bad ass bugaloo who spends his evening bustin' heads. The way I see it, King Kong gave the spic a warning, he got told to kiss off, and then it was whack–out time. Not only that, he got the idea of how to kill from you."

"Why didn't you tell that to Jim Doyle?" I said, regretting the words as soon as they were out in the open air.

"How the fuck you know what I told Doyle?" said Dom, his dark eyes flashing at me.

I had fucked up. Dom had told me to keep Candy out of all this and I'd let her go and talk to Doyle.

"I asked him," I said, lying.

"The hell you did. You sent the knockout to see him. You're a pain in the ass, you know?"

"So why didn't you tell him about the brucine?"

"What would I tell him next? That coalmine got that shit from the corner drugstore? Here I am tryin' to keep your ass in the clear and you're hell bent to get our balls busted," said Dom.

"So what you do if you arrest J. P.? Won't he tell that he got the brucine from my lab?"

"That's why I'm here. I'm givin' that some thought."

"Anything you want me to do?"

"Go home. Let me handle this. Tell the knockout to forget what she found out. You two are professors. Let me handle this."

"I got something else."

"You always got 'something else.' Ever since you became a professor something else is all I get from you," said Dom, rubbing his hand over his face. I checked out the hand. There was no shaking involved with it.

"The One Percents are into it with the Seoul Brothers. There was a fight yesterday at the college. A black girl beat up a Korean. Two hours later, the black girl was missing a finger."

"This is Jimmy Fisheyes you're tellin' me about?"

"You know about him?" I said, surprised.

"I ain't a moron, Richie. Yeah, I know about him. Another present from the immigration department. Look, you think I give a fuck if a slant kills a zulu? Both of them get offed? Okay by me. That about it for 'something else?'"

"That's it."

"So go home, snuggle up to the knockout, but do me a favor: try to button your lip around her. There must be somethin' better you can do with her other than get her young, shapely ass in the middle of some race war."

With that, Dom got up and left. I worked on my coffee. Then I, too, left Harry's. On the corner, I saw the two transit workers. They could now purchase the filth they craved, probably eyeball it while they were tooling normal citizens around Brooklyn. I headed toward my car. I'd learned nothing. I didn't have the energy to check out my lab. What I needed was a good night's sleep.

# Chapter Fourteen

Light streamed into Candy's house, entered her bedroom, chasing the darkness from the room, shining on Candy, who was still asleep. I watched her sleep. I wondered what she dreamt about. She'd done better with her past than I had with mine. She'd gotten somewhere while all I did was wallow in despair. It must be her age. Candy was in her 20s. I was twice that. Two decades older. A long time. In my 20s, I thought I was catching onto the gravy grain, that I had it made, which showed how sharp I'd been back then.

The sunlight was welcome. Yesterday had been a gloomy day in more ways than one. I wasn't about to wake Candy. I'd let her sleep. I'd take more of this on myself, try to keep her on the sidelines where no one would go after her as part of Bucceroni, Inc. Detective Specialists.

I left her room. I knew nothing more now than I did yesterday. Last night's brief sleep had not brought me illumination. What I did know was that Dom was zeroing in on J. P. Carlisle. No point in waking Candy, I thought again, coming to doubt how I could function in all of this by myself. No. It was better for one of us to be rested and ready to go.

Back in the living room, I started in on my morning routine, calisthenics, stretching first, warmed up my legs by working in the Ben Gay that I always carried with me. Candy teased me about my carrying the ointment, commenting on its smell.

A few hundred sit–ups I did, coming at the stomach muscles in a lot of different ways. My gut is still pretty hard for a guy my age. Maybe I should run away, join the circus, and charge customers five dollars for a punch in the tummy. Then again, maybe I won't. It was Houdini who got a big head about his cast iron tum–tum, shot off his smart mouth, until someone took him up on it, let him have a good one, with the result that Harry H. got finally stuffed into a pine box that even he couldn't escape from, up until now.

Thirty minutes it took to do my sit–ups, fifteen to take a shower. This is how I live. I script my whole life. Gaps are bad. Filling up the present with a large shitload of piddly assed little jobs kept my mind from getting frisky.

In the shower, I sang, taking care not to get too loud on account of Candy sleeping. My old man, Butcher, could really sing. He had opera records of all kinds. Italians are funny like that. Use a stiletto on someone behind on a payment one minute, then sing about a clown who'd gotten down on his luck the next. Go figure.

Dressed, in yesterday's night stalker clothes, which weren't too snappy, I stood at Candy's big living room window. From there, I could make out my own house. Even with the leaves on, I had a pretty good view of the third floor of my place. I'd watched Candy from there in here. There's a law against that, you know.

In her kitchen, I put on coffee, took a seat, close to the window, lining up the day, getting straight on what I had to do. I had to do this right. Forget the past, focus on the present. The present was easy. All I had to do was to link up the snuffing of a crumb of a crack pusher with the running murder of a too–handy professor of classics. Duck soup. Nothing to it.

The coffee was ready, spreading its great smell throughout the house.

Three cups later and nowhere nearer an explanation of fixing a clear connection between the deaths of King Gomez and Walt Brzenk. While I was musing, Candy walked into the kitchen, wearing a white bathrobe and looking good. She smiled at me and brought over her own cup of coffee. She sniffed the air.

"Greased up and ready to go?" she said.

"You smell the Ben Gay?" I asked.

Candy coughed, then pinched her nose with two fingers.

"You sit, I'll fix us breakfast," I said, which is what I used to do on Sundays for Carmella and Rich Jr. Not that I did it because I was such a nice guy, it's just that when you do the cooking you can eat as much as you want.

"So, the light of day help you see anything?" I asked her.

"I think so. I'm worried about your friend Dom," she said.

"Worried how?" I said, cooking bacon, five big pieces, I added one more, just in case Candy wanted one.

"He's not doing things by the book. That bothers me. Also, he seems to be closing you out. That's not like him. He ok?" she said, sipping her hot coffee.

"You mean, is he still off the hooch? Hard to tell. It's true that he's not what he used to be. His wife's leaving him worked on him pretty good. He doesn't talk much, but it tore him up inside. It hasn't been but a few years ago that I was tracking him down in Tenth Avenue gin joints when he was totally out of it," I said.

"There any chance that he's running scared, that he just wants an easy answer to this murder, so he can get back on the inside with his captain?"

"We all run scared. Dom was nearly canned for his drinking. This precinct's the end of the line for him. He flops here, he's out. But that doesn't mean he's not on the case. It's just that he wants a clean cut. Nothing wrong with that."

"Nothing right about it either. All he's done is to establish that a dope dealer died from his own dope. Big deal. Why isn't he interested in the poisons and who had access to them?"

"Let's give him a chance," I said, avoiding telling her about my midnight chitchat with Dom. Keeping her out of this wasn't easy.

"What did Dom tell you last night at Fat Harry's?"

I splattered sizzling bacon fat on myself.

"How'd you know I talked to Dom!"

"I saw you."

"I thought you were asleep. You were here when I got back.

"Then I must not have seen you," said Candy, smiling, sipping her coffee.

Candy had backed me up. She'd followed me to the college, covered me in case I was being tailed. Not a bad idea. I'd been a sitting target. Easy to hit. Large, old, dumb, and slow.

"He's after J. P. Fat Harry gave him a history of the One Percenters."

"So what now?"

"Gonna see Dom. Last night he was in a foulass mood, so I said nothing about Brzenk. You still going to the police lab?"

"Yes, I'll go, and then head for work. Let's meet. Let's run the samples from Brzenk."

"Dom knows you talked to Doyle. Be careful."

She ignored my fatherly warning.

"Why's he closing you out?"

"If I was him, I'd close me out. Dom's a pro, I'm a half–ass. Everyone I see becomes a suspect. Last night, Mac was down there doing his after hours work in his office," I said, bringing over to the small table two heaping plates of food and one saucer with one English muffin on it.

"Thanks for the muffin," said Candy, looking at the two, mounded plates of eggs, bacon, cheese, toast, jam and butter in front of me.

"They're starving in Somalia," she said.

I ignored her assessment of my diet.

"Mac and Maria Perez, that's what I was thinking."

"Mac's interested in sex and drugs," said Candy, nibbling on her muffin.

"Yeah, but there was an operation goin' on. Maria Perez was the King's girlfriend. Gomez gets snuffed. The question is, what about the operation? It still on? And if it is, who's running the show? Could it be Mac?"

Candy said nothing. She sipped her coffee, her grey eyes didn't blink.

"So Mac's screwin' the students. So he's up for tenure. So he's takin' chances. So he's got a fancy car. Those are the facts. What they mean is another matter. You need to keep all options open. Nikki and J. P. are easy to finger for this. Nikki is someone to worry about. We're now a threat to her. It's our lab, she can't believe she'll fool us forever," said Candy, passing over my great insight about Mac.

"There's something else we need to do. We need to see if there are any pictures of the actions going down at the college. Pictures taken by Buffalo Pang, the neighborhood's legal dope dealer, the wino's friend," she said.

"I'd forgotten about him. Another sweetheart. You know why he's called Buffalo Pang?"

"He's got this buffalo head. He wears it when he does one of the girls himself."

"How do you know?"

"Some kids were on the Tenth floor one day, looking out the window, down into Pang's 'studio.' I chased them away, took a look myself. There was the old boy, pumping away on Rowanda Simmons in front of his own camera."

"Pang's camera can shoot right down into the girls' restroom. Maybe Pang got a good shot of Perez doing her dealing. Maybe he's got some shots of Mac in his office. We need to do some looking," I said, noticing how many 'maybes' I'd just used.

"Maybe all of this is just bullshit. Maybe it just what Dom said it was at first. Maybe this is just one self–doped dead, dope dealer. No more, no less," I said, continuing with my case of the maybes."

"It was you who said Nikki could be trouble," I said, shoveling food into my mouth a mile a minute"Facts before theory. Let's find out how Brzenk was killed. Let's see if it was brucine and not cocaine that killed the King," said Candy.

"But let's do it like this. You go to the police lab, I'll meet Dom. At the college, we'll link up. Then we can run the samples Wooley gave me."

We cleaned up the kitchen together. The killing was close to home. Too close. Maybe it was J. P. and Nikki, maybe not. Maybe Mac was involved, maybe not. More maybes than I needed.

I got Dom on the phone, made an appointment to see him. He didn't sound like he wanted to see me. Last night, he'd brushed me off. If I wanted to run what had happened to Brzenk past a real detective, I'd have to put up with Dom's manner.

Candy and I went our separate ways. She drove off for the city to examine King Gomez's autopsy report. I, too, would've gladly driven away, but my car wouldn't start. I waved at Candy, but she was speeding away. She always drove fast. I tried my car again. Nothing. I thought about calling Candy, having her come back. Bad idea. We were going different ways. No need to slow her down.

Riding the bus to Bensonhurst, I planned out how I would deal with Dom. He worried me. Candy was right, he was closing me out, ignoring what I told him, making it difficult, if not impossible, to talk to him.

The bus filled up, made its way slowly down the street. Time dragged along. I was running a little late. Dom had told me to be there at noon. I blotted out everything else on the bus and went over how I was going to talk with my old pal.

# Chapter Fifteen

Brooklyn doesn't have many places anymore where I feel at home, but when the bus dropped me off at Bay Parkway I was one of the crowd. Two blocks from the elevated was Dom's place. Not the biggest house in the world. His father had been a cop, bought the house after the war, raised kids there. Lived within his means. Not like my old man who'd moved us to Bay Ridge where we could hob and nob with the hoity–toities. Who said crime didn't pay?

Walking down the block, the past came alive for me. Dom and me, Mr. Inside and Mr. Outside. In close, I was a load to handle while Dom was handy with a knife. All of that seemed a thousand years ago.

Dom's home wasn't a place to spend a lot of time in. Dom's mother was in her eighties, pretty feeble. His father was dead and his sister was at home. She was always at home.

A long time ago, Immaculata Mancini had been my first, which is something you don't forget. Dom must've known I was banging his kid sister, but he never said anything. I was his pal, so it was ok. If he'd told me to knock it off, I would've because being Dom's pal was more important to me than even that, which, if you think about it, is saying something.

What hadn't been ok was when Salvatore "Piecetime" Pizzimente had Immy when she didn't want to be had. She'd tried to fight him, gotten away, opened the car door. He'd pushed her into the street. A speeding car had done the rest.

It was a long time ago that she'd been run over. She'd not taken a step out of her house in a long, long time because now her means of transportation was a wheel chair. A hard life for her. One minute, all the guidos in Bensonhurst crazy about her, the next she's a cripple. Her phone had stopped ringing.

Dom and I had gone to the hospital. Immaculata told him what had happened. Dom never missed a beat. He told everyone who would listen that this was a terrible accident. "Piecetime" wasn't blamed for anything. This was an accident pure and simple. He'd repeated himself. Everyone got the point. Dom was like that: he talked, people listened.

Dom had worked it all out. He used no part of our gang of street crazies. There had been no Jimmy "Ten Inch" Torricelli, no Vincent "Blueberries" Bonanno. Out of the loop had also been "Big C" Petrocelli, "Crazy Joe" Simmonetti, Louis "Double L" Lobasso, Anthony "Tiny" Schiazza who had more chins than Fat Harry the deli owner and Paulie "Too Pretty" Perrone was also not in. Dom had done it right. Just me and him and Mendy "The Cup" Levy.

At first, Mendy tried to talk Dom out of it.

"This is your whole life, Dominick. You go down for this, what will happen to your sister?" Mendy had the makings of a lawyer in him. He made his points: clear, concise. Perry Mason couldn't have done it better. Sounded good to me. Dom didn't buy it.

"Fuckin' cocksman fucked up my sister. He's fuckin' dead."

Mendy had canned reason. There was no reasoning with Dom.

Piecetime had pursued the wrong piece. He would have to pay the price.

We'd waited for several months. Let the air clear. We would see Piecetime in the neighborhood and talk with him, hey, how you doing Piece, you getting' any? Like nothing had happened. For all Piecetime knew, Immaculata had kept her mouth shut about what really happened.

It'd been about this time of year. Indian summer. Nice. The leaves about to change. Mother Nature at her best. Piecetime had an aunt upstate. He went there to hunt. He would stay overnight with his relatives, go out in the woods, bag some birds, bring them back to Bensonhurst, show everyone on the block what a hotshot hunter he was.

He went to hunt birds. We went to hunt him. Dom leg shot him, then cut him apart. I never heard so much screaming. At times, I can still hear it. Dom didn't seem to hear. I'd brought lye. We buried Piecetime's pieces. Dom kept one part for himself.

Dom's mother saw me coming and met me at the door. My mother had been like that. One eye on the kitchen, the other on the street. Nothing happens in Bensonhurst without an Italian mother knowing it first.

"Hello, Richie, Dominick he no here."

"We were supposed to meet today."

"Ma, is that Richie Bucceroni? Richie! Richie! Come see me."

I walked into the house, through the living room to where Immaculata Mancini always was. In her wheelchair, before the tube. Watching soap operas. She could give chapter and verse on what was happening on *A Guiding Light*.

It took me some time to get away from her. I really didn't try all that hard to get away. Time was when I would've kissed Immy Mancini's feet if she would just look my way. A few minutes out of my life now was nothing. I sat on the couch next to her. This was a newer version of the couch where we'd done it. On and on, she talked, putting her small, cold hand on my forearm.

Leaving the house, I looked back. Mrs. Mancini waved. I waved back. Her husband had been dead for many years. A cop. On a pension. Dom had taken care of his family for a long time. Dom had married, lost his wife, hit the skids. I'd helped him back to something of an even keel. Dom did all right by his family.

Back at the college, I eased my way into my lab. Checked the piece of paper, I'd put on the floor. No one had been here last night.

"Candy, you back there?"

"Candy?"

No answer. The student lab was empty. So was my office. She wasn't back yet. I hope that she was out in the world getting something done, which would be one up on her boss, the Sicilian Sherlock.

I'd struck out. All the way over to Dom's for nothing. Left him a message. I've got something. Call me. One left message. I was rolling.

Already the afternoon, the whole day, going down the drain. I had work to do. Samples to run, papers to grade. It would be nice of me to do the work that the city paid me for. After a morning of murder solving I had learned nothing. Certain signs on the horizon suggested that my expertise in detection was questionable.

I decided to run. I kept running gear at the college. I wasn't in the mood to analyze tissue and urine to see if someone had slipped Brzenk something. When in doubt, exercise. Work out. Keep fit. A healthy body makes for a sharp mind. I'd do a ten K, take it easy, seven and a half minutes to the mile, come back, take a shower. Candy should be back by then and I could listen to her tell me what she'd got done. I'd then fill her in about my major accomplishments of the day to date.

Stretching, I added up what my morning of hanging around Dom's house had produced in terms of putting two and two together about Walt Brzenk. I could run a little faster than Brzenk. Point one: I knew that Walt was in good shape. Point two: he shouldn't have died while running. Point three: weekend joggers who go from nothing to running hard, they're the ones who end up at room temperature. Point four: Walt had dropped dead while running. Point five: I didn't know why he had died. I was getting somewhere now. Candy would be impressed.

Stretched, limber, ready to fight wildcats, I took my running water out of the refrigerator, which wasn't really water, but a mixture of Gatorade and water used by Mac, me, and Brzenk. I made it up for them and kept it in the lab. Both had a key so that they could get it anytime they wanted.

Someone had spilled some water. Opening the fridge door, there was a small puddle. Just two bottles were inside. Mac's was red, Brzenks was green, mine was blue. No green bottle was there. I picked up Mac's red bottle. Full. I picked up mine. Felt it to be half–full. I opened it, not even half–full, maybe an inch of water left. I took one drink, then sloshed water around in my mouth and spat into the sink. There was something of an aftertaste.

All of a sudden more than just an aftertaste. My heart took off, like a Porsche off the line, revving up to triple digits.

I staggered across the lab, banged into table, went down hard, my shoulder getting acquainted with the floor. Hot all over, face felt red, dry throat, thirsty, my heart felt like it would blow apart. Pressure in my chest, a deadly squeezing, air hard to come by. I rolled over onto my knees, crawled to the sink, pulled myself up. I took on water, used it to wash out the mouth, no swallowing, trying to count my pulse, too fast, racing, nearly two hundred heats a minute. More water, still not drinking, rinsing out my mouth, better now, the heart backing down.

I made it to a chair, collapsed into it, tried to think what you're supposed to do when you've been poisoned.

Aqueous slurry. Empty the stomach. One mg of physostigmine every fifteen minutes. Catherize. Flush out the bladder.

All of which was swell advice and would probably work really, really well, but it was just that I was missing a neat, clean, orderly emergency room properly equipped with about a million dollars worth of drugs and machines and staffed with about twenty hotshots who'd graduated cum laude and who could run all the necessary procedures just exactly right, and thereby save my aging ass from dying.

From my running bag I got out a banana. Pretty brown. Used it to swab my mouth. My heart was getting itself in control. My mind produced a memory tag:

"Hot as a hare, red as a beet, dry as a bone."

I could add one more phrase: "Then dead as a fucking duck."

I took on some water from the tap. This time I swallowed. It felt good, cold, easing the extreme thirst. I was dizzy, but I was alive. Not like Brzenk. Now I knew the score about him. Donald Wooley was full of it. Walt hadn't run himself to death; he'd been given a helping hand by someone who knew a thing or two.

I lurched back to where I'd dropped my blue plastic running bottle, walking zigzag, and with legs of sand, like a drunk on an ice rink. I knew what was in the bottle. Just like I knew what had been given to King Gomez. This was also a good one. Dope up a runner's water bottle. The runner'd take it with him to run. It'd blow the heart and no one would be the wiser. That had nearly happened to me. I was ready to run, grabbing my bottle and off I'd go. It was just that my trip would be one way.

I could've spent some time and done some T.L.C. to prove my emerging thesis. T.L.C. is thin layer chromatography, but I knew what I'd find. Atropine. Another one of those drugs/poisons, like strychnine and brucine, which I'd lectured about. A killer was paying real close attention to my lectures and my papers. Maybe I should charge admission, hire myself out as a consultant for Murder, Inc.

There was a paper in my file, done a while ago, published in a first rate journal. There'd been over one hundred requests for reprints. There were three names on the paper. Bucceroni and Dwyer; primary; Nateal, Nicole Ann: secondary. Nikki knew all about atropine. I thought I was helping out the problems of the underclass by including Nikki in my work. It just goes to show you where good intentions will get you.

Atropine used to be called deadly nightshade. I'd put that little bit into the paper. I'd established what it used to be and what it did to the unsuspecting. I'd pointed out that it was probably the drug used to do in Hamlet's pop. In my wonderful, illuminating, killer essay, I'd gotten the goods on old Hamlet's nasty kid brother Claudius. I'd solved a crime which was over four hundred years old. Maybe that's who's after me. Old Claudius, the clever bastard. Maybe he, too, had come back as a ghost. This final observation, I said out loud and really loud, the sounds bouncing off the lab walls. One effect of taking atropine was delirium. I should tape this, send it to the Journal of Chemical Education, and combine a publication with an epitaph.

I reread my paper. ATROPINE IS STRONG STUFF. IT IS FREELY SOLUBLE IN WATER AND VERY SOLUBLE IN ALCOHOL. IT COMES IN TABLETS, INJECTABLE SOLUTIONS, AND OINTMENTS FOR THE EYES. Nice style.

Plain, strong, lots of low level verbs. In my paper were specific references to brand names. I even had some in my lab. Good for me. EMS would also have some. Good for them.

Back to my own lab, slowly, moving at less than light speed, back to where I kept my deadly chemicals. A very big deal just to get there, veering into the wall when I first stood up. Dizzy. Lights out, then on, flashing, like I'd walked into one of Tyson's uppercuts.

In my cabinet was a bottle. Neatly labeled. Easy to read. ATROPINE. Whenever I do a paper, I like to have the drugs or poisons on hand. That way, I can get specific about their properties. In the lab was a paper with all of the facts down clearly. In the lab was atropine. In the lab's fridge was a running bottle. Facts, weapon, mode of delivery. Maybe I should just open a vein, take away all the work for the killer.

Atropine is used, by those who are legit, on patients in cardiac arrest. The drug was a stimulant of note, just what wasn't needed by a runner. Brzenk would've stretched out, jogged a little in place, touched his toes, got ready to run, all of which I'd seen him do, as had Mac. Then he would've taken a drink, tanked up, and then good night Irene, so long to this sad assed world. His heart would've raced away, from low doubles to high triples, no need even for him to run, atropine doesn't affect the maximal heart rate, the killer knew his Ps and Qs. The clever, killing bastard. This chemical bomb didn't need running to help it. It was a heart stopper. And now nearly it'd gotten me. I hadn't even drunk much of the atropine. One small drink washed around in the mouth, and I'd nearly bought it.

I decided not to run a ten K. I'd had enough working out for one day. Being nearly dead was more than enough exercise for one day.

I put on some sweat pants and a lyfa over my running trunks and tank top. The atropine went back to the lab. I put a sample of the doped water into a glass bottle, labeled it and got rid of the rest. Later on, when I was more alive, I'd analyze it. Better yet, I'd have Candy check it out to make one hundred percent sure I was right that it was atropine. Now what? Strychnine doing in a street pusher was one thing. That was a death which could be explained away by some sloppy cocaine cutting. But this was something else. This was someone taking care of loose ends.

At my desk, I eased slowly down into a chair. Leaned forward at about an inch a minute, rested my weary head. The wood was cool on my face. Peaceful here.

In my desk drawer were files for each of my students. Addresses, phone numbers, science backgrounds, such as they were. I'd made one for Gomez. Later on, like in about fifteen or sixteen hours or so, I'd look at his file, but for now I drifted into sleep. Not the best of ideas considering that a chemical killer was using my lab as home base.

"Rich, you there?" a voice said. I recognized the voice. I didn't answer. Was I dreaming? The voice repeated itself.

I sat up.

"Come on back, Candy," I said, still not all awake. The drug had done a number on me. I needed some rest to recuperate.

She walked into the room, took one look at me, dropped her purse, came over to the desk.

"What happened? You're all white!" she said, her voice showing concern.

"Nearly a ghost. Sit down and I'll tell you," I managed to get out. I shook my head clear.

I brought her up to speed with a chronology. She listened, saying nothing until I was finished with my near–death story.

"You sure you're ok," she said, putting her hand on my cheek. It was the first time she'd touched me like that. Her cool hand felt good on my still warm face.

"Been better," I said, trying not to let the fear I felt get into my voice.

"Nearly being killed. That'll take it out of you. Where's the bottle? Let's run it to be sure," said Candy, keeping on task. It was a good thing she was here. I could sleep away and the next minute be eyeball to eyeball with someone who wasn't out for my own good.

"Let's not," I said. "Tell me about Gomez."

This I did to change the subject. Look like I was still in control. Machismo dies hard.

"Nothing new to tell," she said.

"Nothing?" I said, feeling my heart accelerate as I became excited, the sensation unpleasant, reminding me of what the atropine had done to me.

"No one was there but some rookie. There was no blood work up. What Dom told them was what they wrote down. Gomez ODed on cocaine. Case closed. End of story. We're still in the dark," said Candy. She, too, had then struck out. The dynamic duo wasn't doing so well.

"Not quite. Strychnine and brucine were educated guesses. There's no question about what killed Brzenk. It was atropine, I can testify to that," I said.

So now what?"

I needed time to answer that one. Like, at least a year. Maybe I would ask Fenner for a sabbatical.

"Did you leave the lab after I went to class?" I said.

"For no more than fifteen minutes. Why?" said Candy.

"How'd this drink get doped? I made it up in the afternoon. It'd been in there for a day before Walt took it out. Who came in here? Was it before Gomez was killed or after?"

"There would only be two time slots. One, someone was in here during the night. The other is during those fifteen minutes when I was out." She said.

It was then that the whole water bottle business came clear to me. I walked over to the fridge, took out Mac's red bottle. Opened it. Full. Before I was really thinking what I was doing, impatient, putting myself back in danger, I dipped a finger in it, wet it, touched my tongue with it. Waited for my heart to explode. Nothing. I went back and sat across from Candy. My heart beat normally.

"You makin' yourself into a guinea pig?" she said, frowning at me.

"Yeah, but a least I learned something. The atropine was meant for me." I said, glad that she hadn't yelled at me for being a risk–taking moron.

"How do you know/"

"There were three bottles. Red, blue, green. All full. Brzenk spilled his, then filled up from mine. Bad luck on his part. I drank from what was left of mine, got a jolt. It was doped. Mac's is clean," I said, noticing that my sentences were a bit scrambled.

"So, at best there were two doped bottles. Brzenk's could've been dirty too."

"Yeah, but mine was dirty, that's all that counts. Whoever did this knows all about me. He knows that I run, he knew which bottle was mine, he knows a lot," I said.

I stood up. I was feeling better. Not a whole lot better, but better,

"I'm feeling better," I said, lying.

"You don't look better," said Candy, not lying.

I began to slowly pace the room.

"I'm in someone's way. That's what this is. Gomez could've been popped, then dumped. There was no reason to use brucine. But the atropine nails it. Someone's after me, someone who's using my own work against me," I said.

"Don't go overboard. Nikki's involved in this One–Percenter stuff. This killing of Gomez is exactly what they would do, kill someone, then stick him out where the world could see, like they used to do with human heads along the Amazon." she said."I'm going to Maria Perez's house."

"You didn't respond to what I just said."

"Someone's after me. I don't care jackshit about Gomez. Someone doped my bottle with atropine."

"You got a suspect?"

"Mac, he bangs Maria Perez, decides to take out Gomez, uses brucine, then comes after me."

"Why"

I didn't have a good answer for that one.

"I'm going with you."

"I've got something else for you to do," I said, picking up the phone. King Gomez had died in Brooklyn. He'd be laid out in Brooklyn. You died in Brooklyn, "Blueberries" Bonanno wanted to do the job. I rang up Blueberries. For the first time in a while, lady luck rode with me. Blueberries did a lot of Hispanic business, he had the King. I told him what I wanted from the body. No problem. I laid it out for Candy.

"I could still go with you. Then we could go get the samples together."

"No time. There's too much to do. The killer made one swipe at me, he'll make another," I said.

That sounded good, but the truth was that I didn't want to go prowling around Brooklyn at night with Candy. I was doing a piss poor job of protecting myself, so looking out for someone else was not on my to do list.

"You sure this is the way to go?" said Candy, her gray eyes fixing on me.

"Look Candy, this is killin'. We've got to be right. We can't go off half–cocked and be wrong. The killer's ahead of us, we've got to catch up."

"So you're gonna check out Maria's place. You gonna carry a gun?'

"I don't need a gun," I said.

Candy didn't reply. She'd heard an edge come into my voice. She didn't argue. She'd probably recognized the source of my tone. Candy knew a lot about men. There was no way to debate testosterone.

"So where does she live?" asked Candy.

I opened my desk drawer, took out Maria Perez's file.

"Off of Atlantic."

"A lovely area. So how long will this take?"

"An hour. No more."

"I best be on my way. Watch yourself."

Candy went over and picked up her purse from the floor. In it was her .38 Smith and Wesson. She was wearing her steel–tipped black flats. Anyone came after her they'd get a handful of trouble.

We went out in the dark hallway. She went toward the women's restroom.

I took the elevator. The college was dead quiet. Down in the lobby, it was also quiet.

Outside, it was hot, humid; it was not the best time for a night stroll. The natives would be restless.

I walked away from the college, my eyes looking about ten ways at once. I hoped I wasn't asking for it. I'd dodged some big bullets, now I had to get sharp and get a line on a chemical killer who knew chapter and verse about me. I was pumped up. Someone was after me. If I got that 'someone' he'd be sorry he'd ever lived. I walked faster.

# Chapter Sixteen

I didn't go directly to Maria Perez's house. That was the start of my bad thinking. Here I'd been preaching big time to Candy about us being on the same page, and I was going off half cocked. I'd headed toward Perez's, then remembered about Brzenk's dying on the promenade in Brooklyn heights. I got a bright idea to go after his green running bottle. I should have known better. Any idea that pops up on the way to break into the domicile of the girlfriend of a recently dispatched dope dealer is probably anything but bright, but away I went anyway, walking lickety–split, as if that would protect me.

I went to the promenade, which actually is a pretty nice place. Over the river, a good view of the city, ships, towers, wall street, uptown, two bridges, to the left the tall lady, the water with waves, the Hudson looking better than it was in reality, hard to tell what was going out downstream. I knew a thing or two about rivers and NYC. My old man had washed up near the battery. He'd made the undertaker work overtime in order to make him presentable to the assembled.

I started to comb the area, head down, pencil flashlight, back and forth, looking under and beside benches. These detective activities earned me a lot of eyeball time from the people who had come there to cool off.

"Sonny! Sonny! You're lookin' for what?" asked one of several old women taking in the night air.

"A bottle," I answer, still looking.

"Of what?" she continued.

"Water," I said, flashing my light past her pudgy legs.

The old woman smiled at me, looked at her friends, got a wink in return. Screw them. On the way home, I'd use my cell to make a call to social security and demand more cuts be made. I'd show 'em.

Starting on the garbage cans I also attracted attention.

"Down on your luck, pal?" said a white–haired old fellow with a pot belly, wearing a light colored shirt, checked pants of the same color, white sneakers, an outfit topped off with a white cap. He looked like he was just back from Boca Raton. He was with a buddy who was attired pretty much the same.

"Here's a fin, get yourself somethin' to eat," said the old man, handing me money. I took it. Upon retirement from the Urban U. there was a future for me in panhandling. I put the five spot in my pocket, waited for the two geezers to move on. Then I explored the cans in earnest.

The garbage of Brooklyn has a great deal to say about the present status of western civilization. For starters, there was a pink card in the shape of an erect penis which informed the curious about the whereabouts of someone going by the name of 'The Teaser', who, like Dominos, would deliver:

HOT TO TROT AND AT YOUR SPOT.

There were a number of pamphlets from the Radical Caucus of Fourth Avenue—the RC4A—demanding that the city dispense clean needles to addicts and insisting that the government allow all foreigners to enter the country. There was a ripped poster of the present mayor, under his honer's picture were anti–Semitic and anti–capitalist slogans. There was a cover of a book with some comments on the author's anatomy. There were soda bottles, cups, food forks, plates, spoons, cartons, all plastic which meant they'd soon be out to sea, then washing up on New Jersey's beaches where some little kid could stub a toe and pick up a disease, courtesy of the Big Apple. There were half–eaten subs and orange peels and the ends of slices which I managed to get on my hands and also on my sweats because that's all I had for wiping off. The topper had been the dog crap that some tidy citizen had scooped up and deposited and which I also smeared on myself. All that I found, but what

I didn't find was the green running bottle of the late Dr. Walter Everitt Brzenk, Ph. D. Princeton. R.I.P.

Doing all that searching had winded me. Atropine is strong stuff, able to do a number on anyone, even muscular Italians. This had not been a good idea, I assessed. I should've listened to Candy. I should have gone home to bed. I set off again for Atlantic Avenue, which was another of my brilliant ideas. It was already past the time when I'd told Candy I would return. She'd be worried about me. Atlantic Avenue was the area I'd run in yesterday, which now seemed like the very distant past.

It looked worse than it had during the early morning hours and the further I went, the worse it got. Evening had now come on in earnest, which meant the night prowlers were crawling out of the woodwork. I was sure they would be glad to see little old me, like Dracula giving the glad hand to Jonathan Harker.

# Chapter Seventeen

On Atlantic Avenue itself, I was in Arab land, the sidewalks full of women in veils and lots of kids, shops full of meat pies and spinach pies and pistachio pastries which put on ten pounds just to look at. I thought about calling Candy, inviting her to dinner at one of the interesting restaurants, putting detective work on hold for a while. The thought passed, I bore on through the swarms.

New York's always been like this; the newcomers huddle together for safety, then take over an area. Pretty soon, they run the show and anyone who isn't one of them gets the fisheye, and sometimes worse. Bensonhurst in my day was like this, with guys like me introducing the unwary to the rules of etiquette. Here, there were probably young studs galore who were just like I'd been. Mirror images of me in my younger days. That was not a comforting thought. They would take a dim view of midnight wanderers in their space.

Leaving Atlantic Avenue, I descended into the land of the downtrodden. Down at the heel stores, rats on garbage detail, buildings with here and there a full pane of glass in a window, a considerable amount of flotsam in the street.

Some of it came up to me, blocking my path. Something in rags. Something with a smell strictly from cat litter. Male? Female? Who could tell?

"Hey, big man, how 'bout I give you one for five dollah? Make it worth your while, man! For jus' five little ones!"

"You want your fuckin' face broke! You want me to rip your fuckin' heart out!" I replied, bulging out my already thick neck, giving my best demented guido impression.

"Hey, man, no problem, maybe nex' time," said the tatterdemalion, stepping aside, giving me a wide berth.

Sweat dripped down my back. I needed the street smarts I used to have. Even something like that could give me an ice pick in the eye.

The hot night was working with the garbage piled up between the buildings to give the area an odor all of its own. In blocks like this, no one walked the garbage down and outside and tucked it neatly inside a can. Here, kitchen windows were opened and the slop airmailed to the ground. Dinner falling out of the sky about five times a day. Rat heaven. The sidewalks were obviously used a great deal by large dogs. I stepped in something. Swore. I wiped my sneakers off on the curb. Pizza it wasn't. Some very big dogs around here. I started to listen for them. Close encounters with pit bulls weren't for me. Down here, no one would call off the monster. A crowd would gather, and they'd be laying eight to five as to how long it would take Fido to chew up the white meat.

I began to check numbers to find Maria Perez's place. Surprise. I walked out of the city of dreadful night and into first a better block, then still better. An area which was being fixed up. Quiet all of a sudden. A different world. Brooklyn's like that. One block a jungle, the next with yuppie types redoing brownstones. Brooklyn is nuts.

A cab pulled up, and a short, stacked, red headed woman wearing tight jeans and a white tee shirt got out. She went quickly from the car into one of the houses. This was the type of place where a professor might live. These old places would look good once they were done over. That's who this person was. She was a professor of Art History. It was Annie Porter, and she wasn't alone. Getting out behind her and paying the cab driver was my old pal and close colleague Dean D. Douglas Fenner, Ph. D. J.E.R.K. I watched Fenner follow Annie up the front steps. At the door, she gave him the keys. He opened the door. I waited for him to carry her over the threshold. She slipped her hand into his. They disappeared. Oh boy.

Seeing Annie threw me. Fenner was in my no–account book. No looks, no build, no brains, no class—a baccalÃ ; yet here he was heading for a hot time in the sack with a wanna be sixty's flower child who had looks, a body to die for, brains, and class. Not so long ago, that had been me instead of Fenner, sniffing after Annie, acting like I was a swinger, playing sex games while my wife was being ripped open by hot steel. I felt my memory click into gear. I clamped down on it, forcing myself to remain in the present. This was not the time for a guilt flashback.

Annie had moved. This wasn't where we'd gotten it on. She was starting a new life, apparently with fuckup Fenner who'd been married for thirty years to a real bitch. I knew. I'd met her at one of the faculty get–togethers. A real piece of work, which was probably why Fenner was after a piece of Annie.

So Maria Perez didn't live in a dump. It took some bucks to live around here. Gentrification or not, the prices were steep. So much for saying "no" to drugs. Perez had said "yes" in a big way, become part of the King's operation.

Now what? I'd counted on Perez's living in a shithole where I could use my handy dandy break in tool to jump a crummy lock. Once inside, I could see if there was something to learn about Gomez and maybe about Mac, figuring that young Ms. Perez would be out on the town, whooping it up with her ill–gotten gains, shedding crocodile tears over her dead boyfriend, who she hadn't liked enough to lay off getting laid by Mac. But this was no area for break–ins. Coming past now, cruising slowly was a small, yellow neighborhood patrol car. They would make a note of me, not that I was particularly noteworthy in terms of detective skills. They'd see me more as trouble. A large, sweating Italian, no doubt a meat eater. Dressed in black. Pale in the face, light in the brain. I'd have to call Dom Mancini as a character witness to get off the hook. But not to worry, if I got nailed I had five bucks in my pocket to make bail.

Heading back to the college, a lot floated around in my troubled mind. I needed to bounce all that I knew and didn't know off Candy. Maybe she could figure out what had happened. I was lost. Didn't know up from down. All of what had happened in this long, long day preyed on me, swirled around and around, freezing my brain from being coherent.

I wasn't paying attention to where I was walking as I made myself go away from Annie's. I was deep in thought, not the best spot for that— this wasn't the Ivory Tower, this was the dirty basement of Brooklyn. Mac and Maria Perez. Mac was asking for it big time. All of his sex action, doing it to as many co–eds as he could, getting more ass than a bicycle seat, chickens coming home to roost, the cops would get on to him. But what if it was more than just sex crimes? What if Mac was the guy? What if the English professor was part of a drug operation? What if he'd lined his running pal up for a hit because I'd gotten too close to the truth? What if's, they'd be the death of me.

# Chapter Eighteen

Noise filled the hot night. Trucks, cars, screams, plenty of back and forth, the f–word used as verb, noun, and adjective, boxes blasting loud enough to be heard in Jersey.

I had blindly wandered onto an all–Spanish block where all the men looked like Roberto Duran, black, stone cold eyes, hair grooming by Valvoline, the type of guys who train roosters to rip one another apart, then bet who'd be king of the cocks. I tried to think of the Espanola I knew—si, no, habla, que pasa, adios. No problem. They would never know I wasn't a native. I had walked back into Shitville from the gentrified area. This was not a good place for me to be.

Into all of that I was heading, like a mozzarella in a mousetrap.

I'd been looking every which way but straight ahead. An error of judgment on my part. About ten meters from me was a group of kids, both boys and girls, using up most of the sidewalk, amusing themselves listening to rap, which no doubt went something like:

HEY MAN HIDY TIDY LETS GO OUT AND CARVE UP WHITEY.

Great stuff, best used for atmosphere during a knifing. The music of the night.

They saw me.

"Hey, Whitefuck, what ya doin' here?" yelled one of the kids, as all seven of them honed in on me, like sharks after a bleeding swimmer. I'd asked for it. Wearing black sweats, white tee–shirt, having white skin, like Bambi with a large, red X on his brown deer ass.

Seven little street punks of the worst kind. If they'd been eighteen or nineteen, then I might've been able to scare them. A kid that's nearly twenty has probably been swatted often enough to know when to cut his losses, but these were vicious little vermin, twelve, maybe thirteen years old, looking for a fix of violence. They weren't going to be scared off.

One kid came right up to me, doing his best, bad ass pimp roll, hat on backwards, shirt out, everything oversized, working his filthy mouth, the words reaching me, f'ing everything about me, my mother, my father, my clothes, my race, my haircut, having himself one hell of a time.

He got too close. I popped him right in his offending mouth. Left jab, straight from the shoulder, the fist turning over, two hundred fifty pounds of agitated Italian behind it. Blood spurted, two teeth flew out, the jaw broke. The kid went back, down, and then under an abandoned car. One down, six street killers to go. This should be easy.

I took off with the pack behind me, yelling and screaming, mostly in Spanglish and largely incoherent to me since most of it was more than si, no,hable, que pasa and adios.

I made like an Olympic sprinter, going full blast, then I tripped, fell, slamming into the concrete, knocking the wind out of myself. I got up slowly, like Marciano after the Mongoose had snuck in a right cross.

The enfant perdus closed in on me, cut off my escape route. Two of them got around in front of me, knives out, holding them like they meant business. One of the gang behind me unloaded, and I took a rock between the shoulders.

The two in front of me had to go. Once past them, I could again run for it. They edged toward me. The one closest had his left arm bent and his right arm cocked and the blade of the knife turned sideways. By his side, his partner in slime was also in commando position. It used to be that nobody knew how to really use a knife, most people just hackers, but these young Americans had grown up on kung–fu movies. They had the moves down right. Who said nothing of value could be gleaned from TV and the movies?

The pukes took too long making up their minds what to do. One of the girls jumped in from my right side and raked at my face with her steel comb. Mistake on her part. I grabbed her by the hair and threw her at the two in front of me, made myself a path, started down it. Now I would run a fast ten K, leave everyone in the dust. I wasn't going to fight this whole pack. Bruce Lee was dead, and I was no Bruce Lee. I was no quail either. What I was, was out of here.

Someone screamed behind me. I looked back and saw one of the kids go down, a gun skittered away from him. He'd been about to shoot me. His leg was bleeding. The rest of the group from hell was looking down the street into the darkness of one of the burned out brick buildings. There was a pop, and one of the girls went down, blood spurting over the shoulder of her floppy white tee–shirt.

Something big and black and low and moving fast shot into the hyenas and latched onto the kid who'd been leg shot. A pitbull, over a hundred pounds. I was glad to see him. He was all right with me. After he was done ripping up, I'd buy him a Milkbone to help clean his choppers. The kid tried to get away, but canis familiaris clamped down on him, pinned him right to the concrete, thrashed its big head back and forth, spraying blood, going after the meat. The kid screamed louder. I didn't blame him. He had something to scream about. My heart bled for him, but that was unnecessary. He bled just fine by himself.

From a fourth story of a building, with the second and third full of burned out windows, a man was yelling a mile a minute, but I could only make out two words: "Mi perro! Mi perro!"

I searched my extensive word bank. A perro was a dog; a dog was man's best friend. Truer words were never spoken.

I left the Brooklyn block party. I felt it was time to go. Never outstay a welcome—that's my motto. It'd been some party. A kindly professor had about got a free face lift, there'd been knife action, there'd been one fast knockout, there'd been a couple of wounds, and now a cachorrito was making a meal out of some street punk's superficial fascia. Nighttime in the borough—how sweet it was! Something for everyone, but all good times must come to an end. It was time to go. I must be going.

No one followed me. The dog was still gnawing on the muchacho and the street was filling up with people who were trying to help and those who just wanted to watch.

The rest of the way back, the streets gradually lessened in terms of action and, lucky me, I ran into no more pre–teens out to make their bones. Hurrying along, I glimpsed, out of the corner of my eye, a bright red Toyota Supra which scooted past me.

I'd been backed up. Good, I'd needed backing up. I made a mental note to change my letter of reference for Candy from excellent to really, really excellenApproaching the college, I could see it was dark from top to bottom. I let myself in through the garage door. I walked past one Beef Patty Norwood, who was practicing false security by sleeping on the job, and rode the elevator to my floor, making a great deal of noise in the dead quiet hallway. I came into the lab and closed the door behind me. Then locking it.

"Hi, you get the samples?" I said.

"I got them. How'd it go?" said Candy.

"Nothing. She lives in a gentrified area. No way I could break in. Also, I went over to the promenade to search for Brzenk's water bottle. Also nothing. I struck out big time. Let's run the samples tonight," I said, talking fast, trying to act normal.

"Tomorrow, I want to be sharp. Also, I found something."

"What?" I said.

"These," said Candy handing me a package of pictures.

The photos featured Dr. Ross McClure, author of Narrative Intent in Dickens and Morality and Our Mutual Friend and The Abuse of Audience in Oliver Twist who was engaged with a variety of women. With Nikki Nateal, with a Jewish girl known at the college as "Anywhichway" and the last one was of McClure and Maria Perez. I had to turn the picture to establish what was going where.

"These were in Brzenk's desk," said Candy.

"How'd that happen?"

"Before I left I remembered something. Last year Mac had room six twenty. This year he moved to six eighteen. Brzenk was assigned six twenty. I broke in."

"So the deliveryman brought the blackmail to the wrong place which means Walt knew about Mac and Perez when I went to the dean's office to be grilled by Dom. That's why he was so quiet. I just thought of something," I said, as insight flashed into my mind.

"What?" said Candy.

"When I came out of Fenner's office, Brzenk was there with Annie and Mac, acting like an oddball, moving his eyes over toward Mac, like he was pointing out Mac to me."

"So he knew. You know, of course, that this is Pang's work."

"Yeah, I can tell by the angle, no pun intended. The old scum had a clear shot into Mac's office."

"If Pang's in this, then so is Fat Harry."

"We need to take a look over there. Tomorrow, that's what we'll do. We'll break in then. Anyone down here while I was out?"

"No one," she said.

"Let's get out of here." I said.

I held the door open for her, being the gentleman that I was. It was the least I could do for her.

"Oh yeah," I said, stepping into the hall with Candy. "Thanks, Tonto, that was a good shot."

"You knew?"

"Six kids cornering me, the one with the gun gunned down, leg shot, nothing but a 'pop.' Then a girl with a knife taken out. Yeah, I knew."

"I got worried."

"I told you to stay put."

"I know that area. They were after you. I did what I had to."

"Why didn't you kill them?"

"Killings attract the cops' attention. In that area, shootings are a dime a dozen."

"Well, youse done good. You saved me from being carved into little pieces. That gun's safe, right?" I asked.

"Right."

Candy and I left the lab behind. It'd been a long day, but probably nothing like full of the stress professors experience at Smith.

# Chapter Nineteen

Getting to the elevator should've been easy. Simple. A piece of cake. Just leave the lab, look left, then glance right, check out to see if a sidewalk lunatic had come in to the college in search of a flop or maybe to use the john. Candy used her eyes, I sniffed the air. My nose is not only just big; a beagle, he could do worse than to have my nose. Some of these homeless had their last bath in the last century from mommy, so you could smell them before you saw them. Another long sniff, but there was no one. We had a clear coast. Smooth sailing. Five meters of open lobby, a little dirty, but still open. Strictly very easy. No problema. I should have known better.

To our right, the door to one of the classrooms opened. Nikki Nateal and J. P. Carlisle stepped into the empty, night hallway.

Both were dressed in basic bed–sty street bad black. Both had chains around their necks. Both had only two pieces of jewelry attached to the chains. One was a number one. The other was a percent sign.

Suddenly, the journey from the lab to the elevator seemed a tad more difficult to traverse.

"Need to talk with you, Doc," rumbled J. P.

"Sure," I managed, wishing I had a weapon with me, like a rocket launcher, a few armored, Stormin' Norman on my flank.

"She ok?" said J. P., inclining his big head toward Candy, who had moved slightly behind me. It was a face–off. Nikki and J. P. weren't placed very well. They were side by side, maybe three feet apart. I could slam into J. P. Nikki would get caught up in the action, Candy could shoot both of them. Ideas like that flashed through my mind. Student counseling: a little different at the Urban U. than at Illinois Urbana.

"She is a professor. Like me. What do you want?" I said, an edge coming into my voice. I wasn't in the mood for more of this street crap. If they had come for trouble, they'd find it.

"Mac's a problem," said Nikki, her voice suggesting tension.

"To whom?" I said, proud of myself for speaking in the right case. Grammatically correct; rhetorically direct. They'd probably put that on my tombstone:

DR. R. V. BUCCERONI : CORRECT, DIRECT, AND DEAD.

"To us," said J. P., his voice deep, a growl in it, like a panther clearing its throat. He was trying to sound tough. Maybe he was tough. He'd better be because he was about to get a lot of hurt. J. P. was tall. I wasn't. I'd go into him low, dig one into his balls, and see how he stood up to that.

"To what we believe in," said Nikki, looking at me.

I felt Candy move behind me. I knew what she was doing. In her purse would go her hand. Long fingers would wrap around the pistol. She could shoot them through her purse. Ok by me. I'd spring for the bucks to buy a brand new one. A bargain; cheap at the price if she saved my life. J. P. and Nikki had better be good. And they had better be fast. Candy was both good and fast. Me? I was just the man in the middle.

"You ok, Doc. You do your job. Mac, he do our women," said J. P., letting a hint of Bushwick slip into his speech.

I looked at Nikki. I had evidence in my briefcase that she knew firsthand about Mac's doings. Did J. P. know how far she'd gone in her investigations of Mac? Could that be used to separate her and J. P.?

"Nikki here check Mac out. He thinks he the man. He's wrong," said the big man.

That answered that. So much for my complex Roman strategy of divide and conquer.

"So now what? What are you going to do?" I said, edging a step closer to J. P.. Thoughts flashed across my mind. Scenarios of how I could take him down. If push came to shove, I wanted him at close range. At a distance, he could stick and move and cut me up; but up close I was still something of Mr. Inside, and might still have the stuff to nail him good. He was younger and quicker, but stronger, maybe not, and meaner, we were even. I would see how this warlord reacted to his ear being bit off. That'd been my trademark back in Bensonhurst in the last millennium. Not many guys have much of an appetite for staying in a fight after they see their opponent chewing on what was once their ear lobe.

"When the time right, we act. But we don' act till we think all this out. You know Mac. He talk to you. We give the motherfucka one las' chance. He don' zip it up, then we cut it off, make him eat his own dick," said J. P., his voice loud in the empty lobby.

This conversation should be burned on a CD. I would get a standing ovation at the NSTA convention.

"You expect him to listen to me?" I said.

"I listened to you. I came to work in your lab," said Nikki, her large brown eyes open wide. Nikki was one of my pet projects. I was supposed to be taking the street out of her. I would not give myself a passing grade as of this instant. That's the trouble with pets, sometimes they don't want to be petted.

"This got nohin' to do with you two. Mac, he jus' got to stop," said J. P., his eyes never leaving Candy. He recognized a threat when he saw one.

"The college doesn't need any more violence," said Candy, her voice calm, no quaver in it. Candy didn't lose her cool. That meant there were three cool customers in the lobby. And then there was me. I was also in the lobby.

"The college got to be clean. Our black women, they come here to improve theirselves, they don' need some whitey humpin' them for his fun," said J. P.

"And they don't need that little slant next door either," said Nikki., meaning she knew what was in my briefcase.

"There anybody not on your list?" I said, backing down from my plan of attacking J. P.

"Right know you two is at the top of the ok list," said J. P., lowering his voice.

"I'll talk to him," I said.

"When?" said Nikki.

"Tomorrow. I'll see him tomorrow. You want me to talk to Pang too?" I said.

J. P. laughed. At least that's what I thought he did. His lips parted, a sound came out., but it wasn't pleasant. It was more like the noise the head lion made while it turned a slow antelope into dinner for one.

"No, Doc, you don' got to talk to the slant." Nikki laughed too. I was a hit. The crowd wasn't so tough after all.

"One thing, do you care if he does all women or just black women?" I said.

"He hump all he want, he jus' leave our race alone," said J. P., turning away from me.

The two of them left, used the stairs, leaving Candy and me alone in the lobby. I took a deep breath. It was good to be still in one piece.

"Life sucks," said Candy.

"Yeah."

"They're trouble. Big time," she said.

"Yeah."

"You going to talk to Mac?"

"Yeah," I said, extending my list of affirmatives.

"Think he'll listen?"

"No. You said he was a sex addict. How well do addicts listen?" I said.

"They don't. But this is simple. He fucks the blacks, he gets chopped up."

Candy had a way of cutting to the chase.

"One thing: Did you reload?"

"I always reload. Having an empty gun reduces me to using my lipstick in self defense," she said. I thought about patting her on the back but, somehow, a pat didn't seem appropriate.

I punched the buttons for the elevator. I felt like I was a thousand years old. Tomorrow should be a fun day. Run a race with Mac, comment on his athletic prowess, keep him in front of me just in case he's the killer who's after me, then work into the conversation a warning about he could come to lose his dick.

Down we rode to the parking garage. My car had been fixed. The battery had been the problem. Triple A had come through for me. Maybe I should hire them to go and talk to Mac. Someone needed to take the juice out of his battery.

# Chapter Twenty

Candy and I went out to dinner. She was surprised when I brought it up. We'd never done anything outside the college. No dinners, no movies, no shows, no drinks, no nothing—all of that leads to trouble. I should know; that's how I got mixed up with Annie Porter. A little this, a little that, then a roll in the hay.

This evening would have been more of the same old, same old: her to her place to do whatever she did, me to mine to feel sorry for myself and plot revenge on the world until Jack Daniels closed me out for the night. That I would've done, except for the fact that I spotted a tail as we drove up Atlantic toward the BQE. I didn't want to head home with a killer on my bumper.

I'd been lucky to get onto the tail. On Atlantic, I'd slowed down to stop at the Damascus bakery to buy a Syrian pastry, which was right up my alley, about five hundred calories in a one–inch square. I'd hit the brakes, swerved to join the double–parkers, looked in my rear–view mirror, and there it was. Three cars back. A small car, something foreign and cheap, pulling over as I did. For once, warning bells went off. This time it didn't take my getting poisoned to see the light.

My eyes weren't keen enough to give me a read–out as to the driver as male or female. I said nothing to Candy. If I told her, she'd turn and look. It's a reaction, can't help it, and then the tail would have us. Right now, I was in the cat bird's seat. I was in control. I knew all about tails. Dom had taught me. I'd rode with him at times when he was new on the force as a detective, younger then, full of piss and vinegar.

"Come ride with me, Richie, show you how it's done. I'm the best tail in the precinct. This guy we're followin' is a real big time, fuckin' ladies man, flashin' the folding stuff all over town. A fuckin' jerk. Small time. A dope peddler, still you got to nail them one at a time. This guy thinks he a fuckin' slickster. You ride with me. I'll be right up his ass, and he'll never know it," he said, bragging.

Dom had been good then. He had a wife he was crazy about, and vice versa. She was also a looker. He was climbing up the ladder at work, had a shot at being a captain. Dom had been showing off, letting me see how good he was at his job. That was ok by me. Dom had reason to be proud of how far he'd come. From the wrong side of the law to the right side had not been an easy journey, but he'd done it.

The tail kept back five cars when we were local, three on the BQE, as much as seven or eight when we hit Manhattan, where the avenues were long and, at this hour, the cars were mostly cabs. This guy knew his onions.

I pulled into a parking garage in the fifties, going east. the attendant came over, I gave him some bullshit about making a mistake pulling in, drove through, came out into a westbound street. The tail didn't show. That was a good one on my part. The tail had two choices. Set up a stake–out from the street, find a parking place, wait for me to come out, follow on foot or drive inside, park in the same place as me. Either way the tail was out of it. I wasn't coming out, and I wasn't in. Candy and I were away clean.

"You lost him," said Candy.

"Lost who?" I said, innocently, being coy, fooling not even myself.

"The tail you've been drivin' nuts since we left Atlantic Avenue," she said.

I could feel her smiling at me.

I needed to have more respect for the talents of others. Candy was the daughter of a cop. She'd probably been taught tailing as a toddler.

"Who was it? You get that too?" I said.

"Had on a hat. Car was a Nissan. Old, New York plates, easy to ignore. Your trick worked. Nice foxhole."

"Foxhole?" I said.

"My father told me that foxes always have an escape hole. You did it just right."

"Thank you. You didn't happen to see any moles or face warts did you?"

"No. Any idea who it was?"

"The killer," I said.

"And that is?"

"Let's eat, I can't solve crimes on an empty stomach," I said. This night would probably get worse, but I was going to die full and content. I wheeled my Toyota into a parking space. Ahead, was my favorite steak house. Porterhouse, crisp on the outside, pink on the inside, enough fat to keep me warm all winter. If I lived to see the winter, I'd die happy.

# Chapter Twenty–One

"Penny for your thoughts," said Candy after we'd ordered. She'd been sensible. It was late to be overeating. She'd chosen a salad and a white wine of some sort, a Riesling, I think. I, on the other hand, had not been even close to sensible. Bass Ale, backed up by a Dew. Porterhouse. Potatoes. The dead man's diet.

"I'm tryin' to think of how many small people I know who want to kill me."

"The driver might just be some nut," said Candy.

"I'd thought of that. A bumper car devotee. Pick a target, tail, ram, I pull over, he pulls over, I get out my insurance card, he get outs his .9mm, I get whacked, he gets away. Another shitty story in Shittown," I said, drinking, then chasing. "But that type of thinkin' gets me nowhere. Nuts aren't my problem right now," I continued.

"There are just three who fit the bill," said Candy, sipping her wine. She looked good in the night world of the restaurant, her blonde hair light against the dark of the walls.

"Let's hear your candidates," I said, taking my second swallow of my Bass. More than a swallow I must confess. I told the waiter to bring me another. In fact, I told him two others. I love waiters, they do as they're told as long as you paid them. I finished my Due. I felt warm inside. The evening was an infant.

"Nikki," said Candy.

"Nope." I replied, eyeing the waiter, making sure he was following my order to the tee.

"Jimmy Fisheyes," she said.

"Also a nope," I said, tanking up with the best Ireland had to offer. The waiter had returned, earning his tip, no doubt knowing an easy mark when he saw one.

This was not so bad. Drink; listen to Candy figure all of this out; correct her lapses in logic, then shove in a side of beef; head for home, sleep the sleep of kings; tomorrow kill a killer. Easy. Simple. Cheers.

"You have some reasons you'd like to share with me?" said Candy, again sipping her wine, watching as the waiter sat some more elixir in front of her boss.

"I'm in the middle of something. Someone wants me out," I said, slowing down as I reached the end of my very short speech, my line of reasoning seemingly a bit fuzzy; strange, in my mind, I'd been clear as a bell. I blamed the Bass for waylaying my logic. I looked around. We had the place pretty much to ourselves. I had a table with my back to the wall. No one could get behind me. I was really clever. I took on more Dew.

"So those two don't fit the bill?" asked Candy.

"They're missionaries. Nikki's on her One Percent kick. Jimmy's the Asian Avenger. Why kill me? Nikki told me about Mac. She as much as admitted they were going to slice him. She had to trust me that I wouldn't tell Dom and finger her. It wasn't her, makes no sense. I'm doing what she wants. It's not her," I said, aware of my repetitions once they were out and away from me.

"And the inscrutable Mr. Fisheyes?" said Candy, running a long, slim finger around the edge of her glass. I liked that finger. It'd been able to direct two good shots into a pack of creeps. That finger was Jake with me.

"Also a definite no. He's after Nikki and J. P. The three of them are strictly street gang. I'm not a blip in their plans."

"Wiant," said Candy, introducing a new candidate in the Murder Bucceroni Contest.

"Now you may be on to something," I said, moving my pints of Bass and my Dew over so that there was room for a large, filling–the–plate steak, potatoes, creamed spinach, and garlic bread. Candy's side of the table had plenty of room, so I put some of my food next to her. It looked good over there. Nicely balanced out the table. She took a small bite of her house special salad while I filled my mouth with a generous part of the better parts of an Angus who'd died for mankind. It tasted good.

"Good?" she asked.

I nodded. I tried to smile with a mouth full of rare beef. She smiled back. She was probably glad to see me eating. Without the steak, I would drown myself in ale and saturate my brain cells with Dew.

"Wiant's a maybe," I said, with food in my mouth. My mother had tried to correct that flaw in me, but she wasn't around now.

"Wiant's a creep," said Candy, not smiling.

"That's why he's a 'maybe.' This has CREEP written all over it. Brucine and atropine are creep tools. This is, number one, a ruthless bastard who's a hardass about the bottom line. And, number two, this is someone who doesn't mind doing a number on someone. Wiant's a definite maybe," I said, without a single speech slur. I would've patted myself on the back, but that would've slowed down my eating.

"Who else?" she said.

"Mac."

"I thought Mac was your friend. He that devious?"

"Look, I'm not ruling out anyone. Mac fucks his students. Nikki and J. P. were dead on about him. He's got no business turning his office into a fuck farm. Who knows what else he's got into? He did Maria. What else did he do with her?"

"It was someone small in the car," said Candy, finishing her wine. I raised my hand to get her more. She shook her head no. This was the first disappointing moment of the evening. Drinking large amounts was one thing; drinking large amounts alone was another. I took a drink.

"It was someone small in the car."

"The car was pretty far back to tell exactly the size, that's for starters. Second, if Mac is the one, then he could've sent Maria after me. She could have tailed us out of Brooklyn," I said, my words a little uneven as they struck the open air.

"Running a drug operation? That's stretching it for Mac"So, anyone else you got in mind?" I asked.

"No one." She said.

"You want some steak, its good," I said, generously offering a sliver of steer. She declined. I didn't offer again.

I was in no hurry. I needed to build up my killing strength, get in shape to bring down a clever chemical killer. The atropine hadn't completely left me. I felt a little off, like I was getting the flu. I ate more and drank a lot. Fat and alcohol. The flu wouldn't have a chance.

# Chapter Twenty–Two

The night turned out to be like most nights. I'd hope that companionship and a belly full of beef and a gallon or so of good booze would be just the ticket for sedation. No such luck.

Candy drove back from the city so that we could both live. For once, she kept mostly within the speed limit. No one accompanied us on our return to the borough. She dropped me at my door. She would leave my car at my place in the garage then walk home. Bay Ridge should be safe, although safe is a relative term in Brooklyn.

"You want me to walk you?" I said, not being really in shape to walk anyone, including myself. I held on to the front door of my house. The world seemed to be moving up and down.

"I'll be fine. You get some sleep. Tomorrow'll be a long day. We'll run the samples," she said.

I watched Candy walk away. She looked like she still had some pep. Hooray for youth! I opened my front door, went inside, moving at glacier pace.

The house seemed to have gotten larger and darker. Staying with Candy the other night had been a step into the light. Being with her this evening had been living. My return to my castle of gloom wasn't exactly a pick me up.

Something red was blinking in the dark foyer. I flipped on a light. There was a phone message on my recording machine. From my dean, no less.

"Hello, Rich. This is Doug. I'll be at the college early. Let's have a talk. Goodbye."

I played the message back three times so that it could make an impression on my alcohol soaked brain. I didn't trust my own ears. Was this a joke? Was someone impersonating Fenner? Playing a fast one on me?

'Rich? Doug? Let's talk. Goodbye.' This from a guy who usually talked to me as if I were a collie. Sit up; sit down; shut up. What accounted for the difference? What did we have to talk about? It made my head ache to think about it.

The house felt cold. I felt hot, like I had a temperature. This was no time to be sick.

In the kitchen, I took on water straight from the tap. My head still ached, a bit early for a hangover. My legs itched. I never should've left the steakhouse. I would've been better off to eat myself into a stupor and then pass out. Have them stack me in the meat locker.

I now headed for the upstairs, which seemed to be a big deal in terms of journey.

To the third floor I went, skipping my nightly ritual. Once there, I stood at the window and watched Candy's lights go out. Living room, hall, a pause. I stood there for some time, swaying a bit. Then her bedroom, now all of it was dark. She would probably be asleep in minutes. I caught myself from saying 'hooray' again.

My mind leaped into gear as to who was after me. Liking Mac made it hard to see him as the guy, but my old man had taught me a thing or two about trusting people. Mr. Left and Mr. Right, those two guys you can trust, he'd told me. All the while he was telling me this, he was punching at me, teaching me to slip a punch, spending quality time turning his son into a dunskey.

My old man was right. Mac could've done this. The fact that I didn't know definitely that he was guilty meant nothing. Mac required some of my careful, sober attention. I wondered if I'd ever be sober again. I was pretty drunk. Mac might be just a professor with a prick problem, but he might also be a guy on the way out of a job/career looking to score big and quickly. Tomorrow would be a new day. Tomorrow I'd give all of this sober attention to Mac.

I eased into bed with my clothes still on. I now smelled of Bengay and booze. Maybe that was why Candy opened her driver's side window while she drove us back home. She'd also kept her keen eyes on the rearview mirror. That much I was not too drunk to see. I'd done my bit by peering out the passenger side window. Nothing. We were clean from the moment we'd got back into my car to the moment we'd arrived in Bay Ridge.

I rested my weary hot head on the cool, soft pillow. Candy was right; tomorrow would be a big day. I hoped it wouldn't be my last day.

I drifted off into an uncertain sleep.

# Chapter Twenty–Three

The next morning found Candy and me back at the college. Candy worked on the samples while I used my master key and 'broke into' Mac's office. This was sex central. If these walls could talk, they could make a fortune with Penthouse.

I took a break from going through Mac's filing cabinets and walked over to the window.

On the street in front of Mr. Buffalo Pang's liquor store was a burned area. I had brought Candy's binoculars in the likelihood that I would need to see across the way where the smut photos had been taken. I focused on the burned area, which wasn't an area but the remains of Pang's big, meaner than death itself dog.

"What're you looking at?" said a voice close to me.

"Jesus! You wearin' moccasins?" I said, jumpy because Candy had walked right in on me. She could've been anyone. Like Mac. Or maybe a killer. I had to get up to speed, and else I'd get run over.

"What's over there?" she repeated.

"What's left of Pang's dog," I said.

She took her binoculars from me. The big Doberman was on its way to dog heaven, or hell, as a char–broil. My eyes shifted to the roof.

"Can I have those back?" I asked, feeling tension take hold of me.

The binoculars were strong, of good quality. Candy didn't own junk.

They worked just fine. They let me see what was there on the roof. Lucky me.

"Let me see," said Candy.

"It's not pretty," I said, trying to spare her the sight.

"Let me see," she said again.

I gave her the binoculars.

She looked. I heard her draw her breath in. Candy had seen a lot of this life's evil, but this would occupy a prime spot in her memory.

Mr. Pang was on the roof. He was tied to a chimney. Naked. He was missing some parts. He was slumped over. Dead? Alive? I couldn't tell.

Candy's binoculars were German. I had seen it all. It took some effort not to heave all over Mac's clean sex parlor.

"If Mac could see this, he might listen very closely to you about his nocturnal activities," said Candy, her voice normal.

"Let's get back to the lab. Dom'll be down here to clean this up. We better be where we have reason to be."

"Should we call it in?"

"Yeah, but use the student pay phone in the lobby," I said.

We left Mac's office and walked down the dirty, dark empty hallway. I went to the lab, Candy headed for the phone.

The night's sleep had not done much for me. My head still ached, worse than last night. I was still hot. I was getting sick, no doubt about that. I didn't tell Candy. She needed for me to be ok. I determined to be ok even if it killed me.

# Chapter Twenty–Four

Candy had laid out Pang's pictures on a table. They were a nice complement to Mac's professional curriculum vitae. Here were the visual goods on a professor who treated his students like they were sexual candy, little chocolate fuck drops. I doubted if this were done at Sweetbriar, but who knows?

Pang was a good photographer. Not only could he get kids to come to his place and strip down and let him pose them, but he'd also been a whiz at long distance photography. The disgusting old fellow had a good view of the faculty offices. He had shot down and into Mac's offices. I wondered who or what else he had captured on film.

Someone knocked at the door, driving my heart up a few million beats, bringing back unpleasant recollections of yesterday when I'd nearly been doped to death in this very room.

Candy scooped the pictures into a plastic bag. She moved to the back of the lab. Her hand went to her purse.

As I opened the door, it occurred to me that I was the one who should be at the back of the lab. Like under a table. Maybe I'd invest in body armor for the lab, trash the white jackets.

I wasn't expecting this to be a pleasant visit. I was not disappointed.

"Hello, Professor Bucceroni," said Jimmy "Fisheyes" Kim.

"Come in, Jim," I said, letting into my lab another of the college's young killers. Mr. Fisheyes was known as a knife man. He had a knife. Candy had a gun. And me? I had wit, and fear.

Yesterday, I'd been up close and personal with the brain trust of the One Percenters. Today, I was face to face with the president of the Seoul brothers. R. V. Bucceroni, Ph. D., chemist and gang counselor. There could be a future in this for me, or it could be the end of me.

Pang saw Candy. He smiled at her. She nodded.

"She is with you, yes?" he said, his voice was soft, measured, but that didn't make him any less deadly.

"Yes, she is with me," I said, being aware of the stilted, formal nature of our exchange.

"My uncle has been murdered by your lab assistant and the African," he said, no beating around the bush for this boy, getting the message immediately out.

"This sounds like police business," I said, keeping my distance from him. Knifers like to get in close, slice open the unwary. If there was anything I was now, wary was it.

Jimmy Fisheyes laughed. His laugh was not any more pleasant than J. P.'s. Laughter was no longer one of my favorite sounds.

"Professor Bucceroni, you are an Italian. I have researched you. You know very well that the police count for very little in this city. In your day, your people, how do you say, 'took care of business.' Now it is our day. We are much like you. Did your father believe in the police?"

"No, that's why he got killed," I said, impressed by what he knew about me. My publications may not have made me rise in the Korean's eyes, but having a wiseguy for a father did.

"Death does not scare me. Fear is a luxury. To be afraid is to believe that one can run away and be safe. There is no place to run away from your Miss Nateal and the head of the One Percents. They must be confronted. And removed," he said, making a fairly long speech. All of it done without raising his voice. J. P. would have a time of it with this boy.

"You came here for a reason. What is it?" I said, cutting to the chase, not wanting to hear any more killer Zen.

"The One Percenters have completed an operation. They have been quite ruthless. I must retaliate. You have been just to my people. Fire Miss Nateal." Bam. Bam, bam, followed by a request.

Why me? All I had done was my job. Now, I had the blacks and the Asians acting like I was the great white hope. I was too good for my own good. I had to give some serious thought to doing a thoroughly shitty job.

"You come in here and tell me you're gonna whack Nikki and J. P. and you're not worried that I won't tell the cops?" I said, staring him in the eye, an old trick for sometimes the eye moves before the hand strikes. His eye moved I'd flatten him.

"No, I am not worried. You know what is, as you say, 'going down.' You will say nothing. Remove Miss Nateal from her place of employment. Thank you," he said. Clearly and distinctly.

Fisheyes extended his hand. We shook. He had a strong grip for a slim man. He bowed to Candy. I don't know what she did, for I kept my eyes on the cobra in the room. I held the door open for him. He left. I shut the door, resisting the urge to nail it shut.

"Jesus!" said Candy, removing her hand from her purse.

I sat down at my desk. I felt weak and sick. I didn't want Jesus to help me. That would probably bring a pack of angry atheists after me.

"What we gonna do?" said Candy, letting some Bensonhurst back into her usual controlled speech.

I paused for a moment, summoned the strength to continue with all of this.

"My old man had somethin' like this once. Two sets of wiseguys got after one another. He used them," I managed to say. The feeling of sickness was spreading over me.

"How you gonna manage this?" she asked.

"Look, we have some things on our side. As of now, neither of them is after us. This war can't last forever. Sooner or later, there has to be a showdown between the two at the top," I said.

"Why does the Seoul King want you to fire Nikki?"

"How the hell do I know? Sorry. Sorry," I said, holding my hot head in my two hands.

"Maybe he plans to kill her down here. He didn't elaborate. Maybe he wants her to have no place to run to," I went on, forcing myself to remove my hands from my head. I couldn't look sick in front of her. This was just getting started. I had to be ok.

"It's crazy his coming to you like this," said Candy, looking closely at me. I could hear what she was thinking. He looks sick.

"Not from his point of view. These clowns are into being warlords, so this is a power rush for Fisheyes. In his way, he's letting me know he could take me out anytime he wanted to," I said, hoping my voice wasn't croaky.

"We've got no place to run to," said Candy, her voice even and steady, her eyes dry. Candy didn't cry. That was too bad. Right now, a good mutual boo–hoo would feel good.

"I want to tell you something," she said.

"Be careful?" I said.

"No, this is serious. What I want to say is that you can't trust anyone. This is just the two of us. No one can help us but us," she said, her gray eyes fixed on me, holding me in her steady gaze.

"What about Dom?"

"You listen to Mr. Fisheyes? Some of what he said made sense. The police are out of this? Did the police save Mr. Pang?"

"So it's like I said. Let Fisheyes and J. P. kill one another, reduce our problem to one. That's killing number one solved. But killing number two is what worries me. Mac still could be the guy."

"There's a time problem with Mac. Remember, Mac had to dope the bottle either Thursday night or during the day on Friday. That means, Mac had to find out that Brzenk had in his hands the pictures meant for him. Then he had to decide to use atropine. Then he had to come in here and dope the running bottle. Quick thinking on his part, then fast acting."

"Yeah, but one thing I learned from my old man is that first you decide who's the guy. That's the hard part. Then you get down to figuring out the details. How close are you there?" I said, the talking and my not wanting to be sick in front of Candy had helped me. The sick feeling had lessened.

"Let me get back to it," said Candy, pulling on new gloves. She settled back in to her analysis.

It would take an hour to drive out to see Mac. In the back of my mind was what J. P. had told me. I was supposed to warn off Mac. That way, he could live, and have a dick. The flip side was that with no warning Mac could end up hung out to dry like old man Pang. A chain of events was forming. A sequence of killings. And if it all worked out, then I was in the clear. Somehow I believed that was not the type of mind puzzle that occupied the professoriate at Penn.

While she worked, Candy talked. She was separating, probing, looking for traces of brucine.

"You willing to listen to some criticism about your Mac theory?" she said.

"I guess so, but I think I'm right. The use of atropine, that's right out of my papers. Mac knows my work. We've talked about it. Whoever did this also knows running, and this someone knows the particular details of my running. Mac fits the pattern."

"By why couldn't it be Fenner? He has his tenure down here. You told me that after doing nothing for too many years, he was sent down here as the dean, which shows the regard held for this place. It goes under, he goes down with the ship. Why can't it be him?" she said.

"Fenner? That's a reach," I said, watching her work. She was doing it all just right. I couldn't have have done it any better.

"It doesn't take a genius to poison a drink with brucine or load up a running bottle with atropine. All it takes is your work."

"Yeah, but fingering Fenner is pretty far off track. He's a fuck up. Always has been. No way he could run a crack operation with King Gomez. You're going back to square one. I think we've got three killings here. Pang, Walt, Gomez. One of the three was definitely done by J. P. and Nikki. Mac is the guy who came after me. Not Fenner."

"You in the mood for some criticism?"

"Let's hear it."

"I'll take that as a 'yes' even though it sounded like a 'no.' You're negative about Fenner. You don't see him clearly. You're squinting the facts if you dismiss him as a suspect because you don't like him."

"It's got nothing to do with 'like' and 'dislike.' Fenner's a type. College teaching's full of them—a dead out failure. He couldn't organize his sock drawer, let alone a crack operation. He's got no track record of ever doing anything right," I said, the anger pepping me up. I now felt half way well.

"But what if he had a partner like Mac. We know Mac did Maria. We know Maria was tight with Gomez. Was Mac part of the action, taking his cut, using it to buy a fancy car, then deciding to put Gomez under? And Fenner was there to help with the chemistry when it came time to kill you. At some point, someone had to see you as a threat. If you knew enough about Gomez to send a report to Dom, then it's possible that Gomez suspected he was being watched. You were/are in the line of fire. Fenner hates your guts. Fenner's a creep. He seems the type who'd give someone a brucine cocktail and not blink an eye. Mac and Fenner could be partners."

"I knew it was a mistake to take you on as a partner. Here I've got this whole thing nearly lined out, and here you go messin' with my great theory."

"I'm not saying you're wrong. All I want is to keep all options open. We've got no margin for error."

"So we shouldn't go to Mac's?"

"I didn't say that. My point was that I don't want you to look so hard at Mac that you get blindsided by someone else."

"What about the danger of going to meet a guy on his home turf?"

"That doesn't worry me. Too close to home. If Mac is the guy, he'll come after you down here."

"So let's do it. I want to know where an assistant professor gets the money for a Mercedes. I'll run the race with him, you talk to his wife. Maybe she'll say something."

I got McClure on the phone. We kidded back and forth about the race. All seemed normal. He was looking forward to beating me.

"You about done?" I said.

"There's something here. It could be brucine but I can't be sure yet. Time has passed, and your Mr. Blueberries has treated the body."

"How much longer?"

"Pushy pushy. Who once told me never to rush science?"

"Sorry."

While Candy finished her work, I decided to stop hovering. I would go down to the fourth floor. I'd forgotten to check my mail. Seeing Old Man Pang turned into an anatomy lesson had made me forget.

# Chapter Twenty—Five

I usually avoided the fourth floor when there was a chance of meeting someone, checking my mail on the weekends or at night, selecting times when Dean D. Douglas Fenner and his weird–ass assistant Winston Wiant H.E.O. would be elsewhere. This was all part of my grand strategy to prevent my breaking Fenner's neck or shoving Wiant through a window. Now, the outer office door of Fenner's deanspot was open. Turning toward the mailroom, I saw Mr. Wiant inside putting envelopes into faculty mailboxes. His fish belly white face was highlighted by a black suit, a bright white shirt and a black tie. The boyfriend of Bela Lugosi, that was him.

"Why are you here?" said Wiant, looking at me, his eyes inset, beady, black against the pallor of his skin.

"I work here."

"Today is not a work day."

"And they say administrators are morons. But here's you who knowing what day it is, you probably know what tomorrow's gonna be." I said, smilng at Wiant. I now felt ok.

"I suppose you've heard?" said Wiant, not reacting to my sarcasm, which is like the undead who care nothing about mere words.

"Heard what?' I said.

"Walter Brzenk is dead."

"Yeah, I heard," not liking to talk about someone I liked with someone I didn't like.

"The dean's on campus. We're arranging for a ceremony," he said. I removed my mail from my box and turned to leave. Fenner was standing in the doorway.

"Can I talk with you in my office?" said Fenn"Dracula's baby boy gonna be there?"

"Dr. Wiant is my assistant, he's part of the administration of this college."

"In that case, I gotta go. I have to change the oil in my car."

Fenner didn't move out of the way.

"Then just the two of us can talk. Come to my office," said Fenner, who stepped back, pivoted, headed toward where he did business.

"Gold's Gym, they got sun lamps," I said to Wiant, who didn't reply but went back to stuffing envelopes in mailboxes.

In Fenner's office I closed the door then took a chair in front of his desk.

"It's time we had a talk," said Fenner.

"Why?"

"Look, Bucceroni, you may be in for some trouble. You'd better find out who your friends are," he said, his voice rising, his face going red.

"What trouble?"

"You know very well 'what trouble.' That Gomez was a dope dealer. I know it. You know it. The police know it. Your lab is probably where the crack was cooked. Doesn't that sound like 'trouble' to you?" said Fenner, who looked steadily at me.

I didn't like Fenner's appearance. The long gray latter day hippy haircut, the jeans, the broadcloth shirt and tie, the bifocals low on his nose, peering at me with cold, blue eyes. But looks were one thing, words were another. Fenner had put two and two together. If idiots like Fenner were onto what had gone down, then sharp detectives were no doubt typing up arrest warrants, checking to see how many vowels were in my name.

"No, it doesn't sound like trouble to me. It sounds to me like you're tryin' to give me to the cops," I said, playing for time, getting a line on what Fenner was up to.

"Why should I do that? Look, Rich, you and I have never gotten on. Ok, fine, so be it, but I know what you've gone through, and I have no interest in adding to your misery."

Sarcasm I could handle, also antagonism, but this I had a problem with. Human kindness coming from an enemy was hard to deal with.

"Let me put my cards on the table. Here's what I think happened. I think that one of your lost soul crusades backfired on you. I think that one of your students got on how to make crack and that your lab was used as a factory."

"And who's the student?"

"Nikki Nateal. She's in league with J. P. Carlisle and I'll bet good money that both of them were partners with Gomez," said Fenner, giving to me a theory which was about one hundred percent dead wrong.

"You told this to the police?"

"No, I have not. Look, this school's on thin ice. We don't need bad publicity. Gomez is dead, found outside the college's wall. That's where I want to keep this whole business, outside, away from us. And you can help me."

"How?"

"This whole business will go away if the drug dealing stops. I see that you have changed the locks on the lab. Good. Also, you'll have to get rid of Ms. Nateal. Take away her excuse to be around the lab."

Fenner was the second person to suggest that Nikki be fired. I doubted if Fenner had the same end in mind for her as Jimmy Fisheyes.

"And that's it? Changing locks and firing lab assistants? That'll solve a murder?"

"To be blunt, I don't care about the murder. All I care about is this school."

"And your job?"

"You're damn right 'and my job.' I'm sixty–two. I've paid my dues. I need to keep on working. Therefore, I want this whole business over and done with. Let the drug dealing go on somewhere else. All I want is for us to be in the clear."

168

"I've already done some work with the lab. No one will get in. As for firing Nikki, I'll have to think about it."

"Think quickly. She's not just a dope dealer. She's a killer. Gomez didn't die from a cocaine overdose. That's just the police looking for an easy answer. I've read your papers. He was given brucine, which is another point. Don't you see how close you are to all this? It's your lab, your students, and your poison delivered in a manner described in one of your papers. Do you now see what I meant about trouble?"

I saw.

"And what about Walt Brzenk?"

"Tragic. I don't know if you have all the details. He was jogging and his heart gave out. A young man like that, one would never guess heart attack. I'm organizing a ceremony."

I said nothing about what had really happened to Brzenk. Fenner had enough evidence against me as it was.

"I think you're right about Nikki. I'll fire her tomorrow," I said.

"No, no. Don't fire her, that'll make her angry. Take it a step at a time. Close down your lab. Say that repairs have to be made. Say there's an asbestos problem. In the meantime, I'll send you a memo about inspections that you can use to tell her that her internship has to be canceled. That way, she'll go away and all of this will be settled."

"Sounds good," I said. And I meant it. I was lost, grasping at straws. This would buy me some time.

Fenner stood up, held out his hand. I shook it.

"This has cleared the air, Rich. We're on the same team. Both of us have an interest in taking all of this off the front burner."

I nodded my head in agreement and left the office.

Walking up to my own office, I felt sick again. On the sixth floor I went to the restroom and splashed water on my face. Fenner was right. I needed no trouble. I needed rest and peace of mind. I saw myself in the mirror.

"You lookin' at yourself, Valentine?" said a voice.

I turned quickly. There, by the door, was Dom Mancini.

# Chapter Twenty–Six

Turning around to face Dom, I now smelled the cheap, definitely, non–Havana cigar, but he had walked right up on me before I'd known anyone was around. J. P. Carlisle didn't smoke, didn't announce his presence at all. Neither did Jimmy Fisheyes. These thoughts were not comforting.

"Been lookin' for you," he said, looking closely at me. Dom missed nothing. He no doubt knew that I was less than chipper.

"So you found me," I said.

"You ain't all I found. Next door, the chink is dead, and he looks like a Thanksgiving turkey at the end of the day."

"I looked over there, I saw..."

"I know, the knockout tol' me," he interrupted.

"When did you see her?"

"Up in your lab. I come lookin' for you. Why the fuck you down here? What the fuck's the matter with you? This what you and her do on a date? Break into other professors' offices, then stand there and eyeball stiffs? You're fuckin' askin' for it, you know that?"

"How'd you know where I broke in?"

"The knockout, she tol' me. She's ok. She's got a head on her shoulders. I get the feelin', I give her some good advice, she might listen. Not like some people I know."

"What you want me to do? Hide under my bed? Someone's after me!" I said, my voice and temper rising.

"Who?"

"Yesterday, I almost bought it. There was this bottle of water in my lab. Someone had doped it with atropine. It came close to checkin' me out. It's what killed Brzenk," I said, the words coming out in a rush.

"Hey! Hey, hey, slow down. What's this about Brzenk? He's the tall skinny prof who was with you when you found the spic, the one they're makin'a big deal over down here? You're sayin' he was murdered? What the fuck is atropine?"

I took a deep breath. I wanted to lay this all out nice and clear.

"In my lab, I keep water mixed with Gatorade. When I run, I carry my own water. Brzenk took some of the mixture from my bottle when he went runnin'. It was doped with atropine. It's a drug which accelerates the heart. He took it with him to run on the promenade. He died right there. Yesterday, I drank some of it myself. Almost killed me. The dope was in my bottle, it was meant for me," I said, my speech a bit repetitive, but still understandable.

Mancini walked over to the window, looked out, relit his stinko cigar, then sat on the ledge.

"Richie, I want you to listen to me, and I want you to listen real good. This ain't some fuckin' professor talkin' ok? This is Dom, ok? This whole deal is lookin' bad for you. A long time ago, the two of us learned to trust no one but us. That still goes now," he said.

"Yeah, ok, so?"

"Look Richie, this case is getting' away from me. At first, it was just one dead spic dope dealer. Big fuckin' deal. Next, it's a chink who takes shunt shots and he's found on his own roof with his eyeballs cut out and missin' his dick. And then…"

"Why didn't you tell Doyle about the brucine? Candy said he told her that it was cocaine overdose," I said, breaking into Dom's speech, something which didn't go down well with him.

"See what I mean about you fuckin' askin' for it? See how you're fuckin' hell bent to get your balls busted? Now you got the knockout doin' your legwork down at the police lab. Look, there was an easy way to handle this case and a hard way. The easy way was the way I was doin' it, which was to treat all of this as a bunch of drug dealers after one another. That was how I played it. Told my captain that what we got here is some guy who ODed on his own dope. He bought it, and the case was well on its way to bein' closed, and you were home free. These other killin's will change all of that. We're not careful, there'll be detectives all over this place, and sooner or later someone will line up the three stiffs. When that happens, your ass will come in for some major league trouble."

Mancini drew on his cigar. It was getting close to be smoked through.

"Let's start over. And, this time, try and keep your mouth shut. Over at Pang's I found a shitload of pictures. He took a lot of shots of the action going on in the offices over here. I looked to see if he took any of that Gomez doing some dealing. You find anything when you broke in?"

I was hoping he wouldn't ask that. But he had. Now I had a choice. Tell Dom about Mac. Or clam up. I had a way to deal with Mac if he was the someone after him. J. P. Carlisle was my hitman. The problem was I didn't know what Candy had told Dom. Lying to him now would get me nothing.

"I found pictures of Mac and Maria Perez. Here's what happened. Someone tried to blackmail Mac, only they fucked up and delivered the pictures to the wrong room. Brzenk got them. The way I figure it, Brzenks's havin' those pictures got me on a hit list."

Dom drew on his cigar. He said nothing to me for maybe thirty seconds. The room felt hot.

"Look, Richie, I've been keepin' an eye on this place. This is what you got down here. You got a dean who's a Nervous Nelly about his job. You also got his douchebagflunkey who looks like he's a fuckin' funeral director. I gave some thought to those two. This smells like a drug operation. Who knows who the head guy is? So there's two to watch out for. Then you got two hard ass One Percenters, that big black bastard J. P. and that hot lookin' little black number who works for you. That's two more who could have done this. Then we got the Seoul Brothers. It'd be all right with me if the One Percenters and the Seoul Brothers fuckin' destroyed one another. Finally, we got this guy McClure. He's the guy I'm linin' up. He's fuckin' everything in sight, comes in at night to screw these college broads. I been watchin' him. Last night, he picked one up, drove around the corner, hit the lights, banged her lights out in the front seat of his big Mercedes. What can you tell me about him?"

"Mac's an assistant professor. He's about to get fired. He lives out in Jersey. Candy and I were going to check him out today," I said, keeping my answers short and sweet so that I wouldn't get yelled at.

"Whose idea was that?"

"Candy's."

"Well, she on the right track. He ain't a right guy. Your tellin' me that he was gonna be fired is the clincher. He's the type of guy who could run a drug operation. Nothin' to lose. One thing, how would he know about these drugs?" he said.

"We team–taught. He reads my papers. Making these types of chemical weapons is not that big of a deal, have to be careful with the brucine. So what do I do?" I said.

"Do what the knockout says. Get a line on him," Dom said.

"You the only cop that's pulled all of this together so far?"

"Who knows? For now, this is my case, but who the fuck know's who's checkin' up on me. But I'll tell you this: we don't need to make it easy for no one. We don't need for you to go sniffin' around Jim Doyle to find out about no autopsy. We need to close this down to just us. And right now us includes the knockout because I know you blab everything to her. You get me?"

All of this from Dom, bang, bang, bang, with an edge coming into his voice, his eyes boring right into me. I was getting tired of getting grilled. First Fenner, now Dom.

"Goin' out to Jersey is what Candy wants to do. We want to know where he gets the moolah for a Mercedes. One other thing, J. P. told me to tell Mac to stop his fucking of the black women. Nikki was there too. They made it very clear that he doesn't stop, then he gets it like old man Pang did.

"So use your brains. Time was that you could take care of guys like McClure with no trouble," Dom said.

"Your tellin' me that I may have to let the One Percenters do their number on Mac," I said, a chill coming over me that wasn't from any illness.

Mancini sat smoking, looking out the window. I thought I saw his shoulders slumped for a moment like he was tired of all this. I felt the same way. We said nothing. Silence hung in the room.

Finally, Dom spoke. He sounded weary. "What I'm sayin' is that this is gettin' away from me. Someone is giving you some serious attention. This killing of that Brzenk, that bothers me because what that tells me is that you're the target. You gotta stop actin' like a professor Richie. You gotta get with it," said Dom quietly.

He got up, squashed his foul cigar on the dirty linoleum floor. He came to maybe my shoulder. That shouldn't fool anyone. Dom had always been number one and me number two. I'd always depended on Dom when something bad was going on. Now was no different.

"So, let's say it is this McClure guy. What we got on him as of now? That he fucks his students? I'll bet good money that he ain't the only one doing that. And what else is there? You're the chemist. It was your lab where the crack got made. It was also your lab where this brucine shit was stored. And also this, what you call it, atropine. And none of these killin's is easy to trace. This is gettin' away from me," he said. Again.

"My old man used to call shit like this a Mexican standoff," I said.

"Hey Richie, your old man, he knew a thing or two about takin' care of business. I'm a cop, I'll do what I can to keep this under wraps, but I got a bad feeling about all of this. I'll take care of the business next door. It'll go down with a good story. A Turf war. More drug dealing shit. I'll take care of that. You got to take care of your end," he said.

Dom walked over and shook my hand. That was what we did when we were sealing a deal. Many's the times we'd shook before going after someone, but that had been in the streets of Bensonhurst a long time ago, like in another life. Did I still have what it took to take on this type of action? He left.

I bent over the sink and splashed water on my face. I was no longer a young man. I'd spent most of my life trying to be anything but what my father had been, which was a world–class wiseguy. As a kid, I could remember my mother pacing from the kitchen to the front door, doing the rosary, praying to all who were above that her beloved husband "Butcher" would come home in one piece. I also remember the day my father didn't come home, the day the chickens came home to roost, the day when the shit hit the fan, and any other old expressions you can think of. I remembered seeing my big father in a small coffin. The undertaker had done his best, but a shot in the face and two days in the water didn't make for a handsome corpse. My mother had insisted on an open viewing so that everyone could see what had been done. My mother was also, in her way, pretty fierce. And now here I was—their baby boy. Up against it. Someone was after me. I was in someone's sights with nowhere to run and nowhere to hide. Dom had laid it out for me. If it was Mac, it might come down to taking care of business. Dom was the law. The law doesn't mean shit in Brooklyn. Something would have to be done, and I'd be the guy to do it. There were no other candidates for the job.

# Chapter Twenty–Seven

Candy drove down Bay Parkway, which used to be a lot safer. Back in my day, it used to be that wise guys had a code about the rules of engagement, like for instance not killing off some rival's wife or kids. Not anymore. Two weeks ago, the Mrs. of a squealer had taken two in the back as she was unloading her groceries in front of her very own house. She'd lived, but I wasn't so sure that her husband would survive. Forget the family, they would be the least of his worries; having to face a wife who thought a husband in the business had nothing to do with her would be his biggest worry. She would probably kill the rat with her bare hands even it meant breaking a nail.

Leaving the heart of Bensonhurst, we got on the belt. No tail. All clear behind us. Whoever it was who'd followed us last night was taking a vacation. I let myself relax. I'd need the energy.

"What the quickest way there?" said Candy, running her Toyota supra through the gears. Candy had a heavy foot, which put her in good company on the belt where everyone was a speeder, and, in addition, there were right lane passers and bumper huggers. I was glad she was driving.

"Goethals, then the turnpike."

"Then what?" she said.

"At exit eight, we get off. From there, it's a straight shot to Princeton. I know the way," I said, holding on as she sped around an SUV.

"How did you come to know about Princeton?" she said, seemingly unfazed at driving at light speed.

"A guy I used to hang out with teaches at Princeton," I said.

"You never mentioned that to me before."

"No reason to. He used to run with Dom and me when we were kids," I said.

"From Bensonhurst to the ivy league. That's a real climb."

"Yeah, it was. His old man was a doctor, got himself into some trouble. His son got out of Brooklyn. His name is Paul Perrone. Back when I knew him, he went by "Too Pretty" Perrone," I said, still holding back some details from her.

"How long will this take?' said Candy, driving faster, changing the subject.

"An hour. Depends on how fast you drive. With you at the wheel, we may make it in ten minutes. That's if we live."

Candy didn't respond to my criticism of her driving habits. She cut into the far right lane, causing a guy in a big Ford with Connecticut plates to hit his brakes. He gave Candy the horn; she ignored him as she made a beeline for the verrazano.

Crossing the bridge, using the top deck, leaving behind Brooklyn and a killer who had a yen to kill only me, I looked to the right and saw all the way up to the city, the statue in the river, the sun hitting wall street, the trade center no longer the tallest thing around. We should have know that terrorists have a way of keeping after a target, then uptown to the place where King Kong had made his last stand. All of that I glimpsed as we whizzed along. It felt good to see New York fade away. I used Candy's rear view mirror and watched Brooklyn recede.

"We're still at square one," I said.

"Not completely. I found some traces of what could be brucine. That and Gomez's smiling appearance give us a match. You were right."

"Yeah, but how did he get it? Carelessness or a cocktail? That we don't know," I said.

"It'd be nice to run away for good," said Candy, again changing the subject, but echoing my own, troubled thoughts.

"Yeah," I said. She was right about that. Brooklyn was trouble, someone had me in the cross—hairs, and it was hard to miss large, lovable me. I had to get sharp about all this, reverse the process, and become the hunter.

"Hey, don't you got somethin' smaller?" said the toll–taker, whose prostate was no doubt bothering him, this on account of his sitting on his dead ass doing a for–morons job.

"No, I don' got nuttin' smaller," said Candy, smiling at him.

The guy gave her a look, then took his sweet time counting out the several bucks he had to hand her. Shame on us for making him do his job.

Candy took the money, counted it herself"See what you get for doing poorly in school?" she said, then sped away while he was responding to her rhetorical question with adjectives and nouns which linked parts of her anatomy to her manner. I think I got included also. What had I done?

"That make you feel better?" I asked.

"Yes, it did," she said, speeding up, the Staten Island Expressway no different than the belt parkway in terms of her violating the speed limit by a considerable number. We zoomed off, her with her hands firmly on the wheel, me with my white knuckles on the passenger seat.

I checked my watch again. We were making good time. How could we not at this clip? The race would begin in the early afternoon, so I would be able to warm up before it began. Today, I was determined to get something done, like get a line on Mac. Although I had some large doubts about how fast a ten K I would be able to run. The flashes of sickness were still with me.

"Shit!" exclaimed Candy, hitting the brakes as a car cut in front of her.

That was the last thing I heard for a while. It was also the last thing I saw because the world went dark.

"Sir. Sir, are you ok?" said someone. Something, maybe a hand, nudged me.

"Talkin' to me?" I said, but I heard no words. I opened my eyes. I could see the sky. Relief. I was at least alive. More sensations. My back felt something hard and unforgiving. I was on the ground. I could feel my hands and my feet. That meant I still had working appendages. Two faces looked down at me. I blinked to bring them into focus. They were EMS, 'That's not good' crossed my mind.

"Where's Candy?" I said, this time hearing the words. Good. At least I wasn't deaf.

"She the driver?" one of the EMS, a woman, said.

"Yeah," I said, scared, waiting for the worst in terms of a reply.

"They had to cut her out of the car."

"Bad?"

"She hit her head on the window. Some cuts. She been in an accident before?"

"Yeah, where is she?" More and more with each word I was coming back to the horror of life.

"On her way to Brooklyn hospital."

"She ok?" I said, my voice laced with fear that I would lose her too.

"Don' know," one of them said.

"I have a concussion?" I asked, moving my hand slowly around my head. I felt no blood or missing parts.

"Don' know," another of the EMS said.

My sense of being cared for was being challenged by these exchanges. I rolled over, got to one knee. The world remained in focus. My hands felt like hands.

"Easy, big man," one of the EMS said.

"I'm ok," I said, slowly getting off the ground, standing, the scene around me coming into focus. I looked to see where the car was. Not much was left of Candy's car. A large Buick was attached to it. Apparently, we'd been rear–ended. Good. I'd sue the pants off the tailgating bastard. The car looked like someone had died in it. Maybe someone had.

One of New York City's finest walked over to me.

"You the passenger?" he said. A handsome young fellow. He smiled at me, didn't look away, which meant I wasn't a mess.

"Yeah," I said, using my tongue on the inside of my mouth to make sure I still had teeth, and a whole tongue.

"Come to my car. I need some information."

"The woman who was drivin', she ok?"

"Her face is pretty cut up."

"Which side?"

"The one with the scars."

"I need to go to Brooklyn Hospital." I wanted to see for myself how she was. I wanted to be with her.

"You come with me, this won't take long. Then I'll drive you." That was a bargain. A few words for a free ride. I had no idea how else I would've got back into Brooklyn. Hoof it? I don't think so.

I went with the cop. Our investigation of Mac would have to be put on hold. We'd been at the mercy of one of life's little accidents. Candy and I were lucky to be alive.

# Chapter Twenty–Eight

A huge death's head was gaining on me. Its mouth open, the teeth bright white and sharp. The skull was bigger than me. I was running fast, making my way through a dark, narrow alley. The skull closed on me, the thing lining me up, surging to catch up to me, the jaws open wide. I turned, looked. Inside the mouth was King Gomez, like he was trying to get out, eyes bulging, lips peeled back. Blood streaked his chin.

I sprinted into the darkness, but cold teeth latched onto my neck, clamping down on me. The cold, sharp points worked into me. The alley ahead was darker still. The skull had me. I thrashed back and forth trying to shake it.

"Dom! Dom! Get 'im off me! Dom!" I screamed, louder and louder, then coming awake, eyes wide open, at first seeing nothing. Where was I?

I was in an all–white room in Brooklyn Hospital. I was alone. I rolled over, putting first one, then two, bare feet on the clean, cold white linoleum floor. I sat up. Not dizzy. I was ok.

I'd been dreaming. There were no death's head, no razor sharp teeth, no nothing. Dreaming, just dreaming. I hate dreams. The devil made dreaming to torment the living.

My white hospital gown was soaked with sweat, but my head no longer felt like I was being used for batting practice. Yesterday, I'd come to Brooklyn Hospital to check up on Candy. She'd been cut up on her bad side, the jaw cracked, some damage to her eye. A concussion. Donald Wooley was the doctor on call, and he'd wanted her in the hospital for a least a week.

Wooley'd taken me, looked at me, tested my vitals and slapped my car–wrecked carcass into a sick ward, which was just the place I wanted to be in Brooklyn. I had a concussion. Dizzy. Which meant that the two hotshot amateur detectives were both on the shelf. Running Mac to ground as the head honcho of Drug Inc. at the Urban U. would have to wait while Batman and Robin recuperated.

It would take some hospital time for me to get up to speed, like a few long years. Time was what I needed to mend, but time was just what I did not have. There was no time for lying up in a hospital. The killer, who was after me, was out there, lying in wait, still in the killing business. Twenty–four seven was the motto for murderers.

I drank water from a container by my bed, drained it, sucking on the straw, refilled it with ice, put some in my mouth. The water tasted good. I was ok. I stood up. I felt like a stale cannole. I sat down. I still felt like a stale cannole.

Light was in the room. I'd slept for most of yesterday, which was an eternity for me, the Insomnia Kid. Sounds came from the corridor. The night shift of the hospital was closing down. A new set of nurses was taking over. Soon, they'd check in on me, see if I was still breathing.

Standing, a little wobbly, I made my way slowly to the one large window in the room. The leaves were off the trees, and last night it had snowed. Nutty weather. It's not supposed to snow in Brooklyn at this time of the year, but it had. A cold northwest wind, what the weatherman called an 'Alberta Clipper' had slammed into the borough and coated it. Not much snow, maybe a half inch, but it looked like Christmas. All that was needed was Bing Crosby.

Looking across roof tops, I could see the belt parkway, bumper to bumper at this early hour, the cars inching along, the snow, small as it was, doing a number on the borough's commuters. I wondered how Candy was doing. I'd call her room as soon as the day shift was on.

"You're better," said a voice behind me.

"Yeah," I said, turning around slowly, coming face to face with Dr. Donald Wooley. Strange to talk with him under these circumstances. Someone I'd taught. I remembered him as a bright kid, someone who was a pleasure to teach, not like the sand in a rat hole work that I did for the most part. Now he was in charge of me. Nothing stays the same. Maybe that's for the best.

"No dizziness?" he asked.

He had me sit on the bed, used light to peer into my brain. Based on my detective work so far, I was not sure his light would pick up anything but bone.

"I go home?" I said.

"You promise to take it easy?" he said, no doubt knowing what he'd get for an answer. Donald was ok, a sharpie. You didn't have to talk much until he got the point. He'd helped me out the night that Brzenk had gotten his. He could probably guess that I was up to something. What he didn't know was that I was largely chasing my tail and barking at shadows.

"No," I said, opting for the truth for once.

"That's what I thought," he said, smiling at me.

"How's Candy doing?"

"Her jaw's not broken. Her cuts are superficial, but they're in a bad area. It'll take someone who knows his stuff to work on her."

"Her eye?" I asked.

"Too early to tell," said Wooley, who then left, after saying he'd sign me out.

I stripped off the hospital gown, and dressed myself in running shorts and a tank top. My Uncle Sam exercise outfit. What I'd worn on the day when I was supposed to run with Mac. Such a costume would make me the center of attention today. The north wind was still having at Brooklyn, so a large Italian in a colored playsuit would be noticed. I'd draw a crowd, and the killer who was after me could fire into the middle and put an end to my misery with one clean shot. Or maybe he'd just clip me and leave me a cripple, then smother me with a pillow. I stopped entertaining myself with such cheery thoughts and finished dressing.

Maybe I'd just stay here in the hospital after all. Injure myself deliberately, like lop off an ear. Here was a good place to hide out. Here was warmth and water and help came if I pushed a buzzer.

There were no help buzzers in Brooklyn. I couldn't stop on the street and have an army come to rescue me when the going got gruesome. It was a good idea to stay here. That was a real working idea. In here, the killer would have to get by Malvina "Heavy Duty" Moore in order to do me in. Easier said than done. Yes, it would be best if I just stayed here. With that established as the thing that should be done, I left the room and made my way to the nurse's station where I would get checked out. The wise thought had not tarried long in my mind, maybe a minute—Sherlock Holmes, I bet he held on to his wise thoughts longer than that.

# Chapter Twenty–Nine

Getting home had not been all that easy. I'd been eyeballed by a nosy cab driver who smelled. He'd looked me up and down in my Yankee Doodle running togs. I was about to call him a fuck of a foreigner when he offered me his coat, making me feel like a jerk. In Brooklyn, we were all foreign once so who was I to get high and mighty. Finally, I was home. It was not fun to be back inside my own house, for it was like climbing down into the remote parts of my mind. I'd been living in the present with Candy, but now she was laid up, and I was back doing too much of what I used to do, which was to mope.

I drove to the college. The roads were slippery, which helped immensely the driving experience on the streets of Brooklyn. So, there was a lot to whine about. So I whined.

A half inch of snow is nothing in Marguette, Michigan, but, since it had come on so early, a very big deal in Brooklyn. Snow disguised Brooklyn, made it look a lot better than it, in reality, really was. I'd read once, in my youth, that Martin Luther had said that people were snow–covered shitpiles, something like that he'd written, when he wasn't having at the Catholics for being Catholic. Martin Luther knew a thing or two. Underneath the pretty, white snow, Brooklyn was the same as always—dirty, dangerous, deadly—a shitpile.

Candy was on my mind. She'd be back home in a few days. Her eye injury was turning out not to be as threatening as first thought. Her jaw was in one piece. We'd talked. It was nice to have her right there, in my ear, all to myself. I'd filled her in about the accident. She blew that off. She didn't want/need me to go hunting without her. I'd promised to not to. I'd lied. What was building in my mind was to handle all of this on my own, draw everything to a conclusion, have it all done when she got out of the hospital. Our talk came to an end. I'd promised to call her again in the evening.

I wasn't the only one at the college who was sick. Beef Patty had the flu. That little tidbit about the large man I'd learned when I was at the hospital. His girlfriend, "Heavy Duty", had visited me. After telling me how sorry she was that I was under the weather and how glad she was that I hadn't been killed, she brought up the fact that her sweetie pie Lester the Large still wanted to talk to me. Said it was important. I hoped it wasn't about a co–ed. I knew way too much about Beef Patty's nocturnal activities. The girls at the college took turns. It was a turn–on to them. I must be missing something. Being butt slammed by Beef Patty's nearly four hundred pounds on an unforgiving metal desk didn't square with my idea of a romantic interlude. Maybe Beef sang to them. Then again, maybe he just grunted.

At the college, in my lab, I sat wall staring, giving the murders at the school my top of the line, very deep Sam Spade thinking. Mac would have to wait. I was in no shape to go prowling around the city of Princeton where I would stick out like two sore thumbs. So, move him down the 'possibles' list of who had a good reason to snuff out kindly old me. Jimmy Fisheyes hadn't been around for a while. He was no doubt plotting against the One Percenters, which was fine with me. So, as for him, out of sight, out of mind. Also, down the list he went. This was easy, in no time I would have no list at all. Nikki and J. P., them I could investigate.

I left the lab, walked across the small sixth floor lobby, encountering no college killers and pushed the button for the fourth floor. I looked toward Mac's office. A light could be seen underneath the door. Mac was conducting office hours. Good for him. That's what I wanted him to do. I resisted patting myself on the back for being so clever.

The elevator door opened, revealing a passenger. I looked at the passenger, but said nothing. The elevator stopped at the fifth floor.

Annie Porter got on. She had on a suit, light gray, white blouse. Her hair was neat, pulled back, professional. She looked good. She also smelled good.

"Hello, Winston. Hello, Rich," she said, an order of greeting that I didn't really like.

"Hello, Dean Porter," said Winston Wiant, who was wearing his usual clothes of death attire.

"Hello, Dean Porter?" I asked.

"Yes, I'm now assistant dean. Doug promoted me," said Annie.

"Congratulations," I said, my mind giving me a picture of Annie and Fenner going into her brownstone. I smiled at one of the two administrators. One of them smiled back. The other looked at me like you'd look at a dog you didn't much care for.

We went down one more floor. The elevator stopped. The door opened.

"Good bye, Dean Porter," I said.

"Good bye, Rich," said Annie Porter, her green eyes sparkling. I watched her walk away with Wiant, who looked like he had two, maybe three, terminal diseases. The two of them set off for Fenner's office. I thought for a moment about what might go on in that office.

I rode to the first floor. I needed coffee. I would go to Fat Harry's to get it. The coffee on the tenth floor of the college was not fit for human consumption, which was why the students could drink it.

The lobby was full of students. They were smoking, talking, playing music, no doubt taking a break from a rigorous examination of their studies.

Across the street I went, slick with snow, ahead of me was a short, red-headed girl with lots of hip action. She went into Fat Harry's where Fat Harry himself the philosopher was in attendance. The fat man stood behind the counter, sweating into his chins.

Harry smiled at the girl as she wiggled toward him. He must've been watching her since she left the college. Fat Harry didn't miss much. He was usually all eyes.

"'She walks in beauty like the night,' and now she is walking into my place. What can I get just for you, my dear?" said Harry.

There were seven men sitting at the counter. I could hear seven pairs of eyeballs click as they looked at the girl.

"Regular coffee," said the girl, who had a husky voice.

"Akman, one regular coffee, on the double, for this beautiful young woman," said Fat Harry, loudly relaying the order to his counterman who was two feet away.

"I heard her when she said it, Harry. It aint like she's in Queens, you know," said the worker in something of an aggrieved tone.

Harry ignored his helper, treating his eyes to an up and down of the girl. Then he finally saw me.

"Ah, professor. Sit down, sit down,"

"Thanks," I said.

"You are now well?" Fat Harry didn't miss a beat about what went on at the college. Maybe I should take him on as part of my detective team, add some heft to our detecting.

"I am ok," I said, falling into Harry's mode of expression. I hoped he would not start one of our long conversations about life in and around Brooklyn.

"Out for a few days?" said Harry, who probably knew what my fever was.

"Yeah," I said.

"But now well."

"Really well," I said, growing weary of this back and forth. I had no time for this. I had crimes to solve.

"Regular coffee to go?" asked the big man.

"Yeah."

"That'll be a dollar," said Akman to the hottie of a student.

"No, no, Akman. There will be no charge. Enjoy, my dear, enjoy. Return soon. I'd like to see more of you," said Harry, being about as subtle as a sledgehammer.

I knew what Harry would like to see more of. Harry had been Mr. Pang's partner. No doubt Harry would take over as the photographer, the message of Mr. Pang's tragic demise having little effect on the bottom line—which was moolah. The girl would be squeezed into a thong, instructed to fake it for the camera. Pang's being dead did not bother me a whole lot. Harry's being next wouldn't bother me either.

"Oh, I'll be back," said the girl, leaving the coffee shop, wiggling her rear quarters just enough to make eyeballs click once more as she moved toward the door.

I took my regular coffee with me. Outside, it was cold and windy. On such a day, one would not expect the down and out to be up and about. One would be wrong.

Ahead of me was Nikki Nateal. Two pieces of waste saw her too.

"Hey, little baby, walk this way," said one bum.

"You one fine lookin' chickie, you wan' some of my wine?" said the other.

Nikki was almost up to the two of them, regulars, their job panhandling, their home abandoned cars. One was sitting on his humble abode; the other was standing, drinking, his fly still open from his recent relief action on the wall of a building. Nikki said nothing. She kept on walking. This ignoring of them did not sit well with the street citizens.

"You hear me, bitch! I ask you if you wan' some fuckin' wine!" said one, getting agitated by her lack of response.

Nikki walked faster. A delivery truck was parked on the street, and it prevented her from crossing at this point. She'd have to pass by the two.

The one standing street denizen moved in front of Nikki, blocking the sidewalk.

"My frien' talkin' to you! You know what's good for you, bitch, you better listen up!"

The present owner of the thoroughfare had just made a major league mistake. Words were nothing to Nikki Nateal. She'd probably heard them all too many times. Words just used up air space. But the wretched of the earth was now taking up real space. He would have to go.

Nikki shifted her weight to her left leg, found firm footing on the sidewalk, which had been somewhat cleared of ice. Her left hand dropped the coffee she was carrying. It hit the concrete, splashed onto her shoes. With her left foot set, she cocked her right leg all in the blink of an eye and executed a front kick. The leg whipped like a cobra striking, the steel tip of her shoe hitting the bum high on the cheekbone, catching him while he was talking, like Ali had been caught working his big mouth at Ken Norton. I would guess that the side of the slimeball's face broke in probably three distinct places. He went down hard, his heading slamming into the curb. Superfoot Wallace would've scored Nikki's kick a ten.

Nikki followed through, the right foot coming down, touching the pavement, pivoting quickly, turning the left foot parallel. She was ready to strike again.

The friend of the man with the damaged jaw was not a fast learner. What he had just witnessed should've set off a warning light in his booze–soaked brain, but he instead moved off the car, big, over 200 pounds, no doubt muscle still there under the decay and fat. He broke his wine bottle. He wasted no time talking. He came directly at Nikki, swung at her face. He missed. He was in for it nowNikki Nateal had a choice. She could step back and allow the man to recover for another cut at her. Instead, she stepped forward, moving inside the arc of his swing, drawing in a breath through her nose, the left arm out front, the right ready, loaded. She struck at bum number two with the heel of her right hand, at the last moment turning the hand, using the side. She broke his nose east to west instead of north to south, which would've driven splintered bone into the brain and sent him on the way to skid row heaven. Blood spurted over his face. He also went down hard, smacking his head on the pavement. Nikki walked slowly over to him as he lay bleeding. She put a steel toe into his ribs. He screamed. She walked away.

A cheer went up from a group of students across the street, who were on their way to Harry's, sort of like the kind of whoop when Yale scores against Harvard. Sort of.

"Down, down, both down and fuckin' out!"

"She bad! Double bad! Street bad!"

I followed, at a safe distance, Nikki as she now crossed the street and walked through a small crowd of congratulating students. She entered the college, making her way to the back stairs. The elevator was full. She started to, I thought, climb to the sixth floor. I was still behind her. I wanted to talk with her. Apparently, she wanted to talk with me, for she began the conversation.

"I got a note from the dean," said Nikki, turning around. She was much shorter than me, but I had just witnessed how violent she was.

"About the lab?" I asked, although I knew that this was what I'd cooked up with Fenner previously. Our lie was to be that the lab had failed an asbestos test and that her assistantship would be put on hold.

"Yeah. Does that mean I'm done for the semester?" she said.

"Looks that way. Sorry." I said.

"Not your fault," said Nikki, who waited a brief moment, then looked up at me, straight into my eyes.

"You talk to Mac? You tell him to stop?" she asked.

"Yes," I lied, for I didn't want her to kick me in the face for giving the wrong answer.

"Right now he's doin' Jamela in his office."

I said nothing. Nikki went into the library on the second floor, which was a relief that we didn't have to continue on together.

Climbing the rest of the way to the sixth floor was not easy. The atropine must've still been in my system, that's what I thought, making me less than one hundred percent. I could not afford to be less than full steam. I had just seen up close and personal what it took to survive on the Brooklyn streets. My way of dealing with those two bums would have been to offer to buy them a gallon of really cheap hooch, something I couldn't even have done since old man Pang had departed this sorry planet for a circle of hell. Right now, Pang was getting toasted for how he'd spent his three score and ten in this world. Yeah, I was less than one hundred percent, but I was still more than Mac was going to be. Nikki would not wait. She'd go right to J. P. with my news. They would not hesitate. The first time that he made himself available, Mac would come in for it. The vision of Mr. Pang hung up and sliced up flashed before my eyes. Soon, there would be a caucasian to add to the trophy case of the One Percenters.

# Chapter Thirty

In my nice, peaceful, quiet, not full, at the moment, of crack–cooking killers lab, I tried to do some of my own work. My mind flitted back to what I was doing. It wouldn't take Nikki and J. P. very long. I was setting Mac up, using Nikki. I was also setting up Nikki. A real double cross. She'd kill Mac. Jimmy Fisheyes and his Seoul brothers would come after her, and old Doc Bucceroni, that prince of men, would be free at last, free at last. I don't think MLK had me in mind.

Someone knocked at my door. A loud rapping. It startled me.

"It's Mac, what're you doin' in there?" a loud voice said. Everything was loud to me. I was lost in thought, not connected very well to the here and now.

I let him in.

"You got any water made up?" he asked.

"No," I said, thinking about the brass ones Mac had. He didn't know I'd found out, nearly the hard way, about his doping up my water bottle with atropine. He was coming after me again, establishing a pattern.

"You up to running? You missed a couple days of school," he said.

"No, I had the flu. I can't run today."

"Oh, chickenshit, huh? I'll see you later. Maybe late this week we can run. Can't wait to kick your tired old ass again," said Mac, smiling at me, ribbing me, acting like everything was ok, like we were pals.

"Lookin' forward to it," I managed to say, watching as he walked away. At the elevator, he waved to me. I waved back.

At my window overlooking the street, I watched Mac jog slowly away toward an avenue. We had mapped out a run, a one mile loop. We'd do it five times. It was a good way to get your running time down. The run wasn't so bad. The natives thought we were nuts but mostly did nothing more than yell at us. I checked my watch. Mac would run the first mile in eight minutes, the next at 7:30, moving down thirty seconds a mile.

Dressed in bright blue, he stood out against the dirt streaked snow.

Behind Mac were two figures dressed all in black. They followed him, walking slowly, just two people on the street, not doing anything to draw attention to themselves, other than being dressed like ninjas on parade.

Mac was someone I knew. He was supposed to be a pal. But he was the one. There was no other way. Dom had been right. I had nothing of note on Mac, nothing that would hold up in a court of law. The time had come to take care of business. I was the jury and on the street were the executioners.

I decided to look at my lesson plan for today. I read it. The words didn't make sense to me.

Eight minutes later, after checking my watch about five times, I went to the window. Mac was back, he'd completed one lap. He checked his own watch, turned, headed back down the street. There was no following him. They were now ahead of him.

I took out some lab reports to grade. They also seemed to make no sense. My heart pounded. I read over one report three times. It meant nothing to me. My mind wouldn't click into chemistry.

Back to the window I went. Seven minutes and thirty seconds had passed. Mac appeared, right on schedule, running harder, I could see he'd broken a sweat even in this cold weather. Another check of his watch, another turn. Off he went, this time even faster.

I did some straightening up in the lab. I moved some stools around. I checked the gas lines. Long minutes passed.

The bottle of brucine was still on the shelf. Mac had read my paper. He'd come in here and coated a glass with the poison. Taken it back to his office. Poured a drink for his partner–in–crime Gomez, then watched as the "King" squeezed himself to death. Dumped the stiff body outside, ripped out a tooth to cover his tracks. More minutes had passed. I walked to the window.

There was no sign of Mac. It had now been six minutes on the nose since he'd done the last loop. Another ten seconds went by. Then twenty. Thirty. Forty–five. I put myself in high gear, left the lab, across the lobby, used the stairs two, three at a time, more or less in a controlled fall, out the front door. If Mac was the guy, I would take him on face to face. This was not for me. I was many things, but I was, not yet, this.

Running down the street in my white lab jacket, I provided some entertainment for the crackheads.

"Slow down man, ain't no Olympics 'round here."

"Run your ass home, whitey."

"Hurry get you nowhere, big man."

All of this wisdom from men who spent their life either up or down.

All of it came from out of the burn–outs in the burned out buildings.

"Mac! Mac! Hey, Mac!" I yelled. Mac came around the block, running hard. He came over to me. Stopped. Out of breath.

"Nice running outfit, Rich...,you a trendsetter?" he said, gasping.

"Let's go back to the college," I said, trying to appear in control.

"Something wrong?" he asked.

"Yes, something is wrong," I said.

"You ok? You said you'd been sick. Why'd you come after me?"

"I want you to come back inside," I said, slowly and distinctly.

"Why?"

I repeated myself.

Mac wasn't stupid. He didn't need life in Brooklyn to be spelled out to him. He looked around at the crummy area. He looked back at me. My face probably told volumes.

Mac and I started back to the college. It was a short journey. I hoped we'd make it in one piece.

Ahead of us, two black figures came out of one of the buildings.

"I'll see you inside Mac," I said, watching as J. P. and Nikki closed the distance between us. If Mac would walk now, he had the angle to make it home free.

"There some problem with them?" he said.

"Go inside, Mac," I said, an edge in my voice. He got the point. He left. He walked quickly. He made it. I was now alone.

I walked over to Nikki and J. P. I was cold. They wore leather and an attitude. I had on a white shirt, black slacks, wing tips, tie, and a lab jacket. Dr. Bucceroni paying a house call. I looked professional. They looked professional. We had different professions.

"You come after him for a reason?" said Nikki, her voice angry.

"Yeah, what you doin?'" said J. P.

"Go home," I said.

"No one tells us what to do," said J. P., his voice a growl.

"I do," I said, not raising my voice.

"Why you protecting Mac?" asked Nikki.

"Why did you kill Pang?" I said.

"We dint kill that slant!" said J. P., his voice loud on the empty street.

"Then who did?" I said, lost for a moment as to what to say. I had to keep them talking or they'd come after me. I did not have Candy behind me. It was just me.

"Not us," said Nikki.

That threw me. If not them, then who?

"Go home. Forget Mac. He'll stop. If not today, then tomorrow. You two have a whole life to lead. Don't waste it on the street," I said, doing my best Father Flanagan.

"We're not punks. This is what we believe in," said Nikki. Everything was a "we" with her. She'd bought into gang think.

"Killing Mac will put you on Rikers. What'll you do there? Nothing. Go home."

"Why you doin' this?" said J. P., again. Was this his last word? Would action, fast action, come next? Could I handle him? We'd have to see.

"I ever advise you wrong?" I said, hoping that our past relationship counted for something. It did.

"No," they said in unison.

"Go home, and watch yourself. Jimmy Fisheyes is after you. He thinks you killed his uncle. He's got blood in his eye," I said, feeling that I'd turned the corner, gained the upper hand.

"We thinkin' about him, too," said J. P.

They went their way. I went mine. I felt like I'd run a marathon. It felt good when I was back inside the college. It was warm as I climbed the back stairs to my lab.

Mac might not be the guy. If Nikki and J. P. hadn't killed Pang, then who had. Mac? Could Mac slice up someone like that? Hard to believe.

I had a class to teach. Mac would still have to be dealt with, but I would do the dirty work myself.

# Chapter Thirty–One

The next morning, I was up early. I'd gotten my first good night's sleep in about a year. Yesterday had ended on an uneventful note. I had taught my classes, graded some papers, called to check on Candy, who was asleep but doing ok, then I'd left for the day. Mac had left when I did. He said goodbye. I said goodbye. He said nothing about our encounter with Nikki and J. P. I also said nothing. He had gone to his aged wife in Princeton. I had gone home to my own, clean, white, snug, safe, warm bed. It had been a good day. No chemical killings, no slice ups of local entrepreneurs, no more gang encounters. Nothing. A normal ending to a normal day. I hoped this was the start of a trend.

From my third floor bedroom, I could see all the way over to Candy's. I'd called her as soon as I was up. She was better, able to see with two eyes. She'd been worried about me. Candy had told me they were going to do some more X–rays. She'd also, with Donald Wooley's help, contacted a plastic surgeon about the new scars on her face. She said her room was being moved. She told me she'd call later to give me the new number.

I had a day of work ahead of me. I had to get straight on who'd killed Buffalo Pang. His death didn't fit with the Gomez, Brzenk, me pattern. Linking him with them/me had me in the dark. Mac, Nikki, J. P., Jimmy Fisheyes. About Mac, I still wasn't sure, but about the other three I had a line. They were kids, dunskeys in training, like I'd been. Black and yellow made no difference. They were closer to me than I liked to remember. I had busted my share of heads, and I'd gone with Dom to take care of Piecetime Pizzemente.

Whoever had worked over Pang had been no kid. Had the three street punks grown up, moved up the ladder of crime? Hard to tell. I was back to square one, which was a too familiar place for me. I needed to expand my list of possibles. Someone who knew about chemical weapons had me in their sights. Mac was not the only one to keep an eye on. J. P. and Nikki deserved my attention. So did Fisheyes.

In my kitchen, the coffee was on, an automatic set. It smelled good, it tasted good. I was more my old self. I had to handle this my way. I was a target. When would the killer strike next? And how?

Today, my Toyota turned right over. A good sign. I needed everything to be in perfect working order. Car. Body. Mind. A nice progression.

I backed out of the driveway and drove toward the college. The driver's side window was down. It was bright, sunny, the snow was melting. It was going to be a good day. There was little traffic in Bay Ridge at this hour. The street was pretty empty ahead. I drove slowly, running all of the possibilities through my mind. With no one much on the street, I didn't pay a whole lot of attention to my driving.

At Shore Road, I stopped, bent forward to tune the radio. I wanted to listen to Howard, get in touch with the younger generation, learn some new word combinations. Two things happened at once. Something struck the back of my neck, a sharp pain, like I'd scratched my neck, and the passenger side window shattered. I ducked down as two more shots wheezed over me. With my head below the dashboard, I drove away. No one followed. I was checking to see if the shooter was lining me up again. The back of my neck was wet. I wiped away blood. This was definitely not kid stuff. This was a hit. Professional. Small caliber.

I made two right turns and went back home. A good idea. Better to cut and run than to knock on a neighbor's door and see if some bright eyes had spotted the bastard who had tried to plant me. I walked quickly toward my house. Fighting the urge to hit the ground and crawl to my front door. Inside, I was safe. For now.

I went to the third floor, feeling my neck as I climbed. The bleeding was slowing. The shot had grazed me.

Using a towel, I got the bleeding completely stopped. A hand mirror showed me a small wound. Not much. A scrape, like I'd cut myself on a tree branch. The bullet had gone through the other window. If Candy had been sitting there, she would have taken it. Who was it? Nikki and J. P.? Why? Maybe my Dutch Uncle manner had pissed them off.

Someone had changed the name of the game. Chemical weapons were out, .22s were in. Jimmy Fisheyes was supposed to be good with both a gun and a knife. Maybe he wasn't such a kid after all. Jimmy Fisheyes was now number one on my list. Had it occurred to the cold eyed, snaky fuck that old Doc Bucceroni might've squealed about his plans to kill Nikki and J. P.? Did he have a gang so big he could send a pro with a silenced .22 into Bay Ridge to kill a guy who'd just done what he was told? A lot of questions, not many answers. Loose ends are trouble for killers. If Nikki and J. P. went down, I could finger the Seoul Brothers. To Jimmy Fisheyes, I was probably just one large, Mediterranean loose end. I had to go.

The phone rang. Dom. He wanted to know how I'd done with Mac. This wasn't like Dom. Italians have a thing about phones, especially home phones. Brooklyn's mostly eyes and ears, which means getting a case of loose lips on the phone can result in a one way trip to Marion doing power pushups in a small cell. I wasn't in the mood to let down my hair. I lied about Mac. Mac was nothing to worry about. He told me to keep in touch. He hung up.

Sitting on the bed, resisting the urge to get under it, I gave a second, then a third thought about my closing out Dom just now. My reasoning had a logical progression.

I had just been shot at close to my own house. Thus, I was not safe even in my own house.

In addition, I had no cut and dried opinion as to the trigger man.

In conclusion, I needed help, big time.

The police were supposed to help me. I paid taxes for them to do that.

Dom was a policeman.

Finally, I called Dom back.

He wasn't home. He had a paging system. I used it. He was back to me in five minutes.

"What's up?" he asked.

"Someone took a shot at me," I said.

"In your house?" he said, his voice calm and professional, which is what I wanted to hear.

"No, on the street near here."

"This happened when?"

"Before you called me," I said, moving the phone away from my ear, getting ready for a blast.

"There a reason you didn't tell me?" Dom said, his voice rising.

"I'll handle this."

"Bullshit. You can't handle your dick any more. Look, Richie, with all due respect, you ain't the hardass you once was," he said, telling me something I already knew all too well.

"I thought you told me to give some attention to Mac."

"I was full of it. You're a prof now, You ain't what you was. You better lay low."

"There's this kid, Jimmy Fisheyes. He might be the one who shot me."

"The chink is in my book. I'll check him out. Give me some details. You must've been in your car, right?"

"Yeah, I bent over. One came in, it nicked me. Broke the opposite window. There were two more after that. Whoever it was had in mind killing me."

"But you're ok," he said.

"Yeah."

"How you gettin' along with the Zulu and his snatch?"

"Yesterday, I got in their faces about their goin' after McClure. I had the bright idea of using them to whack him." I said, ignoring for the moment Dom's nasty minority comments.

"See what I mean? You ain't what you was. So lay low. Keep in touch. I'll nose around. I'll get back to you," said Dom, who had taken to repeating himself about my inadequacies. He hung up again. Now I was on my own. No Dom, No Candy, just little old nicked in the neck me.

I was to lay low. Where? I didn't really have a place to hide. I recalled what Candy had said about us just leaving all of this. That still sounded like a great idea.

At least there was one good thing. My neck had stopped bleeding. It was then that I remembered something. Annie Porter had just walked into my lab. She had a master key. Candy had just changed the specific lock to our lab. Annie had a key to the lab. Annie knew something about chemistry, so did Fenner. Annie had said hello to Wiant first on the elevator the other day. Something clicked in my mind. Annie and Fenner and Wiant were a team.

In the night table next to my bed was my gun. It was also a .22 Safe. Clean. Something left from my old man. This wasn't over. Mac was still a possible, I thought, overruling myself again. Mac was either just a guy who couldn't keep it in his pants or he was a world class creep. Annie, Fenner, Wiant, Jimmy Fisheyes, Nikki and J. P. They were all possibles. It could be Fisheyes, but my address was unlisted. Even at the college. That meant Fisheyes and his yellow killers would've needed to follow me. I'm pretty good at picking up a tail. For some time, I'd been looking over my shoulder. Fisheyes I could spot. That left the trio of Annie, Fenner and Wiant and the dark duo. They knew where I lived. They could have done this.

I decided to check the trio out. This would be a new area of investigation for me. Maybe this time, my sleuthing would get me something more than being shot at. Fisheyes and the One Percenters I set on the back burner of my detecting stove. They should be easier to spot if they were following me. The others would blend into a crowd of cars making it difficult for me to pick them out.

This had started out as a nice day. Nice weather, me feeling better for a change, a cup or three of good coffee, heading out in the world. Then BAM BAM BAM, three shots had turned the day into a nightmare. This should be a fun day because out in Brooklyn was a killer with a .22 waiting for his target to emerge. This was also a clever chemical killer who knew a thing or two about drugs and poisons. And I'd been told to lay low and here I was getting ready to stick my wounded neck out again. Maybe I should put on an orange suit with a black bull's eye over the heartI left my house. I Made it to the car. Lucky me. No one took a pot shot at me.

# Chapter Thirty–Two

Walking down Coney Island Avenue, I felt like a stranger in a strange land. This was an area mainly of Orthodox Jews. There were lots of whiskers and black suits and black hats. And amongst them walked me, in gray slacks, black boots, windbreaker, longshoreman cap. In disguise, or so I thought. Two hundred fifty pounds of aging Italian that no one would notice. I would bet fifty bucks that I'd passed at least ten, maybe twelve, people who could draw a portrait of my manly mug and get every detail just right, including nose hairs, the mole behind my right ear and the new white band aid on the back of my overly thick neck.

I was heading for Academic Realtors, which was the real estate company that handled all the rentals and sales for the college. Lots of faculty rented houses in Brooklyn for the academic year, then they retreated to a home they owned in Vermont or upstate somewhere so that they wouldn't get killed during their vacation. Brooklyn in the summer is no place for the civilized. The temperature goes up, the undesirables creep out. This coming ice age, I hope it hits Flatbush first.

Academic Realtors was being run by an old pal of mine named Mendy Levy. In his younger days, Mendy had been known as Mendy "The Cup." The nickname the result of his always wearing a metal cup to protect his essentials. Now, Mendy went by Menachem Mendle Levy, which let all of the locals know that he knew both his Hebrew and his Yiddish.

"Hey, Richie, long time, no see. Come in. Come in. Talk to me," said Mendy, talking a mile a minute like he usually did, as soon as he saw me walk into his office. His secretary smiled at me, no doubt covering a laugh at my attire. I went back into Mendy's private office.

Mendy's office was like him, neat, precise, everything in its place. Mendy was only maybe five foot eight, wiry, still no fat on him, going bald. He was the only Jew I'd known when I was growing up. One night I'd gone with four or five other guidos over to Mendy's to give him a hard time. The Cup was banging this girl named Angelina "Babaloo" Borolino that primo "Big P" Petrocelli had a thing for. Mendy was downsized to Big P's six foot four inches, but he hadn't backed down. Big P. had broken his nose, knocked out two teeth, busted up his ribs, but Mendy hadn't quit. He'd kept fighting the much bigger man. Primo had gotten tired hitting Mendy, asked me what to do. I'd stepped in, called off Big P., shook Mendy's hand for having balls.

After that, Mendy ran with our gang, did what we did, which was to break open parking meters, roll drunks, beat up anyone not like us, do girls, boost cars, and all the time Mendy had on more athletic support than Roy or Yogi.

"So, Richie, you come to see me about listing your house? This is the time to list," he said.

Mendy must've said that to me at least a hundred times. It was always the time to list to him. He wanted me into a smaller house, more modern, a place full of someone else's memories. He probably had something there.

"No, I need a favor," I said, my voice low.

Mendy looked me over. He got up and closed the door to the outer office.

"What kind of favor?" he said, sitting down behind a big oak desk. I was directly in front of him in a comfortable leather chair.

"I got to get inside one of your houses," I said.

"Which one?"

"On Rugby. It belongs to a guy named Winston Wiant."

"He a close friend of ours?" asked Mendy, looking closely at me.

"No."

Mendy lit a cigar. He and Dom were the only cigar smokers I knew. I used to do that. My old man had the real thing when it came to cigars, from Havanna. I used to smoke Havannas myself, got them from a Russian named Yelenovich in Sheepshead Bay, but I'd stopped. Candy had told me it was a good idea. Mendy's cigar wasn't a cheapie. It was a Hoyo. It smelled good.

"Look, Richie, I don't want any trouble. This isn't much I got, but it's what I got. I don't want any trouble. This some type of professor trouble?"

"No."

"So what is this? You're a professor now. this isn't what professors do," he said, looking worried. Mendy ran a small hand through what was left of his red hair.

"Someone's tryin' to kill me," I said, coming right out with it. Mendy was a pal. To him, I'd tell the truth.

"Wiant? He trying it on with you? He doesn't seem like he's got the weight to stand up to you."

"This morning someone shot at me with a .22. With a silencer. Nicked my neck. I need to get inside this fuck's house," I said, moving my hand over the band aid on my neck. A chill came over me as I uttered the words of what had happened. I had dodged a major bullet. I was lucky to be alive. Luck was ok with me. I'd take luck any day, as long it kept me above ground and still kicking.

Mendy squashed his cigar. He'd just barely started smoking it. Smoke rose from the cigar. It hung in the office air. As did silence. Mendy said nothing, I said nothing. One of us was doing some deep thinking. It was not me.

"This goin' inside Wiant's house, it'll go down how?" asked Mendy.

"You got a master key, right?'

"Right."

"All you got to do is let me in. You need to keep an eye on the street in case weird–ass shows up."

"How long you gonna be in?"

"Could be an hour," I said.

"What do you expect me to tell Wiant if he shows up?"

"You meet him at the front door. I'll go out the back. I figure you can make up some excuse as to why you're there. You always had the gift of gab," I said, smiling at him.

"That's it? Just burglary, nothing else?" said Mendy, not smiling back.

"There may be other houses. Depends on what I find at Wiant's."

"Who?'

"Annie Porter. Douglas Fenner."

"Porter's a renter. Fenner owns his home. He's got a wife."

"Can you get into his house?"

"Yeah."

"So, let's go."

Mendy rummaged around in his office and picked up keys to Wiant's, Annie's and Fenner's. He then told his secretary he was going to look at my place.

I'd parked my car a block or so away from Mendy's. Walking outside, I gave the area around me some close attention. It was clear. That was good. There were no Seoul Brothers parting the Jews, honing in on the sole Italian.

Mendy had a big Lincoln. I liked the car. My old man had one like this, a Caddy, a guinea gunboat, more fins than a flounder.

"The knockout in on this?" said Mendy as he got behind the wheel. I buckled in. Mendy was like Candy, a fast and reckless driver.

"No," I lied.

"Good. Leave her out, Richie. This don' sound good. This sounds bad. You talk to Dom?"

"Yeah."

"And what did he tell you to do?"

"That I'm on my own. Look, Mendy, I don' know how much you want to know, but here's the situation in a nutshell. There's been three killings. Three. I'm close to all of them. One of them was meant for me. It was the use of my own work against me. Dom can't help me. I'm on my own."

"Not quite. You got me to help you do break–ins," said Mendy, laughing. He was telling me that he'd help me. Mendy was still a stand–up guy. I had three people backing me up—Dom, Candy, Mendy. I could do worse.

Mendy drove over to Ocean Parkway, then up ten blocks. I'd lived around here a long time ago. Mendy went south. I turned to look at my old home, also a big house. Close to the subway, on a dead end, my old man's type of place. He'd liked to control the space around him. We'd lived there for a while then moved to Bay Ridge, all the time putting distance between us and Bensonhurst.

Mendy cut off a car about every block, using his horn, endangering the young and the old and me.

"You always drive like this?" I said, holding on to a leather seat for dear life.

"Time is money, Richie," said Mendy, who had an unlit cigar clamped between his teeth.

"Good motto. So is 'slow down and live.' Ever hear of that one?" I said.

"Only pussies drive slow," said Mendy, driving faster, doing well over 50 mph down a narrow street with cars parked on both sides. I closed my eyes.

A lot of professors lived around here. Wiant, Fenner, plus two or three others. Mendy handled the rentals and the sales, made himself a nice little living. Mendy was a pal. Maybe for once I had an edge in all of this. I hoped so for my sake.

We pulled up to a duplex. Winston Wiant had one side.

"Who's next to him?" I asked.

"Some chink. A math professor. Nice guy. Quiet. Minds his own business."

"Wife? Kids?"

"Wife works at the college. Kids are in school."

We got out of the big car, which should have been smoking from what it had been doing. No one had followed us. I'd used the mirror to check. No need to. Mendy's wild driving would've made life very difficult for anyone doing a tail job. The only way to have kept up with Mendy was to have driven on the sidewalk.

Mendy opened the front door. On the way over he'd used his cell, driven with one hand. Wiant was not at home. He was where he was supposed to be. He was doing his job. He served as Fenner's second in command. In reality, he ran the show at the college. All of the dirty details of the college were handled by Wiant, like telling someone when they were getting the axe or informing a professor that they were over budget for a lab. I'd gone round and round with Wiant about that last item. I envied him. I wished I could be spending my time doing my job instead of prowling around Brooklyn trying to get a line on a hitman. This was the time to get focused.

Wiant had a lot going for him as the guy in charge of all of this. First, he was a creep, just the type I could see using drugs and poisons. He'd not flinch at seeing a guy like King Gomez get squeezed to death. Wiant himself looked liked death walking. Second, he was no dope. I gave him a hard time about his brain power, but he knew how to run the college. If he could do that, he'd be smart enough to run a drug operation. Third, he hated me. It's always easier to kill those you hate. I'd remember those lines. They sounded like they should be in a song.

# Chapter Thirty–Three

Wiant's place surprised me. It was normal.

Which was not what I expected. What type of life would a guy like him be expected to lead. At home, he was Ozzie to some nice little Harriet? No way. Anyone who went out in public looking like a backup singer in "Rocky Horror" could rightly be suspected of having an abnormal home life. So, I was thinking that this break and entry would be a visit to whackoland. I was dead wrong. The first floor of his abode was just furniture: tables, couches, wall pictures of recognizable things, rugs and a TV. There were no torture instruments. No stuffed animals (or people). No photos of mutilations. Nothing out of the ordinary.

Mendy took up watch at the front window while I started with the living room. Rubber gloves on, going into cabinets, opening drawers, checking out silverware, looking for anything off the wall.

Wiant fit my criminal profile of the type of creep who'd kill with chemical weapons. It takes someone full of misdirected hate to kill like that. Guns, knives or even clubs aren't as nasty as brucine and atropine. Those two chemical weapons were both connected by one thing—dishing out pain. I could vouch for one of them. Atropine had nearly blown my heart. Brucine had snuffed the King, putting out his candle for good. Pumping a bullet into someone is one thing, but loading up the unsuspecting with drugs is a whole different ball game. Wiant made a match with the weapons. He was the guy to start with

Then I'd do Fenner, who also fit the bill. Finally, there was Annie. Could she have done all of this? That was hard to believe, but the fact is that she had the knowledge, the question was did she have the will?

The duplex had a living room with stairs at the side, a dining room full of heavy, old furniture and an all white kitchen. The whole first floor was neat as a pin. The kitchen didn't look like it got used a whole lot.

"Five minutes in, Richie," said Mendy from the living room.

"I'm going to the basement."

"Anything special you lookin' for?"

"Clues," I said.

"Clues? No shit. And here I thought you were after this doily's love letters," said Mendy, sounding impatient. The basement was big and dry and mostly empty. No knives for ritual disemboweling. No coffins of earth. No body parts on ice. I checked the corners. No little old ladies full of formaldehyde. It was time to go upstairs.

"Twenty-four minutes, Richie," said Mendy, pointing to his watch."

"Thanks," I said.

"Anything?"

"No."

The upstairs had three bedrooms and one bath, which I decided right then and there to save for last. Finding out about Winston Wiant's personal hygiene was something I'd have to work myself up to do.

Two of the bedrooms were nothings. Bare. One bed. Made. Looking unused. One dresser, in it only a spare set of sheets and pillow cases. One closet with no clothes. That was it for guest bedroom (I could only guess at what type of 'guest' this would be) number one. And number two was the same story. Wiant obviously didn't have many overnight guests. Maybe they didn't last the night. I was getting nowhere fast.

"Thirty–five minutes, Rich."

"Ok, Mendy," I said. Mendy wanted to be out of here in under sixty minutes. I was into the last part of the hour and knew no more than when I'd started.

Wiant's bedroom was next. I took a deep breath, stepped inside. Another normal. No bat cage with a large bar for Mr. Deathface to hang from at night. No earth from his native land to sleep in. There was a king sized bed with big posters, heavy, old furniture, like the stuff downstairs, which probably meant it was from Wiant's parents. If he had parents.

His closet was full of black suits, black ties, black shoes, white shirts, a black sweater, and a black hat. Wiant must've been impressed by undertakers at an early age. The dean's right hand man didn't come home and become a peacock. What one saw of him during the day was what there was.

"Fifty minutes," Rich," said Mendy who was now rushing the time.

"Nearly done, Mendy."

The house had a third floor, and I climbed the twelve uncarpeted steps to it. There were lots of boxes, all stacked neatly. Wiant seemed to have no real life. There was nothing in the house to indicate that he had any interests, any vices, any bad habits. The guy was an automaton. Inhuman. That also fit the profile of a chemical killer. Wiant could watch me die inch by inch and never bat an eye. Plus he would already be dressed for the funeral.

In the corner was a throw rug, on it a desk with a computer, a chair. The chair was placed so that Wiant was facing the wall. The window had a nice view of Brooklyn. Trees. The blue sky. People moving about. Life. Which did not appear to hold much interest for Winston Wiant, H.E.O.

I started to turn on the computer. No need. It was already on. Some of the folders had interesting titles: Fenner, Bucceroni, McClure, Porter. Wiant had a file for every faculty member at the college. I brought up mine. I began to hope Wiant was the guy. Him I could take out and enjoy every minute.

He had chapter and verse on me. About my wife and my boy. Date of the deaths. My reactions. Comments about me made by students. By other faculty. By Fenner. Class days I'd missed. He also knew all about me and my fling with Annie Porter. Times, dates, places. It was all organized into categories. Personal. Professional. Wiant had been a good observer.

The file on Fenner was also well organized. One item caught my eye. A cross reference to A. P., who was Annie porter. Wiant devoted most of the file to Fenner's sexual life. Apparently, Annie and Fenner got it on with regularity. Wiant had the when, the where, and he knew the why.

Annie Porter had done Fenner to get herself a safer job. Being an administrator made her more marketable than being an art historian professor. Which is probably why she did me, no doubt she had in mind something I could do for her. I was no better than Fenner. Wiant had it all down. When it started was established clearly. Where was in various locations, including Fenner's private office. Wiant even had some details about the how. Technical. Read like a manual. Annie had gone out of her way to be accommodating.

Wiant, the weasel, also had some entries which nailed Fenner for violating about ten or twelve of the college's rules on tenure and promotion. He'd doctored Annie's teaching observations. He'd filled her in about the type of questions that the tenure committee would ask her. He'd fudged her record, giving her credit for committee work she'd never done. The decisions would be made in the spring. I'd bet a dollar or two of good money that Wiant and Fenner would have a heart to heart chin/chin about the helping hand that had been given to Annie.

"About done, Rich?" called Mendy from below.

"No."

"How long?"

"I'll let you know."

"You find something?"

"Yes."

Mac's file was just as full. Wiant knew all the girls. Mac had been a busy guy to say the least. Maria Perez, Nikki, young Ms. Sung to name a few. The list went on. Candy wasn't on it. I checked my watch. Before the afternoon got completely used up solving crimes, I'd call my place to see if Candy had left me her new phone number at the hospital. Nothing had come through on my cell about it.

I'd read enough. Wiant was not the guy. He was someone who was getting ready to do some blackmailing. I was looking for a dope dealer who'd killed off one of his own kind and who had then started to take care of loose ends. Wiant was not that guy.

Downstairs, Mendy gave me a dirty look.

"You done now?" he said, testily.

"Yeah," I said.

"Let's blow," he said.

We walked outside. Mendy locked the door behind us. We crossed the street slowly. Mendy was in front of me. We were just a rental agent and his customer looking at houses. My eyes swept the street. There was no sign of James "Fisheyes" Kim, nephew of the chopped–to–pieces Buffalo Pang. There was also no sign of the two black avengers—Nikki Nateal, former lab assistant and J. P. Carlisle, current ass kicker.

Inside his big Lincoln, Mendy lit a new cigar, throwing away the one he'd been chomping on. The smoke soon filled the big car. He rolled down a window. I asked him to drive away. Sitting in a car in Brooklyn is dangerous. You're immobile and a killer can walk right up and put two or three, or even four, into you.

"What now?" said Mendy, pulling away, heading for his customary light speed of driving.

"You took keys to Fenner's house, right?"

"I got the originals, but he might have changed the locks." If that were true, I'd have to use the pick set I'd brought with me just in case. I'm a just–in–case kind of guy.

"I want you to call Fenner," I said, smelling the good cigar smoke. This was not a Hoyo, but a la Gloria, which also was no cheapie like Dom rolled around in his mouth.

"I bet you want me to ask him if he'd like to sell his house. I bet you then want me to find out if his wife is at home. I on track so far?"

"Yes, you're getting into the spirit of things, not like back inside when you were pissed at me for going overtime. His number at the college is 951–5543."

Mendy dialed the number. He had a Blackberry, which meant he held most of his office in one of his small hands. He got right through to Fenner, put his phone on speaker so I could hear. Mendy was slick. He played Fenner like a fish. The housing market was rebounding because of interest rates and tax credits. Fenner could make a killing right now. Fenner bit. Maybe he figured he could live with Annie, after he dumped his wife. Mendy then reeled him in by asking if his wife was at home. No. She was upstate. She was with her sick mother. She'd been there for several months, which meant that Fenner had free time to feast on Annie. Mendy told Fenner he'd be back to him about an appointment. Mendy hung up. He blew smoke my way. I'd have to tell Candy that I had not relapsed and smoked a cigar while she was laid up and unable to monitor my ways.

"He's at work. His wife's gone. So I can get inside?" I said, sitting back in my seat as Mendy rocketed through the narrow streets of Brooklyn. I would either solve this crime or die. The way Mendy drove, the dying might come sooner rather than later. I thought about asking him to slow down, but he'd already been pissed once. I didn't want to lose his help.

"What's stopping you?" said Mendy, reaching into his pants pocket, driving with one hand, not slowing down one iotaI got the point. Mendy had stuck his neck out for me. We'd been in, we'd gotten out. No one had spotted us and called the cops. Wiant hadn't shown up unexpectedly. All had gone well. Luck was riding with me.

Mendy was right. He had a nice little business, used it to feed the wife and kids. He didn't need to lose all of that by helping someone from out of his distant past. He'd done enough.

From now on, I was totally on my own. Fear started to work its way back into me. Being with Mendy was like being with Dom. I felt safe with them. Being alone was now doubly worse because I didn't have Candy to pick me up. The last time I was on my own I'd nearly been picked off by a silenced .22 and sent to Brooklyn Hospital as a D.O.A. Dom was right. I had to get back to what I was. I hoped it wasn't too late for that.

# Chapter Thirty–Four

Mendy drove off hard, leaving behind about five thousand miles worth of tread from his expensive tires. I walked along the street, alone, the hair up on the back of my bandaged neck, my hand in my jacket pocket, resting on the safe .22 I had with me. There would be no hesitation. Any sign of cultural diversity on this block, and I'd start firing. Jimmy Fisheyes was moving back to the top of my carefully crafted list. Wiant was now out, and what was left was the sexual team of Annie and Fenner. What I had on Annie was that she was doing her dean and that she'd let herself into my lab after Candy had changed the locks. With evidence gathering skills like that, I would've be a terror at Nuremburg.

Fenner had a real house, not a duplex. It was all brick. Nice. Around the small yard was a wrought iron fence. I'd never been inside it. I knew he had a wife, but I'd never met her. The Urban U. is like that. The faculty doesn't know one another from Adam. I had known next to nothing about Walt Brzenk. It wasn't a place that was made for having colleagues.

It would be nice to run away from all of this, but Candy had been right. There was no place to run and no place to hide. This was strictly a matter of who was the better hunter. Time was that I prided myself on being able to track someone down. Back in Bensonhurst, Dom and I had a street reputation for keeping after those we thought needed some attention. Mancini and Bucceroni were known to have long memories. Never forget. Always get even. We probably thought we were in training to be wiseguys. Two young jerks. But Dom had become a cop. I went into the professor business. Both of us could've ended up as wrong guys, but we'd gotten ourselves lined out. We'd made something of ourselves.

Mendy's key worked. I just walked up to Fenner's front door, used the key and in I went. There was no hesitation, no standing around. It would take a busybody working full time to spot me breaking in.

Fenner's house had some class to it. Good furniture, all light colors, matching carpet and wallpaper, prints hung up in each room. A nice looking place. His wife must have good taste.

The house looked pretty unlived in. The kitchen had no food and no food smell. The fridge was pretty empty, just coffee–mate and some milk. There was no atropine chilling. The cupboards were bare. No jars of brucine next to the salt shaker.

The second floor had four bedrooms with one big master bedroom which looked like the downstairs. Neat. Unused. Like its owner was on vacation. Of the three other bedrooms, two were just rooms, nothing to draw attention to the trained eye of R. V. Bucceroni, sleuth extraordinaire, but the third wasn't. The third guest bedroom was where Dean D. Douglas Fenner was spending his off hours away from his professional duties at the college. He was having himself quite a time.

Next to the bed was a VCR. On the ceiling was a mirror. Under one of the pillows were two pairs of panties, red and black, initials A. P. on them, used, their purpose apparently to keep the scent of Annie close to Fenner at all times.

The VCR had one tape in it. I flicked it on. Good quality tape. Well placed camera. Excellent sound. All of it had captured Annie's entertaining of the chief executive officer of the college of the Urban U., a man of sixty, given power, in a position of responsibility. This the proof of how he was using that power.

On the tape, the dean was in a lot of places, but I wouldn't say he was being responsible. Front door, back door, over, under, beside, straps, restraints, moans, suggestions, pleas, curses, crescendos. Annie deserved more than a promotion. She should be made a full professor for what she was doing for Fenner. I rewound the tape. Pocketed it. I thought of using it to enliven a college meeting, offer the antics of Annie and Fenner as TQM with a twist.

I'd struck out again. These weren't dopers turned killers to get a larger cut. This was an over the hill professor, a baccalà who'd never accomplished anything of note doing a power bang on a woman who was about to be kicked out of the college and down the academic ladder. Annie Porter had put on a good show, but her face had a smile frozen on it. She'd done Fenner, said what he wanted said, put herself into positions that turned him on, worn the secrets from Victoria he'd no doubt bought for her, but she hated both him and herself for doing it. I wondered what she had thought about me. Was I any different than Fenner?

It was time to go. I'd seen more than enough of the two of them. I took one pair of the used, red panties into the master bedroom and placed it carefully into one of the drawers of Mrs. D. Douglas Fenner, Ph. D. I made sure the A. P. was clearly visible. I'm sure this would help relations in the Fenner household.

Downstairs, I checked the street from inside the house of my esteemed dean. It was quiet. I went out as quickly as I had come in. I made my way slowly away, crossing the street, heading toward Coney Island Avenue where I'd parked my car. I stopped quickly, crouched, tied my shoes, and used the down time to look over my shoulder. There was no one. There was no tail creeping up on me getting ready to blow my so—called brains out. I was in the clear.

At the corner, I used my cell. There were no messages on my tape at home. I called Brooklyn Hospital. Candy had checked out. The receptionist wasn't sure if she had left in the morning or at noon. I hung up. I phoned Candy. No answer at her place in Bay Ridge or on her cell. I didn't like this. Candy had said before that we needed to be together. The night of Brzenk's murder she was one spot and me another. Bad news. The two of us needed to be in sync.

It started to rain. Nutso weather. Heat, then some snow, now rain. Mother Nature had a sense of humor when it came to Brooklyn. So does God for that matter.

I took off for Coney Island Avenue, my hand back on my .22. I'd go to the college. Jimmy Fisheyes might be there. I hoped so. I wanted to see him.

# Chapter Thirty–Five

Walking back to Coney Island Avenue was a lot of fun. Just terrific. I directed a few words at Mendy for leaving me out here on my lonesome. The rain water worked its way down my neck, seeped into my shoes, soaking me from top to bottom. Donald Wooley would be real happy to see his just released patient doing a Gene Kelly up Avenue L. At least Gene had the sense to have an umbrella. Not me, plus I was not trying to get wet like he had.

Coming up to Coney Island Avenue, I looked left, right, forward, backward, up, down, but I did not drop to the ground on all fours and listen for approaching horses.

It took me more than a little time to get my old car going. The ancient Plymouth was temperamental. I didn't drive it a whole lot. Today, in the heavy rain, on a street where I stood out like Madonna at a monastery, its tired iron decided not to start. Lucky Me. I gave a brief thought about asking Mendy to give me a ride. I nixed that thought quickly. One, because he was probably still on edge. Two, because his driving in wet weather would be really, really dangerous as opposed to just dangerous. I instead called Triple A, who got lost twice. The guy eventually told me his Garmin was broken, and arrived in an hour and a half, but he did get me going. I even tipped him. The ninety minutes was spent by me looking about every which way at once for Asian killers who specialized in heavy set Italians. There was still no tail. Maybe they were banking on pneumonia.

Finally, I was off, on the way to the college with a lot moving through my mind. The Plymouth chugged along, but my brain was in fast forward.

Wiant; he was just a blackmailer.

Fenner; just a horny old bastard, with too many fetishes for his own, or anybody's, good.

Annie; just trying to get by in this sorry life.

The number of possible, realistic suspects had dwindled. It had been easier when just about everyone on the planet had been in the suspect category. Nikki and J. P. and the One Percenters, Fisheyes and the Seoul Brothers, plus colleagues, and my boss. Anyone I'd left out? Bill and Hillary, Cain and Abel? Mac had been moving up and down my list, had been at one time in the not so distant past right up there at the top. I'd done a bang up job of investigating him. Dom was dead on right: I was a far, far cry from what I'd been back in Bensonhurst.

I pulled down the street, passing Harry's, looked inside. What I saw made me jump the curb with the old Plymouth. I wrestled the old car off the sidewalk, hoping I hadn't squashed a derelict, and continued past the deli. Two people had been sitting at the counter, talking to Harry, they doing most of the talking, plus gesturing. Harry's part in the conversation looked like a lot of nodding. I parked the Plymouth a block from the college, got out. The pistol had gone into my pocket. I started toward the institution of higher learning which paid my bills.

What I had seen in Harry's was the obese owner of the corner deli, a talkative fellow immigrant who specialized in pastrami and pornography, listening attentively to one Mr. Jamal Powell Carlisle and one Ms. Nicole Nateal. They, no doubt, were articulating the positive attributes of the One Percenters. Harry was probably hearing from my two students about his use of women of color in his upstairs porn operation.

Seeing them did a lot for me in terms of my mind. My heart was pumping at triple digits, like I'd tossed down a double shot of atropine. My mind was thrashing around trying to figure out if they were just two tough Brooklyn street kids playing at being revolutionaries, or whether they were truly hard asses capable of rub outs. All I had for proof as to their innocence in Pang's killing/slicejob was their word. Being men/women of their word was not a usual thing in Brooklyn.

I was almost to the college, inside of which I would be relatively safe and sound unless there was a killer cooking crack and prepping another weapon just for little me. I was looking ahead, trying to see into the deli. I didn't want Nikki and J. P. to see me. All I wanted was to find my way to my cozy little lab. I was paying less than close attention to the world around me. I didn't see the person standing in the dark of the doorway of the burned out crack house. But he saw me.

"Hello, Professor," said Jimmy Fisheyes, his voice quiet and calm but nonetheless deadly to me.

My hand was on the pistol. I could twist the pistol and shoot without taking it out. I would lose a good pair of pants, but that was one expense I could bear.

"You want me?" I said, moving my body so that I presented a side to him. I anticipated that firepower would also come my way from Fisheyes.

"Want? I do not understand your usage. I wish to thank you. You did what I requested. But it will not be necessary. The two blacks are no longer, how do you say, 'a moving target.'"

"They didn't kill your uncle," I said, my finger still on the trigger.

"I know. I hear they are after Professor McClure. He deserves to be killed. He had sexual relations with my cousin. She is just eighteen years old. She was a virgin. The white devil spoiled her. That is one operation of the One Percenters of which I approve."

"You know they didn't kill Buffa..your uncle?" I said catching myself as to the dead man's moniker.

"I know."

He knew. It must be great to be young. No aches, no pains, no prostate the size of an orange, all of this he didn't have, plus he knew who was killing who. Whoever said that youth must be served knew a thing or two.

My finger relaxed on the trigger. Fisheyes wasn't talking like someone who had just ordered a hit.

"You ever go to Bay Ridge?" I said.

"Excuse me?"

"Bay Ridge, you ever go there?" I said, completing a very clever string of leading questions. He would soon be at my mercy.

"No. That is not a place where people of my color feel welcome. Why do you ask?"

"No reason? Why are you out here? You keeping up with your homework?" I said, deftly changing the subject from an area which could end up with me putting a hole in Fisheyes to one that concerned school matters.

"Three point seven five GPA. The only course in which I received a B was the cultural diversity seminar."

"Why was that?" I said, taking my hand out of the pistol pocket.

"During one of the classroom discussions, I stated that Abraham Lincoln was correct in his desire to send back to Africa all of the slaves. After that statement, the professor, who was herself black, saw me as deficient in terms of diversity appreciation."

"Anyone in the class agree with you?" I said starting to focus on a way to end this fascinating conversation and get my wet ass inside.

"Carlisle did. He said that there were no 'niggers' in Nigeria. He also received a B. The rest of the class was all awarded the grade of A."

"I have to go now."

"You are feeling better, yes?"

"Yes, I am feeling better," I said, hoping I didn't piss him off by re–arranging his words.

"Next term, I take your history of science course. You have a fine reputation as a professor."

"Thank you," I said. It would never end. I nearly had Nikki out of my thinning hair, I had half a term to go with J. P. and now here was Fisheyes, standing out in the rain, tailing a rival gang's senior administration, and, next semester, he would come to me so that he could gain an understanding of exactly what it was that Lavoisier had accomplished. I needed a sabbatical.

"I have something for you," said Jimmy Fisheyes, handing me a roll of film.

"What is this?" I said, taking it.

"This is why I know the One Percenters did not kill my uncle," said Fisheyes, backing away from me, into the shadows, keeping watch on Fat Harry's.

J. P. and Nikki came out of the deli. I wanted no part of them. Behind me was Jimmy Fisheyes. I was two hundred fifty pounds plus, but a .9mm would go right through me. For once, Lady Luck cut me a break. They turned left, not right, and headed toward the subway station. I gave them some time to move away then I stepped into Harry's. Jimmy Fisheyes glided past me, tailing the One Percenters. I wondered if I could get arrested for doing a piss poor job in loco parentis.

Harry was sweated through like he been in a sauna. I would bet a good night's sleep that Nikki and J. P. had laid it on the line for the fat man. Fat Harry needed to sweat. His being peeled and cored by the One Percenters would not cost me a half hour afternoon nap. I smiled at Harry. He gave me a sickly smile back.

"You are better, professor?" he wheezed.

"Yes," I said, wondering if there was anyone in Brooklyn who hadn't heard my lie about being sick. I wasn't about to let anyone in about our accident. The hospital was as close to a safe house as Candy and I had.

"Flu?"

"Flu."

"You want coffee, yes?"

"Yeah."

Harry waddled away between the counter and the kitchen, like a seal in a small tank. Yes sir, Harry had better mend his evil ways. J. P. and Nikki had a thing about turning people into emblems. Carving up Fat Harry would be a challenge for them on account of the tonnage, but I had the sneaky feeling that they would rise to the occasion. Fisheyes was probably full of it. They were the ones who had done a slicey–dicey on his uncle.

My hand closed on the roll of film. What was he up to with this? There was a photo drop two blocks away. I'd tank up on coffee, then head that way.

My suspect list was shot to hell. Jimmy Fisheyes had been numero uno. Now he was in the safe tank. Nikki and J. P. had told me, cross their fingers and hope to die, that they had definitely not done a One Percenter number on Pang. And then there had been Mr. Fisheyes who backed up their story. But I still was not convinced. Besides, who were they compared to my brilliance? I was a Ph. D., a college muckety–muck while they were students, nobodies when it came to high level criminal detecting. I ran a hand through my hair. I wished this would all come clear. One minute, I seemed on the right track, the next I was back in the fog, flailing about, trying to figure out who did what. Maybe I should let Fenner feed his theory to Dom. Gomez's killing could be tied to the One Percenters and Dom could wrap all of this up. There was only one loose end. That was me. Dr. Rchard Vincenzio Bucceroni, recipient of a chemical weapon, master teacher, accessible to the street gangs, and a damn nice man. Who'd doped me with atropine? That was still the puzzle of note to be solved, and I was grasping at straws to come to a conclusion. Whoever it was had a mean streak, that much I knew. Also the person was giving me no safe haven. Relentless was the word for this bastard. I stopped rubbing my head, not wanting to crinkle my scalp.

"Here is your coffee, professor. Regular. Just like you like it. Made by myself personally," he said handing me a cup; his mitt was very sweaty, the One Percenter visit still having at him.

"A dollar?"

"Free. Enjoy Professor. Regain your good health."

"Thanks."

The coffee, considering the fact that Harry had dripped into it, wasn't half bad. That was the story of my life recently, everything about half right.

# Chapter Thirty–Six

Fat Harry went to dispense some grease to his other usual customers. I drank the hot coffee. The heat felt good all the way down. To my left, sitting at the counter, were two skinheads, one with a swastika tattoo. Underneath it a saying: WHITE IS RIGHT

They had on lots of leather. They wore big stomping boots that Goebbels would have approved of. They were probably getting ready to work out on Harry. I'd evened the odds. Two against two was no fun. They left, going elsewhere to hunt for someone they could take. That was the story with these punks. They'd dress up like Nazis on parade, but their fighting was done against those who couldn't fight back. They tried it on with me, I'd rip off the tattoo and make them eat it. I was in a foul mood.

I also went elsewhere. North on the street to an avenue where I dropped off the film. Tomorrow, I'd have it back. Then maybe I, too, would know what Fisheyes knew for sure. The inscrutable bastard. Maybe we then could partner up.

Back to the college, up to my lab, locked the door, safe. Snug as a bug in a rug.

I flipped on my computer. Someone was logged on to MEDLINE. I recognized the code of the user. Nikki Nateal. She was reading an article about anectine, which was a brand name for succinylcholine. This was another drug about which yours truly, a.k.a. the Big Mouth, had given chapter and verse. This was a breathtaker, and it could be, in the wrong hands, just as deadly as brucine. It was less traceable. So traceless not tasteless, those had been my clever words of introduction to the class. I made a mental note to work boredom into my lectures. It might appeal to Nikki. Down the line something might have to be done with Nikki. Graduation, or execution it might come to that.

I signed off. Getting Nikki out of my lab was a big plus on my side of the books. There, she had too easy access to too many gruesome chemical weapons. My mind floated random ideas before me. I'd have to do something about her. Anectine was a good choice for a weapon. Nikki was no doubt gearing up for a shot at someone. Fat Harry was probably at the top of that particular hit list. Maybe also Jimmy Fisheyes. Or Mac. Or, God forbid, possibly, hard to believe, Jesus's favorite guido.

I had an hour to kill. In the evening, there was to be a brief service for Brzenk in the dean's office, after which the dean would shoo away the crowd and do Annie on his large desk. My car was out in the wilderness. I'd go and put it in the garage. On went a slicker and into my pocket went a wrench. Eight inches of steel. A good Brooklyn night street weapon. Geez officer, I just had it with me because of this trouble with my car. It came in handy when I had a head to split. Know what I mean?

The .22 I had put into a cabinet and locked it securely away, where only the killer who used my lab as kill central could get to it.

Riding the elevator, a lot started to sweep in and out of my troubled mind. King Gomez was dead, but that was just one less drug dealer. Walt Brzenk was dead, but that was just a guy in the wrong place at the wrong time. And Pang? Pang had been a world class, over the top slimeball. Maybe some father had learned of how his kid was being used and had paid a call. Then there was Mac who was still porking co–eds a mile a minute and who might still be the guy. Mac was asking for it big time. Mac needed to get on the One Percenters' bad side like Sestak had needed the advice from good old Slick Willy.

No one got on the elevator as it made its slow way to the first floor lobby. The elevator seemed cold. My head still wasn't completely healed. There was probably some seepage, like a few thousand essential brain cells leaking out my ear and into my shirt collar.

On the first floor, I headed for the student banyo, ran hot water over my still bandaged neck, held it there for a while. It felt good. Maybe I would just stay inside here for a week or two. The mirror was cracked, even though it was relatively new, the result of a wag of a student, but I could make myself out. A killer was closing in on me, and I was spinning my wheels. Dom was right, Richie Bucceroni was no longer street time Bucceroni. I was now a professor. How good were professors at getting the goods on murderers?

When I came back into the lobby, there were two white co–eds at the water fountain about five meters from me. They didn't see me. They were talking loud enough for me to hear all that they said.

"You gonna go, or not?" one of them said.

"I don' know," said the other.

"Come on, why not? It's nothin'. Easy money. Come on. Trust me," I heard the two most fatal words in Brooklyn being used as they always were used—to get someone to do something they shouldn't.

"I don' know. My boyfriend, he'd kill me."

"So don' tell him. This is just between the two of us and Fatso. It's ok, we're just gonna fake it. Trust me. It'll be nothin'," she said, again she came on with the trust word.

The two walked away from me. They were kids, eighteen, nineteen, no more. They went out the big glass entrance door. Me about ten meters now behind them, keeping my distance. They headed across the street.

The two girls slipped into an alley, disappearing from my eagle eye sight. I followed. Why I was doing this I hadn't a clue. I flicked my eyes to the left as I passed the alley. The girls were already inside. Fat Harry had adjusted to the changing times. Nikki and J. P. didn't give a wahoo who he filmed as long they were not black. There were limits to the One Percenters' view of what was morally correct and it all boiled down to the race line. On the black side of the line, Harry died, on the other side he could do what he wanted. These were two students who'd come to our place to pick up some culture and here they were off to earn some quickie bucks by peeling down and putting on a show. A short time ago, these girls had been in Mac's literature class, reading his favorite author, Jane Austen.

I know. I'd seen Mac teach. He was something else, getting these kids to listen to listen to advice about matrimony and now here they were, exposing themselves to some obese sleazeball for the sake of a few filthy coins.

Speaking of sleazeballs, Fat Harry himself now emerged from his deli, walking like a guy who did not walk a whole lot. In the alley he went and inside the same door the two girls had entered. Harry was going up to the room that Candy and I had planned on breaking into, but that was before we'd moved the binoculars upward a tad and seen the anatomy lesson done on one Buffalo Pang. Harry was now in charge of the porn shoots. Afterwards, maybe he'd angle his lens at the college itself and catch some bathroom action. Nothing had changed. It was all the same. Co–eds would now come to Fat Harry instead of Pang and act it out with another or do it for real with somebody like the Indian kid or maybe Harry himself would direct some freak poses, script a part for himself. A new crack dealer would soon take up where King Gomez had left off. Mac would continue to bang away until he was put away. Not a whole lot was changed. Well, that was not quite true. I knew that a few things were changed. Nikki and J. P. Carlisle were into change. A new crack dealer could get real deal real quick if he came into their range of fire. J. P. and Nikki were both hunters. Then there was me. I was the hunted. That also had not changed.

Down the block and around the corner I went, my coat flapping against me, head down, watching my step, unaware of the world around me, making my way toward the building where King Gomez had been deposited. Why I'd parked out here was a good example of what a dope I was. I'd thought I was sneaking up on the goings on at the deli. That was not a clever move on my part.

I passed the first one at the corner. He must've been the look out. I never saw him. He got behind me, yoked me, arm around the throat. The other one got in my face, a knife at my nose. The two skinheads from Harry's had found themselves a victim. Or so they thought.

"Gonna take what you got, dickhead!" said the one punk with the knife.

I set my feet and slammed the yoker back toward the wall of the college. We missed the wall but hit the door, hard, the skinhead first. He said oomph! Something wet landed on the back of my neck. The knifer cut at me, sliced into my coat, the blade caught cloth but missed the arm. I kicked him, the steel tip of my shoe making contact with his soft, dangling parts. He screamed, went to one knee. I pumped my elbows back and forth, did a number on the yoker's insides.

The side door to the college opened and out stepped Beef Patty Norwood. He had a stick/club/weapon in his big right hand. He whacked the knifer in the face, drawing blood, knocking him to the ground. The knife skittered away. Patty fell on the skinhead.

"You only got one now, Doc! I done pancaked this cueball motherfucker!" he said.

Only the ends of the arms and legs of the street punk were visible underneath the nearly four hundred pounds of Beef Patty. I came away from the wall where I'd driven the yoker, pivoted, my hand closing on the wrench in my pocket, removing it, the ends sticking out of my big fist, all of this done in basically one motion.

I hit the yoker a good one, a chopping blow on the temple. He went down. His face was red below the chin. He was on his back, struggling to get up, throwing off blood.

I dropped onto him, knees first. The wrench came into play. Lots of targets. Ears first. Ears are easy.

I straddled Mr. WHITE IS RIGHT, who was not a small guy. His mouth came open, drawing in air to scream, in went the wrench, two hundred fifty pounds of an agitated pasta consumer driving it home. I jerked it to one side and then ripped out, bringing with the wrench part of the depressor labii inferioris and a lot more blood.

I stood up. The wrench went back in my pocket. Lester got off the other skinhead who was out cold. The big man hit him again with his club, something flew off the wannabe Nazi's face. There was still something wet on my neck. I reached back with my free hand and picked off whatever it was, which turned out to be a healthy part of the yoker's tongue. He would have a difficult time articulating threats in the future.

"Here," I said, bending over and placing the tongue piece on the yoker's forehead. "Better keep this or the cat will get it."

The skinhead didn't laugh. He did, however, gurgle on his own blood.

Beef Patty laughed. A deep, from the belly, big man laugh, its sound loud on the deserted street.

"That a good one, Doc, 'Cat'll get it.' Damn funny. Damn funny."

I looked at Beef Patty, who had a swelling under his left eye.

"That eye come from shitface over there?" I asked.

"Naw, that white boy never had a chance. Me and Betsy here took care of his ass. That a love bump you lookin' at. Some li' gal laid one on me," he said, still holding his club, a.k.a. Betsy.

"It worth it?"

"She was nice, Doc. Small but sassy. You know me. I like 'em sassy."

I actually did not know the sexual preferences of Mr. Patty, but he'd come to my rescue. I smiled at him.

"Thanks, Lester. I thought you were sick."

"I am, but I gotta work. Need the money, Doc. Say, I still got to talk to you."

"How about now?"

"I'm a little busy now, Doc. Catch you later. It important though."

Beef Patty went back inside the college. I stayed at the door, took a peek toward his office. Sitting on his desk was an all white, all right, all naked co–ed. Harvard should send professors to visit me. I have some unique insights about higher education in America in the twenty–first century.

I really do.

My coat had a new air vent, but that was about it. I looked up and down the street. No one around. Getting dark. The skinheads could've killed me and tomorrow I'd have been someone's good morning surprise, just like King Gomez had been.

The two punks crawled away. One would be a soup eater and not much of a talker, the other would be sexually dysfunctional for a while, but both would live. Fatigue hit me. Vince Lombardi had said that fatigue makes cowards of us all. I hoped Vince wasn't looking down at me just now.

I still had a car to get; I went to get it.

My life was a little gray right now. Here I was, slouching along in life, a guy who'd come within an eyelash of being wasted by two street creatures, and after all of this I was still in the line of someone's fire. These skinheads had been merely a diversion.

I would bet folding money that the professors weren't doin' this at Middlebury.

# Chapter Thirty–Seven

In the nicely paneled conference room at the college, a very fat man in a very ill–fitting, very black suit was reading a very sad poem, poorly. The poem was called "The Darkling Thrush," written by a poet named Thomas Hardy who apparently hadn't had a happy life. The longer you listened to this poem, even if it was read by a moron, the worse you felt.

All of this was what passed for a funeral service for Walt Brzenk. Fenner had made a short speech, the fat guy was now reading, and that would be it for the service.

This thrush poem had been one of Brzenk's favorites, at least that's what his mother had told me. Brzenk hadn't gone in for religion, that much I knew about him.

The words from the reading were loud in the mostly empty room. The service for Brzenk was not a big affair. No students had come. There were just me, Fenner and Annie, and Wiant. Even Mac had not shown, and he'd had least been a running partner of the dearly departed. This was it. Mourning is not part of the contract at the Urban U.

The four of us were standing and listening. I looked over at Annie and Fenner, wondering how long after this was over they would wait until he screwed her up against the wall.

Fenner had come up with the bright idea of having the service piped to Brzenk's parents in Vermont. So here we stood in Brooklyn, the sole "friends" of the dead, and up there, in another state were the old folks and Walt, whose six feet four inches had been burned to a crisp and the tiny, toasted parts jammed into a pot.

Blacksuit Fatstuff was from the main campus, part of the sunshine committee. He'd come to me after my family had been destroyed. "No thanks," had been my response. I'd heard his work before. His reading today was just a recitation, no feeling, no emotion, no soul, nothing human. He read like he was a mortician.

I kind of knew the poem and the poet from Walt showing it to me, so when he went past the part about the caroling, I remembered the end. Also, Mac had read this selfsame poem for my wife and my son, but he'd done a bang up job. There hadn't been a dry eye in the house when he was done.

"'Some blessed hope, whereof he knew, and I was unaware.'"

I hoped for Brzenk's sake there was a kindly God. Maybe then we'd meet up again. What I'd say to him, I wasn't too sure. Brzenk had been in the wrong place and the wrong time and he'd drunk the drink meant for me. The guy, in truth, had been something of a goof, not someone I could be friends with, just another professor.

I took a glance at Annie, standing next to Fenner, both of them in appropriate black, she with her eyes cast down, in grief mode. She saw me looking at her and smiled a small, sad smile. I smiled in return. Her hip was touching Fenner. She'd probably done him in the car on the way from Midwood.

The service, such as it was, came to an end. We then all lined up to walk past the conference phone and say a few well chosen words to Brzenk's mom and pop. I put in my two cents about how much I'd thought of Walt and how too bad this all was. The old folks thanked me. Their life was now over. Burying a child was the end of the line. They would place Walt's earthly remains on the mantle over the fireplace then settle in for the final assault on them. God must have a mean streak in him if he sits around and watches all of this.

I felt myself losing it. A lot was converging in my mind. Learning about the atropine, Candy's accident, calling off Nikki and J. P. from putting the arm on Mac, having night chit chats with Jimmy Fisheyes, all of it whirled around my brain, making me dizzy. I had to get a grip on myself. This was not the time to look like, and to be, a guy out of control. This had to be done right, this was not time for a major league foursquare foul up like me to also become a looney.

"It's time to go," said someone, who then tugged gently on the sleeve of the black suit, my reserve, the one I kept in my office.

"Sorry," I said, then looked to see who was talking to me. It was Winston Wiant. Another suspect. Someone else to be watched. A great way to spend my time, watching a five star weirdo like Wiant.

At the door were Fenner and Annie, like greeters at a snazzy party. So glad you could come. How sad it all is. Talk like that made me sick.

"A sad day, Rich," said Fenner.

"Yeah, I said, I was in no mood to converse with this over–sexed senior citizen who felt the need to document his romps in the hay.

"I have my hands full with the police. Mancini's a friend of yours, correct?" he said, looking down at me, over his bifocals.

"Yeah," I said, looking over at Annie, who had plastered a concerned expression on her face. Her only concern in life was her job, and I had the VHS to prove it.

"Your friend, Mancini, did he say anything about the 'troubles' down here?" asked Fenner, putting a forced smile on his old kisser.

"Dope dealers from the street is his line on all of it. I must've left some keys around. The way I see it, they got in this summer and cooked some crack. Edwin Gomez, my student, must've been involved somehow. That's all Dom told me about how he's handling this. He's giving some thought to Nikki, but Dom's pretty close mouthed about his job," I said, feeding Fenner some facts which were more or less true.

"Let sleeping dogs lie is how I see it. She's out of the lab, soon she'll be out of the school. Good riddance," said Fenner.

"Yeah," I said, rubbing my hand through my hair. This was touch and go. About two more questions and I would strangle the pair of them right here in their own office.

"We all need to pull together to make the college work," said Annie, offering a nine on the ten point platitude meter.

Fenner shook my hand with both of his. Annie smiled at me and patted me on the shoulder. I smiled in return. I allowed myself to be shaken, but I did not return shoulder patting. I was getting good at concealing how I really felt.

I escaped from the two of them. I went to the parking garage. There were sounds of sexual combat coming from Beef Patty's private office. I thought about waiting till he'd concluded. I could then listen to what he had to tell me. I was tired. Beating up street thugs had taken something out of me. We would talk tomorrow. Also, tomorrow, I would get to see Fisheyes' pictures, the ones with his 'proof.'

Tomorrow would be a great day. I wondered how Candy was doing. I'd tried her on all of her phones. There'd been nothing. In a way, I was glad. The accident had taken her out of all of this. That was the best place for her to be.

# Chapter Thirty–Eight

The next day, after a long night of tossing and turning, which I'd interspersed with getting up to check the street for killers with large, sharpened sticks, I was driving through early morning Brooklyn, scrunched down in the seat like a Florida retiree with only my white knuckles showing at window level. I again had two windows in my Toyota. A guy had come to the house, repaired everything, and left me a bill. I was back in the death car.

One bit of information had come my way last night late. The love nest of my pal Dean D. Douglas Fenner and Assistant Dean Annie Porter Ph. D. had been fouled. I'd called Fenner, an unnecessary call, to get a line on exactly what he had sent to Nikki. A woman had answered. I'd said "Wrong number, sorry," then hung up. Fenner's wife had apparently returned, which meant my esteemed leader would have to return to the bonds of matrimony and eschew for a while the bondage tricks he was playing with his sexy subordinate.

At the college, all was quiet in the parking garage. No Neo–Nazis were on the prowl for pain. There were no bums sleeping off a night's drinking in the doorway. Best of all, there was no very large security guard doing the nasty with a co–ed on his desk.

It was like Davidson on a Sunday afternoon. Instead of going directly to my lab, I stopped at the fourth floor. Approaching the mail room, I saw someone who I would've preferred not to see.

"You've heard?" said Wiant, standing in the doorway of the mailroom, blocking my way.

"About what?" I said, contemplating knocking Wiant to the floor, then stepping on him in order to step over him.

"The dean and his wife. They're divorcing."

"Why's that?"

"Don't be coy, Bucceroni. You know as well as I do that our none–too–good dean has been entranced by that piece of fluff," said Wiant, his lips drawn, back into a sneer.

"'Piece of fluff?' Isn't there supposed to be a code of honor and respect among you senior administrators? What're you, some kind of snake in the grass? Shame on you."

Wiant laughed. That was unusual. Usually, he ignored my witticisms and just told me what I had to do.

"Touché. But seriously, I've worked hard to achieve my position She has done nothing but open her legs for her boss."

That was true, but coming from Wiant it still made me want to pop him a good one in his mouth.

"And I guess that Mrs. Fenner found out about them?" I said, joining in the dialogue.

"Yes, she's on the warpath. They're through."

I wondered if my placing of Annie's panties in Mrs. Fenner's underwear drawer had figured prominently in the confrontation. I didn't offer my thoughts on this matter to Wiant, although he might have considered that too to be humorous.

"This happened when?"

"Last night. The two of them went back to his house from here and did what they usually do, only this time Mrs. Fenner appeared on the scene," he said. I started to wonder what role Whiteface here had played in all of this. It would not be past him to have called Fenner's wife and dropped some hints.

"You under the bed, checking to see if the mattress tags were still on and if they were engaging in safe sex?"

Wiant laughed again. I was a hit with the undead, his lips peeling back, showing large white teeth, matching the maggot white of his face. Wiant was standing close to me. He was a good deal taller than I was, not as tall as Walt Brzenk had been, but tall. Could he have tailed me into the city, sat way down in his seat?

"I didn't need to be that close. As you may know I, too, live on Rugby Street. Fenner and his little floozie appeared, lights went on in the upstairs, then off, another car pulled up, out stepped the lady of the house, inside she went, the lights went on. Time passed. Our young assistant dean left in a hurry. She was carrying some of her clothes. I was close enough. "What will all this mean down here?" I said, continuing with this seedy conversation.

"I may be taking over down here. Fenner has been, shall we say to be polite, indiscrete. He's abused his position. That I can attest to. Plus, he's planning on making a big stink about our sex fiend —the honorable professor Ross McClure. He's no better than McClure. Both of them have no self control."

"I didn't know a HEO could run a college," I said, not rising to the bait about Mac, who Wiant no doubt considered to be my pal.

"I have a Ph. D. I could be given a faculty line. This place could do worse than be run by me."

"How?" I said, unable to resist the opening.

"You needn't joke. You would find me a much better boss than Fenner. I'm competent. I'm in control of my, how shall I put it, my needs. In addition, I know a great deal about this faculty."

Wiant was right on several scores. He had a file on each and every member of the faculty. He was just what we needed, a dead–on bureaucrat with no soul and a tendency to get the goods on everyone. Oh yeah, he'd be a great boss.

"Rich, can I see you a moment?"

It was Fenner, standing out in the hall, looking like he was on his last legs, face white, clothes rumpled, red eyed. His wife must've done a number on him. Good for her.

Wiant had his back to Fenner. Wiant winked at me. I was in big trouble. Lestat's little brother was laughing at my jokes and now giving me the wink. By midnight, he'd have a straw in my neck.

I followed Fenner down to his office. This should be a lot of fun. Now I'd have to listen to the sob story of a jerk I'd hated for years.

Fenner motioned for me to sit in front of his desk. It seemed like an eternity since I'd been sitting there being grilled by Dom and his partner. A lot had gone over the dam since then. The chickens were now roosted, and I'd get to have a heart to heart with one of them.

"What was that snake Wiant telling you?" said Fenner, beginning with a bang.

I hesitated before I answered. There appeared to be a rift developing in the administrative ranks of the college. A veritable rift about the size of the Grand Canyon.

"He said you were having some problems at home. I'm sorry to hear that," I said, telling one truth and one lie.

"Thanks, Rich, yes I am having problems. That weasel Wiant, he seems to have a line on everyone down here." Fenner's words were truer than he knew. I'd seen up close and personal the info center that was Wiant's home base. This little exchange was probably being secretly taped by my new pal Wiant.

"Not much else in his life," I said, coming too close to revealing what I knew about the dean's number three man.

"No, this place is his life, but that's not why I asked to see you. The president called me up in arms. He's on a rampage about all of the killings that have occurred close to the college. He wants me to bring in some other people to help with the damage control. I thought of you," he said. How thoughtful. Here I would get to work with an old enemy to get his over–sexed ass out of hot water.

"What do you want me to do?" I asked.

"This means a lot to me, Rich. After all of our problems, we're now on the same page. We'll make a good team," he said. Maybe I should feel guilty about my underwear drawer prank. Then again, maybe not.

"I'm to do what?" I said, hoping to guide him to his point.

"I would like to for you to write a report, put all that has happened down here into some sort of perspective. Of course, be discrete. Don't include anything that'll make the president more aggravated than he already is."

I could do a bang up job with a report. I would explain how the college's drug dealer had been poisoned. I'd need transition expressions in my writing to account for the killing of a classics professor who was dead from a doped drink made for a loveable teddy bear of a chemist, and then insert a line or two or three about the Korean porn merchant who'd been separated from some of his body parts. Oh yeah, this should make for some fine reading. I wondered if I could list it under my publications for the year. Best not to, since the rest of my list had been a blueprint for a chemical killer.

"This report was due yesterday, right?" I said, smiling at Fenner.

"No time to lose. The president wants to put a good face on all of this. He wants the facts. You're the man to tell him what has happened. Of course, you'll need to spin it to keep yourself and others in the clear."

People kill me. They always say they want the facts. They say they want to know exactly what has happened. What they really want is a good, plausible, well delivered lie. If I told the truth about this whole mess, I'd end up in the slammer, looking in the yellow pages for a hot shot attorney who had built a reputation for getting off the guilty. Fenner knew this. I knew this. We were a team.

"I'll have something preliminary on your desk tomorrow at this time. You can review it, then we'll take things from there," I said, speaking slowly, slipping into Father Bucceroni mode, a kindly, reassuring, pillar of the academic community.

The phone rang. Fenner answered. He got that 'oh shit' look on his face. I stood up and left, listening to Fenner's dealing with his wife. He was getting nowhere. She was laying into him. He couldn't get a word in edgewise.

Out in the hall, I lined up my day. Teach, lie, look innocent. Beg for mercy if the killer cornered me. Nothing to it.

# Chapter Thirty–Nine

The hallway was empty, so was the mailroom. Wiant was nowhere in sight. Down the hall came Annie Porter, wearing a nifty gray suit, her wild, red hair neatly pulled back, looking nothing like what she was accused of being. She smiled at me, said hello, but didn't stop to talk. I did the same in return. She was heading for the dean's office. She would have her hands full there.

Before I turned toward the elevator, I looked dead ahead and saw a woman standing at one of the pay phones. She was well dressed, long black skirt, gray hair, and she was carrying a large hand bag. She didn't make eye contact with me because she was staring past me, watching the assistant dean head toward Fenner's reception room. I had never seen the woman before. I didn't give her a second look or a second thought. It's things like this which should tell me that police work and Bucceroni don't mix.

In the elevator, I had company.

"Hello, Professor."

"Hello, Jim."

"I regret to inform you that yesterday you told an untruth."

"Hey, nobody's perfect, Jim," I said, regretting that I had not stopped on Atlantic Avenue and purchased an Uzi from an Arab on the way to class.

"It was not your fault, Professor. You merely relayed incorrect information given to you by your assistant."

"You're saying that Nikki lied to me."

"Yes, I am."

"And this relates to the late Mr. Pang."

246

"Late? I do not understand the term in this context."

"Dead. Killed. Sliced to pieces. That Mr. Pang."

"Sorry. At times your idioms confuse me. Yes, it was about that, that she lied."

"Nikki confess to you personally?"

"No, it was one of the lesser gang members. Rowanda is her name. You know of her, correct?"

"Right."

"This morning, she was bragging about how the One Percenters had 'taken care of' my uncle."

"Why are you telling me this?" I said, having had more than enough of both his racism and his attitude.

"You need to distance yourself from the One Percents. There is no need for you to be, how do you say, the 'man in the middle.'"

"This is just bullshit. They're taking credit to build up their reputation. They didn't do it. Trust me," I said. So, I was now using the 'trust' word.

"Professor, I think we cannot agree about this matter."

"What about your film?"

"That, I am sorry to say, constitutes a rush to judgment on my part."

He smiled, kind of bowed my way, got off the elevator at the next floor.

The Seoul Brothers and the One Percenters were back at playing payback. Anyone caught in the middle would go down from the crossfire. Life sucked and then you died. I think it was Hamlet who said that.

Maybe what I should do for the president was to demolish the college floor by floor, blow to Kingdom Come horny professors, Asian street thugs, African avengers, and one art history professor/ assistant dean who specialized in table top sex with an over the hill about to be divorced dean.

Walking into my class, I took comfort in the one constant in my life. No matter how many people tried to kill me, and no matter who I had to plan to kill, one aspect of my life remained the same.

My students. Bored eyes bored into me. Jaws slack. Ears closed. Brains off.

No books.

No paper.

No pencil or pen. No one who wanted to listen to anything I had to say. No one, that is, except J. P. Carlisle. He was in his usual seat, at the back, all in black. He wrote down whatever I said, especially if it had to do with killing people.

The lesson wore on like any other lesson—Dr. Bucceroni pitching, damn few catching.

A student rushed into the classroom.

"Come quick, Doc! Some shit goin' down. Somebody fightin.' They askin' for you.

The class now showed some interest in me. My knowledge of chemistry put them to sleep, but my being asked to investigate the latest atrocity at the college gave me status. I was a somebody. Colleagues fingered; killers caught, almost. Brooklyn's renaissance man, Dr. R. V. Bucceroni, the pride of Urban U.

The place where I was needed was the fourth floor. I used the stairs, made it down in record time.

Beef Patty Norwood was keeping students away from Fenner's office. Not an easy job. This was what turned on the students. Shakespeare sucked. Rembrandt was a bore. Who gives a rat's ass about Isaac Newton? Listen to Mozart? Fuck You. But seeing violence up close and in person? Yeah!

Jimmy Fisheyes and some Seoul Brothers were at the back of the crowd. Fisheyes looked my way, nodded, smiled his killer cobra smile. Nikki Nateal was with a bunch of black students. Another nod, another smile.

"Someone down, Doc! The dean askin' for you!" said Beef Patty.

"Who wants to see me?"

"Whiteface and the dean. They in there. It pretty bad, Doc!"

I opened the big wooden door of Fenner's office. As soon as I was inside, I smelled it. A gun had been fired. No one was in the outer office. They were all in the other room. Four of them. One shot, one down, one dean, and one Dracula.

"He's here, Fenner. Bucceroni is here," said Winston Wiant, who was sitting on a leather chair Next to him on the floor was a partially nude body. A woman. Blouse on. Nothing on below the waist. She was making noises which, apparently, Wiant was ignoring.

Wiant had directed his comment at Fenner, who was wearing only a clean white shirt, paisley tie, and one black sock. My mostly naked dean was in a corner of the room astride a woman wearing a long black skirt. The woman was trying to move, but Fenner had her, face down, pinned to the oak floor.

"Let me go, you bastard! Let me up!" screamed the distinguished–looking gray haired woman. I recognized her. I had seen her on the way to class. She was the person I had ignored. Of course, she had not been testing her pistol by shooting holes in the wall, so how was I expected to notice her?

"Help me, Rich," said Fenner.

I took over for him, pressed down on the woman with my left knee, twisted her right hand until she got the point. She relaxed. Fenner grabbed at his blue jeans, which were next to his desk and hopped into them. His hot pink bikini underwear was also on the desk. He stuffed it into his pants pocket.

The beat cops arrived.

A big Irish had me get out of the way while he cuffed the woman. The other bent over the figure on the floor. Annie Porter was now on her back, her red hair lying on a green throw rug, Spreading over the rug was blood, from, apparently, an exit wound. Annie'd taken several shots, up close, shoulder, arm, a lot of blood, but she was alive.

EMS jammed into the room. The big Irish removed the woman. Wiant and I were ushered out into the outer office.

"Fill me in," I said.

Wiant motioned me to come to an unpopulated area of the room.

"The old fool never learned his lesson."

"That was his wife on the floor, right?" I said, beginning our conversation with the obvious.

"That is correct. She shot Porter at least twice. She tried to shoot Fenner. He got the gun away from her. I came in, called Norwood, who sent for you." That was not quite the truth from Wiant. He knew too much. He must have some spot where he could spy on Fenner and his 'excesses.'

"When I left him I thought he was on the phone with his wife."

"He was. She must have called him from down here. She was trying to catch him again with our Ms. Porter, which she did. Our little assistant dean had her own way of dealing with his stress."

"I think I saw Mrs. Fenner when she came in. She was next to the phone in the hall. She was waiting there when Annie walked past."

"You didn't see anyone," said Wiant, his dead black shark eyes locked onto me.

"I didn't?"

"No one. Mum is the word. The less you say, the less interest you'll attract."

Wiant had a point there. Cops are funny. They want their cases solved neat and sweet. Opening my big mouth about spotting the shooter right before she started target hitting would put the spotlight in a bad place—on me.

"I get your point," I said.

"Good. I thought you would. This is not good for the dean. He will be implicated in a sorry scandal. The president will not take it kindly that Fenner's sexual adventures resulted in a shooting, and at the college no less." I would also bet that Wiant would use his file on the dean and Annie to nail them further.

"Where were you?"

"At my desk. Mrs. Fenner came in, walked past the secretary, entered the dean's office. The shots came almost immediately."

"What's that," I said, pointing to a purse next to what had been on Annie Porter's desk.

"She was satisfied with her appearance when she went in," said Wiant, as a nasty smile worked its way into his deathly features.

I looked into the purse. There were gum, keys, condoms, a wallet, lipstick, eyeliner, a compact, tissues, Mace.

"This should be given to the cops, they'll want to see her belongings," I said, handing the purse to Wiant, who took it, knocked on the door, and was let in. He didn't return. I left.

Outside, more cops had arrived. The students had been swept from the floor.

"That dean of ours dead, Doc?" asked Beef Patty, standing at the door to the stairs.

"No."

"Mrs. Fenner the one who did it?"

"Yes."

"The dean, he ok?"

"Yes."

"A jealous woman no one to mess with."

"That's true," I said. Beef Patty had better heed his own words. Malvina "Heavy Duty" Moore might perform a similar action if she caught Beef Patty doing his elephant number on a co–ed.

"Need to talk to you, Doc."

"I'm here."

Beef Patty looked left and right, worked his tongue over his lips.

"No one can hear, Lester."

"Never know, Doc. Down here the walls got ears."

Beef Patty was dead on right about that. Of course, if he provided security instead of piling girls, then some of us might be secure and a few of the dead might still be up and about. This evaluation of Beef Patty's job performance I kept to myself.

"You said you wanted to see me. Malvina said you been lookin' for me for a couple days."

"Yeah, Doc. I seen somethin.' Can't figure it out. You a professor. You a smart guy. I needed to talk to someone I can trust."

More trust I had inspired. Trusted by J. P. and Nikki to hand deliver my colleague to them. Trusted by Jimmy Fisheyes to separate Nikki from the college and put her into the line of fire and now trusted by a four hundred pound night watchman whose idea of surveillance was to screw first and ask questions later. Tomorrow morning, I'd look at myself in the mirror while I was shaving and practice looking untrustworthy.

"That Gomez, the spic who got hisself killed, you know?"

"I know," I said, starting to pay attention. Apparently, Lester was not going to ask me to assess his moral stance but instead was going to tell me something about the murder I couldn't solve. Why I hadn't asked him sooner I didn't have a clue. That was me. Old and clueless.

"He down here a lot. Started comin' down here some time ago. Comin' and goin' like he owned the place. He a pusher, you know that, right?"

"Right."

"But he don' act like no street pusher, most of them stay away from here. This dude, he around here all time of day, any time at night."

"He by himself?"

"That what I want to tell you, Doc. No, dude had company. Strange company. I meant to ask you about this before, but I ain't the world's best watchman. Don' want stick my nose in. I see trouble, I hang back. Know what I mean?"

"Know what you mean," I said, resisting the urge to slam Beef Patty's head into the wall. Tell him to get to the point, cut to the chase, that a straight line is the quickest way to tell a tale. But I did nothing of the kind. I said nothing to speed him up. This was his story, and I'd let him tell it his way. I did give myself a hefty mental kick in the ass. Lester should've been grilled long ago. I was a piss poor detective. The killer had counted on my being as sharp as salami.

"First time I seen them, it made sense. Second time it didn't. Second time didn't add up. Shook me up, Doc. I got a record. This job is the end of the line for me. Got to watch my P's and Q's."

I thought about how the big man was minding his P's and Q's. In the not too distant past, he'd been doing his mastodon movements on a small co-ed. Not exactly the actions a parole officer would be happy about. On the other hand, Beef Patty would have some good lights-out stories when he was back on Rikers.

And then he told me. He got to the point. He laid it all out in front of me. Names, dates, places. The scales fell from my eyes, but I didn't see God; I saw the Devil. I give myself credit. I didn't foul up my mind by saying this couldn't be so. Patty had the facts. Facts develop theories. Now all I have to do was lie.

"What it all mean, Doc? This bad news?'"

"No, Lester, it's nothing," I said, summoning up my best voice of assurance. I went on. I gave him a common sense explanation for what he'd seen. He listened as I lied.

"So it ok then, Doc?"

"Nothing to worry about, Lester. But thanks for telling me. Let's just keep this between us two, all right?"

"No problem. I feel better now. Been wantin' to get that off my chest. You goin' out?" he said, stopped in the stairway.

"No...I left something in my lab. Just remembered it. I'll be down later." He went down, I went up, leaving me more alone than I'd ever felt in my life.

My first task was over. I'd lied to Beef Patty, put the kibosh on his saying more to anyone else. Now, I had to get my hands on Fisheye's pictures. All of my detective work had come to naught. Finally, it'd just been a case of someone seeing something.

The crime was now solved. Now came the hard part.

I had a killer to kill.

# Chapter Forty

The floor was bare. There was no cozy rug on it. Every other plank had a split plus lots of splinters. This was not a cared for floor. I carefully stamped my feet to force blood down to my toes. Checked my watch. Nighttime in Brooklyn, a great time to be out and about.

I was in one of the abandoned buildings, sixth floor, on a line with my lab across the street. As of now, it had been several long hours of watching, and, as of now, that's all I'd done, watch. There'd been nothing to see.

A nice place for a stake out. This was a crackhouse. On the floor, crack vials, needles, and rubbers rested on urine, vomit, blood and shit. Contrary to popular opinion, gentrification isn't a bad idea.

The crack freaks were not here. I was the only occupant, which was okay with me. I was not in the mood for crackhead companionship.

No one had come into the college from the side street entrance. The college was dark from top to bottom. Time crept along. For once, I should have an edge. I'd used some red tape to give me targets in the lab.

A light came on in the lab. Someone came in. Someone was on the job I moved close to the broken window, whose remaining glass I'd removed. I had my pistol in my hand, watching the person move about. The person seemed to know where everything was. This person had been in there before. The fucking creep.

I drew a bead on a gas line, which had red tape on it. I couldn't miss. My finger closed on the trigger, applied pressure. I stopped. I clicked on the safety. I wanted an answer. I'd looked for an answer

254

about my family, riding subways, pacing floors at home, forcing my mind to analyze what could not be analyzed. Killing from over here would not give me a final answer. I wanted the truth from the horse's mouth.

I exited the crackhouse, sprinted across the street. Let myself into the parking garage. Beef Patty was asleep, snoring up a storm. His conscience was now clear. The person upstairs had made a mistake because Beef Patty had enough on the ball to see the operation in action. When this was over, I'd buy some Wilt Chamberlain condoms for my good friend Lester.

Up the backstairs, taking two steps at a time. At the sixth floor I slowed down, gulped down air, took out the pistol, pushed the safety off, and stepped into the dead dark.

Down the hall I went, slowly, using the wall to guide me, making a mental note to think better of Stevie Wonder. I inched my way to my lab, put my pistol away, tapped on the lab door which would open to the left. I moved behind where it could swing out. The door opened. Out stepped the killer, holding a pistol. They say a bear can run down a deer over short distances. I wouldn't know, never saw it done, but I've got early feet. I can get my 250 pounds moving in a hurry. I got to the person quick, clamped my left hand on the hand holding the pistol, at the same time slid my right forearm around the neck of detective Dominick Mancini.

"It's, Richie, Dom. I got you."

Dom relaxed in my grip. No struggle. He'd seen many a guy try, to no avail, to get away from me. Once I got my hands locked on, the game was over. Mancini released the pistol. It went into my other pocket.

I took Mancini back into the lab, put him into a chair, stood over him, took out my own pistol.

"So, tell me."

"How'd you find out?"

"You were seen. The night watchman told me he saw you and the King down here together. You're the guy."

"So you know the story, so what you want me to say?" He said, massaging his throat.

"You want to tell me how you got tied up with a scumbag crap pile like King Gomez?"

"Busted him. I nailed one of his street pushers, worked my way back to the head spic. Had him by the short ones, cut myself in."

"Where'd you get the brilliant idea to 'cut yourself in?'"

"From you. You was always tellin' me about life bein' a series of accidents, about how breaks never seem to come our way. This was a break, so I went after it."

"Why'd you kill Gomez?"

"You was onto him. He tol' me that he was worried about you, that you'd been checkin' him out. We worked out a plan."

"That plan was atropine in my running bottle, right?"

"Right."

"He make it up or you."

"Both of us."

"How'd he die."

I could see Dom look me over. He was still figuring he could get out of this. I had his gun, but Dom was like a fox down its hole. He'd have more than one weapon. He'd talk, throw me off–guard, then take his shot. I'd been Dom in tight spots before. Telling this story was buying him time.

"I got him good. Spic thought he was a sharpass. We got done mixing up the shit for you, we went out to my car. Toasted our success. The spic liked to drink, so I gave him a drink."

"Brucine?"

"Yeah, I read your paper. I ain't a moron."

"And you dragged him out of your car, then took out his tooth."

"Yeah."

Dom was looking right into me. His eyes were black, light went into them, but it never came back out. He knew there was one more question I wanted to ask him. He'd let me ask it then make his play. He knew how bad I wanted to know.

"It didn't take long, Richie. That shit is something to watch, hit him in the leg first, then his arm twisted up on him, then his face. Worked on him like one of them big snakes workin' on a rabbit."

"You figured you could palm this off on a gang?"

"Yeah. One Percent, Seoul Brothers, Monarchs, take your pick. It was like fat fuck Harry said, the One Percents make emblems, I would've nailed them."

It was time to get down to what was really important.

"You came after me, Dom."

"You was onto the spic. You was never one for doin' something halfassed. You get a bee in your bonnet, you keep on until you get the job done. Sooner or later you woulda got to me."

"We go back a long way, Dom."

"It was strictly business. You were in the way. You were snoopin' around. It was nothin' personal."

"Why?"

"What the fuck you mean 'why?' Look at me. I'm on my way to the ash can. Who's gonna hire me? A drunk with shakey hands? I'd be a nobody. I made some real money down here."

"You woulda had a pension."

"Yeah, you live real high on a cop's pension. Go to Florida, live in a small ass trailer, place two dollar bets on Jai Ali, try to bang some old broad with blue hair. Not for me."

"And it was just you and the King doin' all this?" I said, finally getting to my real point.

Something came into Dom's eyes. He paused, then spoke. "You think it was just us two? Look, fuckhead, it was me and the spic and the knockout. Your little sweetie, she's the one who knew about the chemistry," said Dom, looking behind me, an old trick, making his move as he looked. Dom's hand went toward his neck. One of his spots, probably a stiletto in there. Dom was quick, but he was not quick enough.

I slammed the pistol into his face. It struck my old pal at the corner of his left temple. Mancini hit the floor, his head whacking hard.

I took his police issue from my pocket, wiped it off and returned it to his holster. I took the stiletto from its sheath behind his neck, took the sheath too.

I took one last look at him on the floor. A life of friendship down the drain. Dominick Mancini, my old best buddy from Bensonhurst had linked up with Edwin "King" Gomez, become a partner in the white poison business. The talk about Candy was just a diversion. Get me pissed off so he could stick me.

I stepped over the body and turned on one of the gas burners. Leaving the lights on, I left.

I walked the six floors to the garage quickly, keeping my mind blank, focusing on action. I had the rest of my life to think about what Dom had done to me.

Below, Beef Patty still slept. He hadn't seen me come in; now he didn't see me go out. Before, when I had gone for the stake out, I'd made sure he saw me leave. The garage got a quick onceover. Solid. Beef Patty's love nest was protected by concrete. He should be ok.

I crossed the street and stepped into the building and up to my stakeout. The lighted windows of my lab made for an easy target. Steadying my right hand with my left, I was ready to shoot. I'd never get to see my wife and son again for doing this. God doesn't like someone else doing the killing. But where had God been when push moved to shove on the New Lots platform? I fired one bullet into the lab which I'd filled with gas, aiming at a specific spot. It'd take a sharp fireman to find the bullet.

The night exploded. A fireball burst out of the college's sixth floor. Bad news for anybody in there.

Once outside, there was no hurry, blend into the darkness, don't attract the attention of someone on the prowl. By the time I was three blocks away, I heard sirens. They could take their time. All the king's horses and all the king's men couldn't put Mancini together again.

To my car, still no hurry. Driving slowly away. Window down listening to NYC's finest on the way to clean up the mess I'd made.

Behind me, a small car flashed its light then pulled alongside. It was Candy.

"What happened!" she said.

"Drive over to Church Avenue," I said.

She did what she was told. I found a parking space. Candy got in behind me. She got into my car.

"You ok? What happened?"

"I blew the lab. I turned on the gas and shot into it."

"Why?"

"The killer was in the lab."

"Who?"

"Dom."

Candy rested her head on the dashboard. She said nothing for what seemed a long time.

"Dom! Dom. How could that be? What tipped you?"

"Nothing 'tipped' me. I'm too dumb to be tipped. Beef Patty told me. We met in the hall, he laid it all out. He'd seen Dom and the King together. I finally saw the light."

"Pretty basic," said Candy.

I listened to the noise heading toward the college.

"I was a clown. Acting like I was a detective. Anyone who knows anything about being a cop starts with the eyes and the ears of a place. The fact that Beef Patty was more dick and balls than eyes and ears didn't mean I shouldn't have questioned him."

"Dom. I can't believe it. What a bastard."

"He was strictly bottom line. He'd busted Gomez, then horned in on the action. I fingered myself by getting onto Gomez, so Dom gave him a brucine cocktail."

"What about the atropine?"

"Dom and Gomez made it up together, then Dom shrank the franchise."

"Dom and Gomez do this all by themselves?"

"Before I knocked him out, Dom blew some smoke my way about having more partners. It was bullshit to buy time."

"You sure?"

"...Yeah, I'm sure."

"We thought it could be Nikki or Mac," said Candy.

"We thought it could be anybody. Annie, Mac, Wiant, Wenner, Nikki, Jimmy Fisheyes, Castro, Santa Claus."

"What about Annie?"

"Today, I broke into some houses. Wiant, then Fenner. Wiant has a file on everyone at the college. At Fenner's I got the proof about what Annie's been doin' with our dean. The only hitch in their relationship was that Mrs. F. came home. Today, she shot Annie."

"She ok?"

"Yes. The wife caught Fenner in the saddle, performing some desktop fornicating."

"Annie alive?"

"Shoulder and arm, she'll live."

"Some day you had. Fenner alive?"

"For now. His wife gets loose, she'll kill him."

"And all of our theories were bull shit, and it was all just Dom."

"Just Dom."

"Who got Pang?"

"That's where I was blind as a bat. Dom was a knife man. I saw Dom use a knife back when we were punks, I should've recognized his work."

"So Dom saw Pang as a loose end? Why?"

"Look at these," I said, handing Candy the pictures Fisheyes had given me. First rate work. Pang shooting down into the men's can. Catching Dom and Gomez together exchanging money.

"Pang was also a blackmailer, maybe he tried it on with Dom like he did with Mac."

"Mistake on his part."

"Yeah."

"We in the clear?"

"Depends how hard the cops look. Gomez hasn't been dead very long, then there's Brzenk, and there's also Pang and now Dom. That's four killings, plus Annie got shot by an irate wife. But the only killing that's gonna concern the cops is Dom's. Cops get real curious when one of theirs gets it. I got to count on the cops being unable to see the forest for the trees."

"Not I. We. This is not you all by yourself."

"I blew the lab. Who knows who saw me? Nothing you can say can change what I did, so why cut yourself in for some trouble?"

"You're not alone anymore. You've got me. Don't close me out."

That sounded good. Being alone sucks. I had been a loose end. Dom had come at me twice, once with atropine and once with a bullet initialed R.B. Ph. D. R.I.P.

"Let's go home."

"Your place?"

"My place," said Candy.

Candy got out. The streetlamp showed bandages on one side of her face, swelling still around her eye. I hadn't asked how she felt. I'd had other things on my mind. We drove off toward "home." Fire trucks were still honing in on the college. I'd made a night of work for the Irish.

Dom was blown all the way to Brooklyn Heights. His death could be passed off as an accident. That's the way I would play it. Dom smoked, the lab had gas in it, bad combination. A real tragedy. The loss of one of the thin blue line. I would rub my eyes to make them red.

I drove slowly. Candy was already out of sight. All of the killings could be explained away. All neat and clean, but I was worried that some slow and steady cop would piece the puzzle together.

The traffic made me slow down even more while my mind ramped up. There was no motive connecting me to any of this. There was no money involved. It would take a really sharp cop to figure out that a college professor had gone into the vigilante business.

I found a parking place close to Candy's. There'd been no tail on me. I saw no one around her place. I would worry about all of this for the rest of my life. Each and every day, I'd listen for the rap at the door, two cops there: "Professor, we got some questions for you." This would never be over. Rule number six had been written in stone. There'd been a reason for doing that.

Outside, I knocked on Candy's door.

Dom's last words were bullshit. There was no way that Candy was back in the dope business. I could trust her. Candy wouldn't turn on me. I believed that.

Didn't I?

# About the Author
# W. J. Reeves

W. J. Reeves works in Brooklyn.